W9-ADD-264

A VOYAGE
TO PAGANY

WILLIAM CARLOS WILLIAMS

NEW YORK

THE MACAULAY COMPANY

1928

Republished 1972
Scholarly Press, Inc., 22929 Industrial Drive East
St. Clair Shores, Michigan 48080

Library of Congress Catalog Card Number: 71-145373
ISBN 0-403-01278-3

CONTENTS

PART III—THE RETURN

To
the first of us all
my old friend
EZRA POUND
this book is affectionately
dedicated

I

OUTWARD BOUND

OUTWARD BOUND

AT ONCE the great sea, never calmed by divine feet, came from astern, a northwest gale that caught the old Rochambeau on her starboard afterquarter in sleet and rain. The wind shrieked as the whipping spray struck the ship's cabins momently all day long for three days; while from the sheltered foredeck the clouds and stars— for the middle sky remained often clear in spite of the storm—could be seen to circle and zigzag overhead. Evans, standing in whatever shelter he could find, was thrilled by that ferocious might of Nature, the ancient antagonist and begetter, green, protean, slippery, yet pointed and personal as a god, while he thought, watching—lace white, spinning among the waves—of white flowers, bunches of them, yarrow, boneset and of the epithet "privet white."—How apt that is for seafoam.

Leaving New York harbor, January 18th, 1924, during a month known for heavy storms at sea, Dr. Evans had acted fairly upon his wish to see the ocean once again, not as a placid millpond, but as he felt it still to be, home of the wild gods in exile.

11

Nothing so delightful to Evans as to be immersed in the feelings bred by a ship's strong run against the seas. He gave himself completely to the ship's contesting motions. Wildly at peace, after America, laying himself down in his salt bath the first in the morning, waiting for the steward's tap each day, each gesture of the voyage during the storm or after it quieted his solitary mood the more. The gulls paralleling the ship's course without a move close by the rail held him at stance, a deep peace washing away the strains of his immediate past. At sea he felt secure, nothing more solid than that turmoil. A great shout of exultation was often at his lips—making them smile alone, with a kindly indulgence.

It was, in effect, to him each day as it had happened to the ship one night, a ten foot section of the handrail forward had been torn off and was gone, only the twisted iron stanchions remained; with him the same, each day something of his immediate past the sea struck at and carried away—to his everlasting relief. Some day, my God, let the whole works go. I should never think of the practice of medicine again. Never! And, in all probability, this was so. Evans had practiced medicine all his adult life, so far, up to his present fortieth year, in a continuously surly mood at the overbearing necessity for it—wanting always to do something else: to write! Why? Because then only, when he was stealing time for his machine and paper, did he live. Why? One thing about the man, he never argued with his instincts. Temporize with them he would, saying secretly to them:

Wait. Some day I will give myself to you, you whom I
love. I should only lose you, myself and the world if I
went faster. Meanwhile, he had gone back from col-
lege to practice medicine in the New Jersey town of P.
where he was born.

But he really loved the irregularity of a suburban practice, rushing out into the weather at any hour; in the
spring stopping his car at four a.m. to hear the hylas
waken, watching the snow figures on the windswept
roadways at night in a blizzard, plunging in his car
through impromptu lakes of rainwater with lightning
flashing all around him and thunder splitting the sky,
dust and mysterious fog banks at sundown, the stars pep-
pering the sky, the new moon coming—and thoughts
flinging up words to that accompaniment, words that
occasionally would have a bewildering freshness upon
them as they rose to his sight, it seemed, from somewhere in the center of his brain. And yet he was a good
first line doctor. But at the next breath he was off. Let
the sea carry it away, all of it, he should never think of
it again. And at that moment, if he had been certain
that he was bound for the sea's bottom, nothing could
have stopped his enjoyment. A dark, medium-sized,
impressionable fellow in very ordinary clothes, he looked
at the sea.

In the cabin opposite his own was that excellent
young American violinist, Marjorie Kent, about to under-
take her first European tour under the chaperonage of
her devoted mother. In that heated young imagination

Evans found some confirmation for his joy. Marjorie played. He had not yet seen her; it was the music which first came to him. He listened a long time. In the first place, it was extraordinary for any one to want to play hard exercises, scales, arpeggios, and passages of difficult bowing during a storm at sea. Yet there was the music. Its insistence struck him with delight. Once he heard a boyish voice admonishing her.—You'll never be a world beater, why don't you shut up once in a while and give us a rest?—But then came the question. Is this it? Is this the real thing? What is this? He listened fascinated by the problem for two days without seeing the girl. There were moments—yes, there were moments. So he could accept and let the player speak. He let her speak. By moments it was the exultation he felt in the ship's solid pitch and roll, of the determination the Rochambeau was offering to the sea, a naked offering, naïve as a ship at sea, the sweetness of sailing through dark and light.

But when in the night of the third day the storm grew heavier he smiled like a baby. With some pains, but resulting in exquisite comfort, he wedged himself into his bunk and listened to the creaking and groaning of the ship while outside the waves brushed or pounded against the heavy glass of his cabin porthole—so near almost one could touch the gods.

An old woman had fallen during the day and broken her arm. Few were at the tables. Thank God it was not a larger ship! One could still feel the sea. The ship was rolling heavily with a steady list to port from the force of the wind which carried her lower to that side on which his cabin lay. Down, down she went without a great amount of pitching, but down, down, down till the trunk near the door squeaked in its lashings and loose objects in the cabin shuttled and slid about the floor. Then with a slight shudder she rose slowly, leaning again for a brief moment to windward—and with this motion and joy in his heart—such a peace as there is not elsewhere in the world—he slept.

His own parents had come to America in ships. His uncle, the doctor, had died in a ship and been buried at sea. To him the sea was the grave of all his cares, the one power hopelessly subtle and uncontrolled, unbridged, unbeaten.

"I am beginning to think we should have no mercy for anyone—unless we love him. Get all you can out of the other fellow before he takes it out of you." Curious bits of conversation he picked up going about from one deck to the other. *"J'étais un homme très vulgair— j'étais un voleur"*—"the twist of years"—"Truth and Beauty married and the child was love." *"Deux cognacs s'il vous plaît. Je suis polis, moi."* French once more! His ear drank it in with avidity. *Benedictine* 10¢. *Fine* 10¢. That's something!

Then the wet and cold of the storm passed but the great waves continued, causing the ship from time to time to give three or four lurches deeper than the rest. The sky was blue overhead, the decks sanded. Evans stood by the weather rail watching the seagulls flying near the ship's side, especially one, a beautifully marked Mackerel gull, larger than the rest, which with motionless wings was gliding, keeping pace with the ship not ten feet from his hand resting on the rail. He watched its eye watching him—and its head shifting slightly from time to time.

There was a hailstorm that afternoon. The wind was now due north, the weather cold and squally.

Then swiftly, the sea, limitless, filling the imagination roundly on all sides, supporting, buoyant, satisfying—was damaged. Forward, to the left, a section of it had changed, the whole mind was changed along with it. As if the work of birds flying out from beyond the horizon, the thought of land! land! The seahold upon the imaginations of the ship's company had been broken.

England was there, little as a boat. One felt all England, all one had ever heard or felt of England, from Old Mother Cobb to the last pantings of discomfort in the daily press. There it was, pathetic, an island in the sea, powerless and naïve as the small strength of a lion, or the boom of a big cannon. From the sea one could come to hold it as a god might hold an infant on his arm, for a moment. Later, the twin lights of the Scilly Islands gave an inkling, the only inkling, of the world beyond them, silent under the night sky.

At one a.m. the last night the men in the smoking room went wild, threw bottles, glasses. Captain G. had to summon sailors to put them out.

Sleep. Then, early in the morning Evans was standing once more by the rail watching, eager for the arrival. He went forward and forced his body into the very angle of the ship's prow so that the ship thus, behind him, remained invisible. The mechanism that propelled him was annihilated by his concentrated mood. And now he felt himself advancing over the sea, alone and unaccompanied, from a height. To the south a long, low, smoky strip of land was slipping slowly back. A narrow steam trawler wallowed in the dirty swell; the tricolor was at a masthead. So this is France.

Land!

Fickle, by nature, Evans longed now to be again on shore. In this desire, everything else melted and was lost. Time too went by the board.—On such a day, on such a day in early spring, on such a sloppy, dirty-yellow sea, the first coracles put out from the bottom of the red cliff there (they were now close in to Le Havre)— and the wind blew them over to England. I am among them.—He could feel the anxiety and strain of that adventure. There we go by the prow of this mythical ship, invisible to us just as to them we, too, are invisible. For there is the land and here is the sea, exactly as then; and this is I, the same. Now am I come home to old Pagany.

In this mood as the ship was drawing closer to the houses and he could see people moving about in the grayish sunlight, standing uncertain along the edge of the dock and waving a scarf sometimes uncertainly, he

was interrupted by the deck-steward who presented him
with a wireless.

> *Greetings. Have reserved room Beausoir.*
> *See you later.*   Jack.

Fine. How in hell did he time that so nicely?

The train for Paris started gently, to a birdlike whistle
from the *facteur,* passing slowly through the back streets
of Le Havre. Like a child, he seated himself at the
window and began to drink in the scene. Everything
seemed afire in that soft-gray morning sun. He was
looking, watching. For what?

Of what importance this small garden of some
switchman, a row of sprouts, a cabbage growing almost
in the cinders? Poor, insufficient, it seemed. Along the
track little boys ran barefooted shrieking for pennies.
They looked sick, poverty-stricken, lost. The whole city
was as if pillaged.—Where *la France?* he cried within
himself, as if expecting to see some symbolic image of
joy rise from the ground and stride forward carrying
flowers in her hand triumphantly beside the train.

Unhappy beggars! He longed to give them—what?
What had he to give? What could anybody give them?
This is France, that's all. But then a remembrance of
the old gods came upon him as the train gained head-
way and between high embankments started into the
country; and this poverty, this loss, he began to blame
on the death of the gods.—And they starve, they starve,

not because there is no food but because there is no one
to give it to them any more.

Then he remembered what Kay had been saying:
These people are clean, hard-working, traditional in
thrift, fixed as the months in the year and the hours in
the day.

The train was moving rapidly now between farms.

He looked and he began in his mind to see how they
are waiting, these people. Waiting. Wise and lost. Lost.
Lost—just as he was lost. Foreign. Inaccessible. Noth-
ings. Just cut-outs from a paper unfurling itself from
rolls turning outside the car windows. Paper people
forever inaccessible. Never to be known.

And now of all times he wanted them, while the
train mechanically ticked off the miles. At a bridged
street crossing there was a boy in a blue jumper looking
up. He was holding a bicycle and turning half around
to look at the train. A fat *gendarme* was standing by as
if he had just been talking to the boy. Gone.

Gone! Whither? Everything went just like that.
Living and dead. Turn the corner and it is gone.

But to his wonder, it being January, the banks of this
winter landscape began to burst into yellow bloom,
flaming yellow to the tick of the train. Whoo! Whoo!
and with a crash the train kept on—to Paris. *A Paris,
à Paris, à Paris*—as he heard the comedian imitate
the train's talk at the "Olympia" when he had gone
there as a boy with his mother and Trufley, in
'98.

Magpies were flying, black and white among the bare trees.

And now sober France began to ply out, field after field of winter wheat, neat, regular; fine farms. Cattle turned and looked at the intruder or browsed on indifferent. The walls of the gardens and houses were covered with bare fruit trees, carefully pruned—neat as a hat.—The French are careful, dextrous, they love to arrange petals and twigs.—Sometimes farmyards were hedged with fences, a moat, a ditch, cutting them out from the fields.

And then at Mobray when they were beginning to slow up near the station, he saw a deserted garden, all brown and weather-beaten. It was the garden of an old square brown house which stood in the background. No one was in sight. The ruined flower patches were covered with winter débris; the garden was close to the track, so close that the railroad seemed to desecrate its graceful humor. But in the corner of it by great trees that looked like elms, Evans saw a small mound. All on it were shrubs, leafless but marking the spiral of a path that wound around three times before the summit of the miniature mountain was reached and there there was a tree and under it a stone bench, perfect. All was ruin, there was not a blade of grass to be seen anywhere, but the little mound seemed to Evans' too willing sense an altar to some forgotten household god.

And again the country seemed ravaged, beaten. Each

man looked to be feeling his destiny there. Waiting.
Encitadeled, waiting. Meanwhile, a garden.

And so going on to Paris, growing night, the train
came to the hollow of Rouen with its great gloomy
cathedral filling the bottom of the bowl: a great pile of
stone, full of death. Evans looked and was chilled as if
it had been the angry center of all this country which it
was depriving silently, sordidly, of its life; as if it were
drawing the life in; stone sitting in state over the green.

But he laughed away his mood, calling himself Anti-
christ and a fool. He remembered Sister Julien, the
Mother Superior, at the French Hospital in 34th Street,
with her sly pride and great vigor—and how, as a young
man, he had loved her.

Oh yes, this is where Pichat was born. And he wondered what effect all this had had upon the mind of
that modern French genius of whom New York had
been ecstatically talking just at the outbreak of the war;
that fine painter whose pictures had been so admired
and ridiculed—and whose influence on several of
Evans' painter friends had been so great. Pichat was
born in Rouen, so Evans had heard.

What should this produce?—And as the train went
on and began to cut the windings of the Seine along its
way, he began to propose what this would produce: or
what it had produced perhaps in the case of Pichat.
—What light does this landscape give upon Pichat?
His character? A land, caged, hemmed, embittered—
wanting to—a land to which nothing has happened in

a long time. A small wet land. Industrious—with the shadow of a great medieval dragon in the center—as in a pit.

"Oh, let's go to Paris. Paris is where one forgets and works and loves."

What does this land produce? What does any land produce?

Jeanne d'Arc—everyone thinks of her—as if expecting something; just because she was a girl. What of it? Jeanne did something in Rouen. Got killed here, I think. English had it in hand then. England over there, still further out, still more needful. Everybody cut off there. Makes them hard, fearful. No use to go in coracles. Jeanne did it her way. Get out. Take a chance. What good? Had to get out. Wanted to get out. Do anything to get out, and by accident do something great, get crowned for it. *Crowned* is right. Did the thing that happened to be handy. But we can't get to it. Can't get to IT—it wants to get out. That's why I'm here.

The train had slowed up almost to a stop. Three girls, crowded into a factory window close to the track, waved quietly and smiled at the "rich" foreigners in the special train, the finest on the Havre-to-Paris line, the boat train. Deep-chested, buxom—naïve, they seemed—with faces of Oreads or field nymphs; one imagined their flesh would smell of hay and animals, sweet. Evans smiled to think what it would really smell like, however.

"You know, dear, all good Americans go to Paris

when they die, and we are dead, as far as they over there are concerned."

"Yes, but are we good?"

Every now and again someone bursts out like Pichat with design. And takes the shape of the moment. But America is off the track completely. But here they are resistant, fastened down by a stone—waiting—as if some power had cast a great spell over the land out of which the people look without means to recall the past or to escape. And this power is beneficent, while it holds them, soothing the irremediable hurt. White sisters are running sterilely about stone corridors; pure, arduous in their devotion, gone in spirit; little plowgirls, diverted; girls from near the sea diverted from looking out at the water.

Time will tell, maybe. And art; maybe.

Or is it alive? It is. My stretching mood is all I am thinking of. America. Here is. Here is. Here is. Dressed in a church.

Paris ahead!

Rouen, past now, he still thought of it—the first of those great medieval fortresses of the gospel of which he would see more—built of stone and pageantry, flowers —in stone. All in a spell.

What kind of people? Something somber, profound, resistant, dextrous.—Swiftly the train swept it up at a pace and crashed bl it all. A few carts and autos going forward went backward on the road while peasants walking slowly moved their legs as if on a cord while they were whirled behind in the dark sunlight.

II

PARIS AGAIN

Paris! where notable Englishmen come to see their illegitimate daughters.

Paris, a place abandoned and serious. What is its tooted frivolity? The froth of serious waves?—In this way, it being now full evening, Evans had been composing apostrophes to Paris for the last twenty minutes of his ride—Paris! Its frivolity, its frantic milling about for pleasure—that's America, not France—*"Jenseits des Lust-prinzips."* These are the evidences of a seriousness foreign to us; this rock sets us spinning as dry land does feet after a ship. From the small cities of the whole world, frivolous from their bedrooms to the ornate corridors of the minds of their—to every little chamber where men and women hide themselves to do business of whatever sort—and no business without first the gesture of hiding—in Paris it bursts out to become serious—

Paris as a serious city, the beloved of men; Paris that releases what there is in men—the frivolity that means a knife cut through self-deception.

He also thought of Paris as a woman watching for a

24

lover. Paris is a stitched-up woman watching the international array that constantly deploys about the Eiffel tower and goes frantically about its streets in the squealing taxis—hunting a lover.

It must be a lover. He must come of machines, he must break through. Nothing will subdue him.

Yes, that is Paris. Nothing will subdue him. Finally he grows serious, finally clear. It expects lovers out of the hearts of machines. Out of the felted chamber of boredom you must come clean. Somehow you must have saved, must have built up a great seriousness.

Good God, Paris—He remembered how he had hated it; just an opportunity to shed the nerves; the cast-off of international malady, like the crutches at Lourdes.

They were passing through the city now. And Evans began to think of the stern morality of certain legendary great French families, the rigid discipline, the cold aloofness from the loose life of Montmartre, bespeaking a solidity of character which permits liberties no other nature could afford. He remembered his mother's stories. And her brother's.

And they are dextrous. To that he added "argus-eyed."

Paris wipes all frivolity aside and stares in. What are you made of? What are you made of? What are you made of? It coincided with the slowing rhythm of the train. Then try it, try it then, try it then.

This is the secret of Paris—and, that if it be a lover, *here* is the reward.

A Voyage to Pagany

Come, you incestuous,
Bald and uxorious.

In the crowd at the Gare St. Lazare the porter was drunk and started to put up a scene. What! only two francs. What! for the boat train!—Evans gave him five and demanded the two in return. The porter gave them back grumbling, and the dilapidated taxi started out madly into the rain in the disordered whirl about the station front. At his time of life Evans was less inclined to stop the parade to think than formerly. He was always straining out of windows. And now for the third time in Paris he stared and stared into the gloom of the rue du Havre in an excited frame of mind. Had it changed?

Had it changed since as a boy Trufley had taken him to the Catacombs and on the great boulevards fed him *syrop de Groseille* while he himself slowly sipped absinthe and smiled and smiled? Had it changed since that day when, a schoolboy from great America, he had sat playing with others on the third floor of an apartment house on rue la Bruyère, and one of the little devils had tried to push him out of the low French window? *Coup de poing americain!* He smiled. Had it changed since he had come from Germany reading Heine; from London where he had seen the literary world just before the war?

What would Jack be like now? And he was anxious to meet his sister. No one had come to the station. Well, so much the better. He wondered what luck he would have on this trip. And always he kept saying: Perhaps this is the time. Something may happen and I shall not return.

But what to do? and what to do next?

Bess, his sister, was in Paris ostensibly to sing. She had the available cash of the family that their mother had left them when she died. Evans wanted none of it; he could work. Bess was twelve years her brother's junior. They had sided together against the old man. Evans was like his mother. "Bess is like the old man—purged," her brother sometimes said.

Marvelous to be in Paris, the air is different; feel it at once. Even that night he had to go out for a walk—anywhere—to the Boulevards.

You must not be afraid.—But Evans was uncertain—and American—and this and that and careless—and amused and lazy and more than a little critical and no drunkard at any time and—hard to crack, a sparrow in short. He wanted to write—that was all, and not to have written, but to be writing. He got his whisky that way, he got all he ever got from that. To be feeling it in his mind and his fingers as it flowed out. And there in secret he lived.

What a life! But Paris understands that too. It did not seem to Evans that he was afraid; it was that he had to discard so much to get at what he wanted that he never arrived anywhere. The whole world is built to keep it from being said. And so he walked admiring the fabric of it—the hateful fabric.—No, he laughed, not hateful, but in the repulsive phase. Every discovery is only a discovery to hide it deeper.—How shall I talk to Jack for instance, when I see him?

III

LOOKING ABOUT

EVANS walked, though very tired, for several hours on the principal streets of the city, up the avenue de l'Opera, etc., seeing the famous dancers on the portico, all verdigris, and dirtied by the birds. Lit dimly from below he saw the lyre of Apollo featured at the peak of the opera façade and remembered the story: When the poet Verlaine had died and from his poverty-stricken room they were bearing his body up the avenue, a state funeral, to bury it, as they approached the Opera, suddenly the great golden lyre was seen to totter in its fastenings and fall!

He looked at the lyre, refastened in its place.

On the boulevard des Italiens, Evans admired the toy-like clocks in the windows of several jewelry stores, their tiny pendulums going, visibly, at a great pace back of a hole in the face—something he had not seen before. But he was filled with a strangeness inexplicable—satisfying —by it all. It was, as far as he could gather it, walking. How much one escapes by just being here, how much of lying, how much of stupidity!

29

He went for supper to a small place next to the Theater du Vieux Colombier. There the waiter brought his Chateaubriand, serving him a portion of it from the plate and putting the remainder of the steak aside, on a shelf—which Evans let him do, half-suspecting he was stealing it, which exactly, he was doing, and did.

A crier came in from the theater announcing the last act of the play.

Waking next morning at the Beausoir, Evans looked out of the window as three planes went by slowly overhead in flying goose formation. The sky was clear, the sun was shining. He flung open the window and saw an old fellow in baggy underwear walking about his room across the court.

Paris! He felt ridiculously delighted. He pried into every corner of his room, the small familiar violin-shaped *bidet* was there. This made him think of Mme. de Pompadour. He smiled contentedly.

Without ringing he dressed and went out. Brioche and coffee on the sidewalk at the corner. Fresh butter. A woman at the *caisse*, prim, neat, keen-eyed. Snappy.

On the street an old woman was selling mimosa from a bunch in her hand.

There was the usual morning market on the boulevard Raspail. Evans crossed over, watching the orderly line of people waiting for the bus, each pulling his serial ticket from the bunch fastened to the post, each waiting his turn. Orderly and intelligent. He needed some fresh collars. Walked over to the Bon Marché. They were having a white sale.

Collars, he said to a floor walker standing in frock coat and high collar facing the door.

To the right in the rear.

All about the floor were heaps of linen and cotton sheets, pillow cases, etc. Even at this hour the place was crowded with women in shawls, poker-faced housewives, going about from place to place. But the heaps of stuff were on the floor, the floor was dirty. Towels were being trampled, the edges of sheets were black here and there.

A wash cloth.—He had a devil of a time to remember what it was in French. Yes. He found what he wanted and found a girl to take it up for him.

Follow me, she said. He did so—delighted, grinning to himself.

She took him to the *caisse*. There they checked off the purchase, took his money and entered the transaction in longhand in a great ledger. He was amazed.

The boy who sold the collars asked him the size, which Evans could not, of course, give in centimeters— so they guessed at it. You have a neck *a peu près* the same as my own.

You have the damnedest way of selling things in this city, said Evans. I should think you'd pass out with all this running back and forth, to and from the cashier's desk.

Yes, I've heard they do it better in New York. He smiled. I'd like to take that place in.

Why don't you? said Evans.

Some day, perhaps, but what can you do?

He was a good-looking kid in a stiff collar and a frock coat. He certainly was earning his money.

And I suppose they—of course—they were balancing as they went.

What a country!

Then he went out with his collars, a wash cloth, a nail brush and a leather purse that smelled to be of goat's hide, in a bundle in his hand.

Delight was his on this January morning. Everything seemed to function with economy and precision: the eggs in flat baskets in the stores, fruit, the neatly cut and tied bundles of meat, the children with blue jumpers over their clean clothes, going to school.

He stopped in at the Post Office on the rue de Rennes and sent a *pneu* to his sister: he had not—purposely— told her when he would arrive.

Then, going back to the hotel to rid himself of his bundle, he ran directly into his friend Jack, looking a little stouter, a good bit wiser, but dressed with the same engaging nonchalance as ever. The two friends, the older and the younger, greeted each other enthusiastically.

Never had Evans forgotten the balance of spirit, the distinguished attack upon life which had charmed him with Jack Murry from the moment of their first meeting in New York. The firm, thin-lipped lower face, jaw slightly thrust out, the cold blue eyes, the long, downward-pointing, slightly-hooked straight nose, the lithe, straight athletic build. The whole picture was there— almost intact.

How would it be inside? for they had had great plans together for rescuing life from the thicket where it is caught in America, the constant pounding on the head. They had worked hard to get to an expression—and Jack had left—to marry.

That night at 42nd Street when they had parted and Evans knew it was all up, tears had stood in their eyes. Jack had showed him his new clothes, they had spoken of continuing a scheme for publishing good writing—and Jack had sailed next day.

Oh well, that's America, Evans had written down in his mind.

Now here was Jack. They shook hands a long time. Dropping the bundle at the hotel, they set out on foot talking as they strode.

You must meet—so and so and so. Van Cleve is not in Paris just now.

They stopped for a moment at the Dome while Evans told Jack his plans. Then they set out again walking and it was important. They went past La Closerie des Lilas. —There's Harland, said Jack. We won't stop now. See him later.

They were no business partners, no members of a cabinet, not even members of a team. How would they get on? How do men ever get on without some business together? Brothers never do. In the same ship, the same regiment—maybe. There is the Field Marshal, the General, the Major, the Colonel, the Captains, the Sergeants and the privates or it is on a ship. The order keeps them down. The order kills it all. But, as Walsh said, you can't even get drunk with a guy any more without having the name pasted on you.

Evans thought of his English father. How the devil do you love a man anyway? Either you slop over or fight or else you avoid each other. He had admired his father, in some things; loved him—for a few things. But here in Paris, nothing to do—he felt uneasy with Jack.

To hell with what anybody else says, anyway. Evans loved his friend, as some one who brought over to him a section of life where *he* was weak to get at it, too shy, superstitious, too stately reverential.

He loved his younger friend for the bold style of his look at life. Often, when Jack demolished situations and people with one bark, Evans smiled to himself at the rudeness of it, the ruthlessness with which so much good had been mowed down. But he himself never could have done that. Jack struck at the false and, in the thicket of good where it lay, it perished—along with a number of other things. But when Jack ignorantly had smitten, he Evans freely could breathe.

God bless Jack, he had said to himself a thousand times, I love him. I stand for him.

But when it came to saying anything to Jack about it —nothing doing. They walked in together and through the Luxembourg gardens, down between the lines of

34

chestnut trees toward 12 rue de l'Odéon, to get the mail.

Evans saw the French children of the better classes playing around the basin. He didn't admire their dolled-up appearance. It isn't the lack of births that keeps the French population down, it's that so damned many of them die before they are five years old. The French are the worst people in the world for bringing up kids.

They went on past the gloomy buildings of the Senate.

If we had anything to do together—anything—

Already Jack was getting on his nerves.

Merely to walk and to talk—What?

The modern ideal is the prize ring. Men soaking men on the jaw. A gentlemanly art. That's all.

But if you want to know a man, if you find him excellent, why you've got to have something to do together. You've got to work.

Why do you have to do anything? Why the hell do you have to work anyway?

Jack and Evans, wide apart as to ages, were not so far apart in general appearance. Evans needed Jack. Jack had rescued him in America, rescued him from much stupidity, from dullness, at a certain time when he needed just that. Evans thought he had aided Jack to get going.

What remained of all that now? One can't go on just beating the air. Was it still there after these three years past?

Each knew the other's antecedents pretty well. Perhaps there was nothing left.

Evans had begun to be depressed without knowing why, at first.

There was no mail at the bookshop. Coming out they hopped into a taxi.

What in God's name did I come here for?

My generation has done one thing, Jack started off, it isn't afraid to be called anything. It—they're not going to be frightened into anything either, by a lot of spineless—just tell them to move along when they get too thick.

Evans didn't know.

He was disturbed, avowedly. The connotations of his affection for Jack with nothing he could do about it— nothing to do—the slipping, slipping way the world has of getting out from under a difficulty and presenting the wrong face of an object, while it gives you, yes, perhaps what you ask, distressed him heavily.

They were lounging in the taxi. Evans looked out across the place St. Sulpice at the façade of the great church which had given the square its name.

How get in? Where was Jack? Why else then was he, Evans, a writer? He *would* do something about it, *something* at least.

Being a writer he could at least make it into a book, a poem, a novel. But he didn't want to make it into anything. He wanted Jack and he did not want a makeshift. He wanted to be let in, he wanted to let Jack in,

Looking About

He grew angry because as he thought, they wanted to make him do what he wasn't even interested in doing, or if he didn't do that, they wouldn't let him speak to Jack. —You might as well pick up a sailor; but you can't find this——

What was it he found in young Murry? What does anybody find in anybody? Something he can't get except through that somebody. The luck of it gave that one the chance to look in and see; to look through.

Evans wanted to be let in.

Was it literature? To hell with literature. Was it to know the details of Jack's life? Evans didn't know he had any. Was it his soul? What the hell is that? It's to get *through* something. To get down to it, or up to it. There wasn't any act, that Evans knew, that would do any good for that. Not that he knew of.

Yes, you shouldn't be afraid, but you shouldn't let them hand you a sack of guts either—or kid you into thinking you want it. Some day, maybe he'd have to come to that but not yet a while, not while there was any chance of getting through whole.

Maybe Jack didn't need him any longer.

A sudden coldness went over Evans. Jack suddenly faded far away. Evans looked at him coldly and asked himself what Jack had ever done to warrant his, Evans', liking—except to be decorative, as he was.

But to get down to what? That was what it amounted to. What to do, not in desperation and whining self-pity but—whole. How are we going to get to know each other again? said he aloud.

What do you mean? said Jack. Then he went on, You've got to see a whole lot of things over here, people first. They all want to know you, they've read your stuff. Like it.

Evans had forgotten where they were going. Oh yes, to the bank. They stopped the taxi. Jack got his cash and they went on to sit for a while at the Café de la Paix.

Then as J. spoke of his plans for publishing, Evans' mood began again to revive.

So it was the desire to get down to some sort of sense about writing, then, that was the cement for their friendship and there Evans decided to stop for to-day. Jack had a fresh mind on paper. He was distinguished—as a writer. It made no difference to Evans that he hadn't done anything much as yet. Evans knew better than that he should fail—and that's love. Yes, he still loved Jack.

That ended that. He got up positively—Let's go. Jack liked that and they set off. They took another taxi, Evans improvising to himself on the streets, staring out.

Now they were coming back again to Montparnasse, and again Evans saw the façade of St. Sulpice with its severe front and wondered what in God's name it signified. *La Cathédrale Englouti*—signified Debussy. He said that. But there, square stone blocks ornamented with carvings. What? You looked at it. Devout people were going in at the doors. Devout? What? Is it a poem? So is the grass. Leaves of Grass: America, because the people are common as grass—and as green; nothing showy; on the ground. True enough, but what of that? Does that help?

Love. Everybody talks about love. It's the commonest thing in the world. There are no two kinds of love. Love is love. The moralist will tell you that. You love some one, that is all. If you love a girl, you want to have a baby. If you love a man, you want to have—what? If you love a girl, you don't want to have a baby at all. You just have one. You love her and after a while you have a baby. He thought of Panurge and the lady of Paris—called her a name.

It's love and how do these medieval church fortresses help? Love. Where is it on them? I don't see any love. Yes, it's one kind, a kind of official love, museums of love! That's what churches are.

This amused him—Museums of love presided over by men to watch the cases so that you don't take anything precious. I wonder if the jewels in the Louvre are real and if they still look as large as ever.—His mind flew off.

He looked out of the windows of the taxi, and wondered which of these old houses of the Latin Quarter it was in which his uncle had first slept soundly.

He saw the Musée du Luxembourg.—Paris is love, Paris is the living cathedral of the world. But what of today? He did not pray for help. He was interested and felt glad he was there.

IV

SIS

BACK in his hotel, Evans felt half sick. If the truth were told, he had fled from Jack. Now he flung himself across the bed, noting as he did so the soft coal smell in the air from the open window and hearing the toylike toot-toot of the taxis faintly beyond the court on the boulevard Raspail, just before he fell into a sleep.—And a dream disturbed him, a dream in which he was dimly aware of the poet Walt Whitman eating at——

With a start he woke to find his beloved sister Bess a few feet off looking at him while the female floor supervisor was standing outside holding the door.

Dev! cried Bess and the woman discreetly closed the door behind her. You darling! And before he could answer or arrange his sleep-ruffled clothes, Dev found himself embraced and shaken and kissed upon his cheeks, his eyes, his nose and finally, swiftly full upon his lips as if it were some fruit it were that Bess was pulling from its twigs by the lips alone.

They fell more than sat upon the edge of the bed. Laughing and a little out of breath, Bess was about to begin it again when Dev caught her arms and held her.

For God's sake, Sis, quit it, he said laughing. But he pressed her hands eagerly and looked long and fondly into her clear gray eyes.

It's a year and a half, Dev, a whole year and a half since I've seen you. And with that she went on to upbraid him with not letting her know the details of his arrival, holding tight to his hands meanwhile and looking long and delightedly into his eyes, brown eyes, in her turn.

Can it be that we are children of the same parents? Dev said to her.

From America expect anything! Bess replied, even a race immune to——

Stand up, Dev commanded her. As she did so, he pushed her away from him to examine her. As she had stood in the doorway, when he had been so rudely awakened, he thought for a moment that this was the most beautiful woman he had ever seen in his life—though he knew his sister, chin, elbows, and ankles from the cradle up.

What is it? he said. Why Bess, what is it? You are transformed, you are beautiful.

It is these clothes, Dev. The clothes fit me for the first time in my life.

No, but your face. Little girl, little girl, he chided her. Something has happened to my little sister.

Bess shook her head. Not yet.—Bess Evans was

41

fairly tall for a woman, straight, almost too straight, with a longish, even countenance and rather pale skin. Dev had never found her especially beautiful before. The high, rather narrow forehead, and the deep-set, clear eyes seemed now somehow to give her an air of unusual distinction. She was her father's daughter while he was of the southern side of his family which was so mixed that no one ever had been quite certain what they were, except that there was a strong Basque strain there associated with the somewhat mythical name of Hurrard.

Nevertheless, differing as the brother and sister did, they had grown up intimately together, almost as one child. They had shared everything with each other, first by little Bess telling her brother all she knew and later by the brother reciprocating when he had grown more and more confirmed in the state of old bachelordom—writing, and living by his profession as a physician. The war had separated them. Bess had come to Paris to stay with her "aunt." And now here they were once more looking into each other's eyes.

The thing which had always kept them together was the total lack of constraint they felt in each other's company—a confidence which had never, so far, been equally shared by them with anyone else. Bess began thumbing through some papers her brother had lying on the table. What in the world is this? The Ground Bean and its Uses—"Among the additional specimens recently installed in the display of Indian foods is that of the ground

42

bean"—and have you still your vest pockets full of Indian arrowheads, silly?

No, I have saved only one perfect one. Come, Sis, continued the brother, let's go and have lunch, then you can tell me what it is all about.

So they went up the boulevard Raspail to the Restaurant l'avenue close to the Gare Montparnasse exchanging all the family news as they walked. There they sat outside for a moment watching the weather—as it seemed as if it were going to rain—while they sipped their Dubonnets under the awning. But, finding it would clear, they went inside and out again into that delightful triangular courtyard so well known at that time to Americans of that quarter, and took a table in the open.

Think of this, in January. Aren't we lucky? And Bess pressed heavily her brother's foot under the table. Her elbows rested on the table top, she bit her lip and looked even now after an hour's reacquaintance thirstily into his eyes.

She had left the meal to him. As he ordered it, consulting her over every item which she ended by selecting with a quiet word, she talked.

Here was indeed a strong contrast in temperaments. If the truth were told, the cause for Bess' excessive pleasure and excitement at her brother's arrival in Paris was not a natural gushiness of temper but quite the reverse. Bess was not an easy person to know. She attracted men but not those who could expect to profit by a nature such as her own. She was cautious and firm. She attracted two kinds of males. Those she impressed by her slight body, clear eyes and fine forehead and who wanted to win that, and those who sought her intensity. Her pleasure in Dev was that of a totally opposite nature to its opposite. She admired his flexibility, his easy access to all kinds of feeling while her own feelings were so stable, so well known to her that she could have told years ahead, almost, what she would do or think on a certain day. But, most of all, her pleasure in Dev was that here, and here alone, she knew a complete breakdown of her reserve. Dev knew her, had known every wish in her heart from the time she first shook with terror and fascination over the fatalism of fairy stories, to the later phases when her wild anger at the political injustices of her country upset her while he smiled and continued his poems.

We shall begin with the hors d'œuvre and a bottle of Chablis.

Yes, Bess assented.

Then, we will have a broiled lobster between us.

No, said Bess, let's skip that and have a Chateaubriand and the vegetables.

With a good Bordeau.

No, thank you, I want a clear head to-day.

A half bottle then?

Have it for yourself, Bess answered.

And then?

A little salad and coffee, that's all I want.

Cognac?

I think so, yes.

So they talked.

The trouble with our philosophy, Dev, and the way we differ from the ancients is that *we*, you and I, are not important people as those masters were, while we still think we are so.

No one is to-day. There is no need. It all goes on mechanically like an advance of trained troops. One drops out and another pops in. There is no sense in it. It's a distinction to be nobody and to do as you please.

Oh no, his sister replied. Some day, I am going into politics. Wait and see.

Dev laughed, rather thoughtfully, however, knowing she'd be a damned sight more efficient at it than ever he would be if she once made up her mind to it.

She continued: You think you are attempting something for America and for the world, you and your literary friends—your artistic friends. You rather look down on the politician and us other poor tongue-tied mortals. But, Dev, you're just kidding yourself, you're just out for your own amusement, that is all.

This was a familiar tune to Dev but it worried him for all that. Well, then, so were Homer and Dante.

No, No. One was a subtle historian and the other a great moralist. You're wrong there.

You think we have no moral purpose?

Do you have the nerve to look at me and say that, Dev? Have you a moral purpose?

Oh, I don't know. It seems something of the sort sometimes.

Bess smiled quietly. Evans remembered with misgivings that she was an M.A.—or whatever it is—from one of the American female colleges.

We have no Christian purpose surely, he answered her.

An international non-Christian purpose, she taunted him.

Yes, and also non-political, he said.

And it is, she concluded, to amuse yourselves. Is that not why you are here in France? You say you are going to Vienna to study. Dev, do you want me to believe that?

Dev, sweetheart, she added, seeing she had hit home, I am not finding fault with you, but sometimes, my dear, you do amuse me, especially when you think you are doing something wonderful.

Sis, if I had your cold outlook over the world, I think I should jump off the Eiffel Tower. How you can go on with life, thinking as you do, makes me shiver. Bless your heart, Sis, what are you made of, anyway? I guess women are the tougher.

I am just the same kind of a fool you are, Dev, in a different way, that's all. And that's why we love each other. Don't we?

Yes, we do.

Only I'm not a poet. Not a writer. I'm jealous of you, Dev, that's all. I wish I could write. It must be a wonderful alleviation.

Lucky for the world you can't. It's lucky it rains water

and not chunks of rock. You'd batter the world into a
pulp with your devastating hardness. You'd freeze its
marrow, little sister.

No, I'd be no realist. I'd just write nice, silly little
stories about true love. And now, what are you really
doing in Paris?

A voyage to Pagany, Dev replied. I'm not staying long.

No?

No.

Dev, why don't you stay over here permanently?

Finding nothing to say, he passed it off, this time,
looking down without a reply. She did not press the
point.

I'm going on to Vienna, he continued.

To Vienna? Why there's nothing there now.

Via the Riviera, and perhaps Rome.

And is that all?

Yes, are you coming with me?

Bess looked at him sharply, then smiled. Dev, that
isn't fair.

No, it isn't, he answered. I'll tell you the rest if you'll
tell me what made you so glad to see me here to-day.

I'm always glad to see you. Oh Dev, why are there not
more men like you? You seem to bring the breath of life
into me whenever I see you.

You mean, I let it out of you, he corrected. Bess, have
you deviated from your clamlike ways at last? What is
it? A man?

No, Dev.

Bess, you've changed.

No, Dev, I'm desperate.

You're not old enough.

Dev, I've got to do something, and you've got to help me. I've got to break myself in. I have never realized how much I have loved you, dear. Do you understand me? I've been a child, a baby. There have seldom been a brother and sister so close as we have been. That's not it exactly. It's inside myself. I'm an American, you know what I mean, a fool, all tied up, letting the wrong things out. I've let you represent things to me, I've written you letters, silly little confessions, newsy letters—you know what I mean, just to keep the thread whole. It hasn't been you, yet you've been the only one there, but something is ready inside me.

Who is it?

It's nobody. Yes, it is. It's somebody. It's a man. I've got to have him. You understand me. Maybe I'll marry him. I don't know.

Dev's heart sank. For a minute he looked at his sister as if she had slapped him.

Don't do that, Dev. Don't do that. You're jealous, that's all. Madly and furiously jealous and I'm as elated over it as if I were sixteen and you were my best beau.

Yes, you're right, I guess.

Bless you, dear old Dev.

Don't call me old.

Nobody could do that, dear, except me, she said reach-

ing over and stroking his brown hair. I've loved you so
long.

Dev was pleased in spite of himself.

Tell me what I should do and I'll do it.

Dev laughed.—No, Sis, you wouldn't but you'd
do it without me. Come on. Don't let's talk any more
about it now. Let's finish this gallows meal and get
out.

What do you mean?

So he paid the check and they went out. Hailing a
taxi, they hopped in and as they passed the Dome,
Evans thought he recognized a girl he had seen on
the boat. Bess looked also and blinked but said nothing.

Is he there?

Yes.

An American.

No.

Young?

Where are you taking me?

To the Louvre.

All right.

The brother and sister sat silent in the taxi, both
felt a little flushed and drowsy from the meal and were
glad to be silent. Each looked out of the window on his
own side. But they clasped the fingers of their adjoining
hands as they rode.

Love, eh?

But Dev was not prepared for the reply.

Coolly, his sister turned around and in a positive quiet voice that had always frightened her brother she said, I shall never love anyone as I love you.

On the Seine, swollen with the early spring tide, men were still fishing as he had seen them in the morning. The view of the Louvre; they alighted and, it being Monday, found it closed.

Well, there goes antiquity—with about as much reason as usual, Evans remarked.

Are you leaving Paris so soon?

He did not reply. They had started to walk.

Crossing the graveled court to the north of the palace they wandered up the river bank under the bare plane trees where the book stalls were closed, to the Pont Neuf and from there to Notre Dame which Dev had not entered in ten years.

They looked at the famous cathedral: It is the lack of solution hardened into this form, twin towered, all the paraphernalia of the aisles. We should not be down-hearted if we can't solve it pronto, he said to himself. Of what else are all the great liturgies built?—the Egyptian, the tribal, the Greek—to hide the difficulty; the Christian to-day, to hide the difficulty; equal, colored glass before the blinding face of—this the me to you, impossible to communicate, impossible to put over anything important—the truth, as they call it familiarly, the heterosexual truth—just children trying to do it all at once. Blood in this street. The Church heads it all, the dead stops of life, everything made static—stopped that is—made into a form beautiful.—It gave him a chill, that word.

Inside, along the east aisle a funeral was progressing, the beadle with his staff marching in front. The body left a bad odor in the place. The brother and sister walked clear around the nave glancing indifferently at the chapels and standing to stare at the great colored windows.

Evans was bored by the lack of light. Yet, it frightened him, too. Such a mass of inexplicable gloom. To what end? It always got him the same way, primitive, savage, cruel. It was like his sister, he thought. A kind of northern gloom. But she was cynical while he was inclined to be impressed. She was a cold Huguenot. The light in her eyes as she passed the tinsel altars was not a holy one by any means. She grinned once or twice in a way that made Evans shiver.

And yet indeed, this dark interior was like his sister. The tall columns, the floor marked with effigies. The windows. Everything still, sure, inexplicable. Dev was always cast into a spirit of awe by cathedrals.

The pagan strength is in them. When the Christian spirit conquered the world, the pagan gods were turned into these stone images. Oak leaves, acorns, the faces of the people of the streets in the forms of devils and angels. Such was it all. It was the power of those racial stocks that built them, gone to sleep there—to go on, to go on, undefeated. He thrilled always at that thought.

It is like a tomb. Here the sun never comes. When they want to do anything that will last they come here. Or they used to. They come here to the early gods masquerading in these stones, for power. Napoleon came here to crown himself. Here the Kings are afraid. The naked spirit has taken this inexplicable shape right from among fauns and shepherds. The——

What are you thinking? said Bess.

That you are a curious phase of the American commonwealth.

I hate America, answered Bess with so much fire, such a cold certainty, that once again he did not answer her.

Are not the windows wonderful? she continued. I could look at them forever.

Come on, let's get out of this damp place.

They went out into the streets.

Let's go up on the tower.—So they began to climb the hundred steps. Dev was surprised that his sister should be frightened when on the winding dizzy steps, as black as if they had both been blind, she called to him frightened not three feet away and made him come behind and rest his hand upon her back before she would go further.

Out of breath at the top they came forth into the sunlight at last. There they saw three smiling Japanese tourists who were climbing around looking with manifest amusement at the devils in stone all about them.

Brother and sister looked at the great bell, Louis the 14th, which it takes eight men to ring. And saw in the distance the *Sacré Coeur*, the modern sanctuary, which Dev thought looked like the Taj Mahal in the mist. The Japs had left. Then sitting down on one of the stones of the cathedral roof, they had their hearts out.

Bess wanted Dev to free her by pretending to take her south with him. Meanwhile, she would go to stay with some friends at Montreux.

Dev's heart sank anew.

Oh Dev, you've got to do it.

All right, Sis, only I could commit murder, God damn it.

Yes, yes, I know. But I can't marry you and I don't want to go home and do the decent thing. I can't and I won't. I'm no fool, dear. Trust me. If I need you, I'll call—I promise that.

Evans looked at his sister and there were tears in his eyes. But she was blazing with heat. Never had she looked so magnificent. Diana, he thought, Diana of the chase, a flat simile, and a wrong one.

But you, Bess, you, of all people.—He felt as though he had lost something of his very life.

Yes, I—of all people. Exactly. Everyone but me is excused. I am *not* excused. Well, now I don't care whether I am or not.

Sin?

Yes, it is a sin and I will commit it. It is the result of your teaching.

I never told you to sin.

Oh Dev, you blessing! You are my liberator. I love you, I wonder if I have ever loved anyone but you, or if I ever shall. Why are there not other men like you, you precious baby?

Lucky for them. You are much the better of us, Bess. Look at my chin and look at yours. You upright Puritan!

Evans was always delighted with his sister's accent. For, though they were but first generation Americans from their small suburb of New York, Bess had gone to school for three years at Sweetbriar in Virginia and the slight Southern drawl she had acquired there had never left her. It amused and tickled her brother.

Virginians, that describes us, Bess. Virginians. A Virginian, that's what I am by selection—not descent, thank God.

He began to tease her: All I am is a ticket to you. You don't care for me at all. It's just that I mean freedom for you from your own miserable conscience—by hanging the blame for what you are going to do on my weak shoulders.

Dev, I want to go the limit. I want to get drunk completely, thoroughly, to forget this sinful world and all its devices.

Do you call it that, Sis?

Yes, sin I insist.—The old fight did not flare up; instead, both laughed.

Would you care, Dev, if I went off? Answer me.— He loved her and was turbulently resentful. He couldn't help thinking of her as little Bunny.

Without answering her directly, Tell me, he said.

Bess watched his face a moment then: Oh you do love me, you do still love me, and she said nothing more. But the brother and sister laughed again together. She threw herself on her knees before him where he sat and embraced him eagerly, kissing him on the eyes, the neck—he held her and was troubled.

And so they went down from the cathedral roof and took a taxi to a small place on the rue du Medicis for dinner, and later to see Aunt K. who had been expecting them for several hours.

V

THE SUPPER

THE third day of his stay in the French capital Evans called, as he would think of it in the following weeks, just Paris. He had had a wildly sleepless night. But in the morning he received a note he had been expecting. It read: Arrived safely. All set. Wednesday evening at the Quai d'Orsay. Signed, Lou.

All right. America to the fore. And with that he put all trouble behind him, arose and went out into the air.

This was the night for which Jack had promised him the literary banquet. At noon he was to lunch with his sister and their aunt. Now he went for a stroll toward the *Champs Elysées*.

As he crossed the river before the *Chambre des Députés* he leaned to watch more closely the fish-catching. The poles were so long, the men so staid-looking, the fish so bright and shiny and so small that he could not but laugh.

Again as he walked he saw men and women greeting each other familiarly with kisses on the street. It was the Paris that charmed him. Just the sense one had of being here—just Paris. But it seemed absurd that the greatest thrill he had that morning was when, still early, he stumbled by chance upon the *place François Premier.*

This tiny gray plaza, but a step from the great *Arc de Triomphe,* did for him exactly what he wanted France that day to do. Standing there he found himself all unconsciously addressing the low gray houses, with the small plot of grass around the statue in the center, as if it were a person.—Where did you come from, you beautiful creature "with the cross between your horns"? —Thrills coursed up and down his spine, tears came to his eyes as if he had been a starved man looking upon a fruitful oasis. It seemed ridiculous even to him to be thus standing there crying; he looked around hurriedly to see if there were any from whom he should hide his tears. But the cobbled streets abutting upon the little symmetrical place were all empty.

And still he stood and looked at the low gray houses ranged around in an hexagonal symmetry and, feeling broken down, low, peasant-plain, he put a pear, which he had just bought, again to his lips like a country bumpkin and looked, asking himself what it was all about. Was it just an *asile,* an escape from roar to quietude and symmetry? This did not seem quite enough. As far as he could tell, it said *Braque.* It linked completely with the modern spirit. It was France, cold, gray, dextrous, multiform, and yet gracious—its smallness, in this case, endeared it to him. It came all pressed up ready to understand, to be understood, to carry away like the bundles they handed you so graciously in the department stores.

He walked thoughtfully on, eating his pear.

But at the bridgehead facing the *École Militaire,* he stopped again at a piece of brilliance unequalled in his experience: there passed a high-powered motor car, a limousine of great size and most immaculate blackness, with two men in staid untrimmed livery on the front seat. But the car shone, the glass flashed brilliantly as if specially polished, and inside Evans saw two boys about twelve and fourteen years of age, blossoms of a stagnant birth rate, males exquisitely finished, sitting in position on the back seat with eyes as brightly burning as the car was brightly polished, but restrained, symmetrical, one like the other: design, intelligence and a cold fire.

At noon he went to keep his engagement with his family, when, with their "Auntie" at the famous *Tour d'Argent,* his sister and he attacked without relish the well-known *canard pressé.* At the same time it must be added that though the duck at the old hostelry was far too bloody a morsel for these two plain-eating Americans, yet the bottle of Corton they had before it Evans remembered as one of those significant minor events which by being perfectly appropriate to the moment remain forever memorable. And here they arranged the trip Bess and he were to take "together"—feeling somewhat subdued and mean about it all.

At four, leaving the others, Evans went to the Dome as agreed the day before. Jack was there with Salter and his lovely wife. Jack at a table next to the open sidewalk beckoned and Dev sat down. The tables were crowded. Jack said little but pinched his thin lips up once or twice and sipped his whisky. People were jammed in, one on top of another, it being a fine p.m. Three "girls," arm in arm, were talking earnestly together at the curb before the tables: Kiki, Zaza and a little Polish model. Jack began pointing out the celebrities, Russian, English, French and American of various degrees of distinction, success, despondency; rich, starving, lewd or whatever it might be. There was a certain type of international Dome face one might have detected in them all, a sort of wary face, a little on parade. There was little vivacity apparent in anyone. Occasionally some woman would come up and be kissed by a man, her husband watching or not as it might be. She would sit then with a little group, a man here or there moving a few inches to give her place. People got up and wandered off. The waiters moved about with glasses. It was as if each group was more or less in its own rooms. One was walked upon without resentment—unless it suited. Some avoided the eyes of others. Occasionally two would look, whisper and stare. All seemed waiting. Not all, for some, inside the windows, were playing chess in what appeared to be complete absorption. Women wandered about. A man would stand in the door staring off down the street.

How is your baby? asked a wealthy married woman of the little Polish model who had come up to greet her.

Very well, now, and how is *your* baby?

In general, it was a well dressed crowd. There is Léger. Evans saw this one, that one. Presently George Andrews came up, then Mary Lloyd and her beautiful daughter. All sat and drank, the women painted their lips.

It was fun. Joyce did not come here. But many Evans had known, whose work he had admired, whether in writing, painting, music, sculpture, seemed to be here or had been here or must be coming here soon.

It was decidedly an atmosphere where conversation could take place. It was an atmosphere, liberal, phoenix young or old, like a park or a place in the woods, or it had an air of isolation, indifference, about it that might have been the atmosphere of a wild tribal village—without the danger of attack. A prince here or there, a prominent figure from some last year's show in New York. All came up to the level of the Dome. One left behind all his "side." One was, at least for the sitting at a table and drinking, equal to any other, while no one presumed to believe it so. One came and went and looked or did not look. One talked. Ah, there's so and so.

Let's get out of this, Jack said suddenly in his usual abrupt manner.

They got up and hailed a taxi.

At the Trianon, where Jack had arranged for the supper, the regular patrons of the little restaurant with the strong cellar smell in the entrance corridor, were departing. In the back room six or eight small tables were placed end to end before the upholstered wall-bench to one side and in a moment eight or ten of the guests arrived. Others followed—more than were invited for this is the custom, it seems, in Paris. These were mostly English and Americans who Jack thought might be interested in Evans; at least, he wanted to honor Evans by having them meet him. For the few things Dev had contributed now and again to the lesser known literary papers had been frequently admired.

Evans was a man who enjoyed writing. He wrote because he loved it and he wrote eagerly, to be doing well something which he had a taste for, and for this only did he write. As far as wishing to advance his acquaintanceship by his writing, or to advance himself, it never entered his mind. If they liked it, he was entranced; if not, he didn't blame them. So that now he felt uneasy. But none let him be so for long.

With the American cocktails the conversation became general and before many minutes it became uproarious. Evans need not have worried about himself. They asked him for a speech, which he could not make. He said something stupid in his embarrassment, however—something he never forgave himself for saying, and Jack heard it. Something about the honor that is done corpses in Paris—where all men on the street doff their hats when a funeral is passing.

But it was a magnificent dinner, wine flowed fast and expensively. Jack sang Bolliky Bill. Others sang. H. tried vainly to shout a sailor story across the table. Some

A Voyage to Pagany

ate for the week, perhaps. But some were silent and looking.

Evans drank. Some one kissed him. He grasped the arm. He was being swallowed. He playfully nipped the tender skin of his admirer below the elbow with his teeth—Is not this what is required?

But he knew Jack was watching him.

To him it all meant nothing, something that might be for some one else; he drank, he was restless. He was glad it was over.

Back to the Dome went many of the guests, others turning home early. For the former, after several high-balls, taxis were chartered when out they all piled at a nigger joint on the other side of the river.

Jack forgot everyone and stood from then on at the bar. He drank.

Evans drank and danced with Delise whom they had picked up at the Dome. He had at once formed a passionate attachment for this sleek-haired American woman. The minute he had looked at her clear eyes, Evans had determined to keep close to her. She was wildly hilarious that night. Before many minutes she was on the table taking off her stockings. One foot at a time she held in the air removing the shoe, then the stocking, then putting back the shoe she repeated the process with the other leg. Dev was jammed in between two others on the cushion side of the table next the wall. Delise jumped down forcing herself next to him and turning at once looked full into his eyes while the others,

62

seeing how things stood, found other interests. They two became oblivious to everyone as he began to kiss her again and again.

No one paid any attention.

Delise jumped to her feet in another instant and seeing Jack at the bar, she ran over and grabbed him by the hand. Out into the middle of the floor she drew him and there they danced—wildly. Several well-groomed men at another table applauded her loudly. She danced like mad, her bare legs flying. Jack followed her as a foil till he was tired and went back to the bar.

Dev, slightly drunk, could not get up and go, he could not. He looked and admired her. One of the gentlemen outside the party got up. Delise accepted his offer. They danced to the nigger jazz all over the place. An American sailor and a French girl now got on the floor; this was the girl Dev knew was going to the tuberculosis sanatorium in the morning.

Delise left the floor and acknowledging the gentleman's bow carelessly she came back to Dev's table, panting, placing her arms out flat on the cold surface and her head over them, panting. Dev stroked her hair.

Dev thoughtfully kissed the back of her neck, tenderly, lovingly—with greatest admiration and tenderness.

What a delightful thing—drunkenness. He grew furious at the damned stupidity of his people. Whose people? Look, he thought, at this beautiful girl, this armed, able woman. Look! compare her with that, that God damned hell hole of a country.—He wanted to be profane. Instead he kissed her arms, admiringly, tenderly again, with intensity, with peculiar heat such as he knew, he knew—but who else would understand it in him? He was a timid fool—not at all; only *he* knew, or could ever know.

He kissed her drunkenly. But she looked up with an understanding smile and taking him with her they were on the floor together, nobody watching them.

But Evans was a poor dancer. The fire was not in him for that. Maybe it was his age. Once he had danced. Delise soon left him and then all moved out once more to the taxis. It was three a.m. Where shall we go now? To the Dingo.

There, there was a crowd at the bar. They sat, Dev and Delise, to themselves in a corner and Dev patted her face between his hands, the drink bothered him a little but it gave, it gave much. There was an English woman in the corner gathering up her man, her man in a dress suit, silly, paralyzed, helpless, drunk. But Dev shook his own head a little to clear his vision and—caressed Delise. She was quiet.

Why are there not more men like you, dear? she said. He looked hard at her clear eyes. You are tender, kind. Nobody else knows how to be so kind.—Dev only kissed her. She leaned over the table into his arms; tenderly he held her as if it were the whole world he were holding. Amazed, puzzled, wishing nothing else, knowing it was nothing.

Leaning closer she confided to him her jealousy over

Garda. Her feeling that when Maurice smiled at her, at Garda, that she, Delise, couldn't bear it. Why are you so good, why are you so good? Why do I tell you this? she kept saying. You ask for nothing.—She leaned over and nipped the graying hair at his temples with her sharp white teeth. You don't ask for anything. What is it?

Dev felt—as he always felt: what? And that's all he could say. What? What? I love you. I love to kiss you, dearest. But what? What?

Then he drank, drank and slept with his head on his arm. Delise had gone to another table and was leaning upon another's shoulders. Later, all went out to a little place near the Gare Montparnasse. They had fried eggs with the laborers who came there for breakfast.

Jack didn't eat. He was drunker than Evans. He was peevish.

They left the others and walked home in the dawn. Jack felt quarrelsome.

The trouble with you, Dev, he said, is that you're a damned fool. Didn't know you were so soft.

Yes.—But it cut deep. The whole thing was clear to Evans. The assinine attempt at a speech, and so forth, and so forth, and so forth. Anyhow, he felt that way. To hell with all of them then.

Why don't you *do* something?—and there were worse things said.

VI

CARCASSONNE

Dev was wakened from a heavy sleep next morning by a phone call from Bess wishing him good-by. She was leaving Paris as they had planned and would write to him from wherever she would be—later. That was all.

Immediately after, he was desperately sick and didn't give a damn where she was going or in fact for anything about her. He felt horrible. After a while he flung himself on the bed and managed to go to sleep once more. At about noon he roused himself for the second time. Things began to come back a little. This was the day. He must get up, get washed, catch the train for Toulouse—or wherever it was he was going. He dimly remembered something about Bess. Bess had called. Bess had gone. Hell, he must get up.

By five, he was at the Quai d'Orsay, feeling rather gaunt, but there was Lou, as planned, standing in the midst of her luggage—hat boxes, tennis racquets and all. She had not seen him. He lit a cigarette before going up to her. She *is* beautiful, a blond beauty. Legs a trifle heavy though.

66

Lou was trying to keep from meeting the eyes of a chap standing by one of the pillars a short distance off. She was very glad to salute Evans with a kiss as he came up.

The thing had been so carefully planned that for the moment neither felt at all the novelty of the situation. Both were dead tired.

I'm so tired, Dev, she said, after they had arranged their bags in the compartment. And so, without further dallying, he went out for a smoke.

Standing in the corridor smoking as, leaving Paris, the train began to assume its rapid country pace southward, the thoughts and events of the day before began slowly to come back to Evans' mind and it dawned on him that at last blessed Lou was here with him on the train and that he was going south and away. At last, he was going away. He was on the train with Lou, going away.

Jack would like that.

Neither he nor Lou had cared for supper, so that when Evans thought she had finished her preparations for the night he went in and sat on the edge of her berth a while, quietly talking. Finally, kissing the tips of her fingers in a sort of daze, early as it was, he, too, turned in, in the berth above and both slept.

It was in the fulfillment of his wish that Evans and Lou were going to Carcassonne. Now they were sleeping near each other on the train, neither knowing what the outcome of this adventure would be.

In the night he woke and looked out at the stars. It

was sparkling moonlight. The stars were big. But on the fields lay a coating of frost. It was getting damned cold in the compartment. There was no hurry. Cold and starlight; fields and still villages. Thank God, Paris was behind.

Carcassonne, the medieval city. And blessed Lou: cool, caring. So he dropped away again half remembering low hills off to the west covered with frost.

And Lou. It was for Lou that the whole trip to Europe had been arranged—with the greatest care. Lou Martin was taking a chance with Dev. She didn't know whether she was engaged to another man or not. Dev, at least, wanted her and had gone to the greatest trouble in the world for her pleasure. Dev would take trouble to please.

Carcassonne, Carcassonne, Carcassonne, said the train.

Still the lovers slept like tired man and woman out of whom all passion has been drained.

Carcassonne, Carcassonne. The moon shining outside, Evans dreamed bitterly of his life. He saw them taking what he loved away from him and he could not open his mouth. They were degrading him and he knew they were right. He looked and looked and seemed to be living in his eyes alone. He smiled to himself, in his sleep.

The Statue of Liberty seemed ten miles high to him. He felt small but fascinated by his own fate. It was not so bad as long as he could see. All he wanted was to see Carcassonne.

Suddenly he had the feeling that the train was going in the wrong direction. He was wide awake now. He half sat up feeling the train rushing north, back to Paris with great speed. Great snow mountains, which he knew could not be there, he saw in the region of Chartres. He felt himself rushing through space feet first, instead of head first as they had started from the Quai d'Orsay. Then he realized what had happened, the train had been turned end for end on a siding in the night.

He looked at his watch, holding it up close to his eyes to make out the hands: 4:15. He had a notion to get down and crawl in with Lou. What in the world did it all mean?

He had come to Europe to be going away. He was going away now as hard as he could, but he knew, somewhere in his mind, that he would be coming back. Too often, he, Evans, had been secretly wanting to turn back—this was what he had been hiding from everybody. Yet they saw it plainly anyhow.

Bess saw it. Bess knew him. Others felt things about him, but Bess knew. Wonder what's happening to her now, poor kid? She'll come through though. Leave it to Bess. She'll come through, all right.

Why not want to turn back? What sense is there in going on? There was nothing idle in wanting, not *wanting* but *knowing* he would be getting out of this, somehow. But he hadn't gone into it that way. He'd gone in, fair and square, not knowing the end, just for Lou. But it was cheating to be pretending to be going on and to be certain, inside, that he would be returning and not have gone really at all. And yet that was not all. That is not all: there's more to it than that.

Where was Jack going, anyway? Damned if he knew. He, too, would go, would be freed from his enslavement, if he knew any place to go to or how to begin. He was trying to, now. But he wasn't going to kid himself; there was nothing in it.

Not yet at any rate. He hadn't seen anyone just go who had kept his, Evans', admiration for long. Just go. Why? He couldn't let himself do that. Why not just kill yourself. It's more sensible. And yet, he dreamed to go, madly, as he remembered at twelve he had sometimes done, madly, with no end in view; that day the kids couldn't catch him at hare and hounds, that phenomenally successful day when he had kept them baffled all the afternoon in a certain neighborhood, running, hiding, showing himself, doubling on his tracks, escaping, running again, showing himself and so on, hour after hour, running on. So, desperately scattered, he had remained *still;* whereas they, Jack and the rest, being always collected, could go loose. But if he should go loose, he would die, of this he was convinced, since to go loose to him was to go totally ungoverned, drunken, syphilitic, starved, jailed, murderous: Finis. The rest were pikers really—careful schemers, really. This had been his excuse. Not an excuse. It was the wall over which he could not climb, short of annihilation. This kept him enslaved.

He could see himself running, hitting against the bushes madly; bruised charging against Moresco the giant back; going against insuperable odds.—Yet that is the only thing worth going against. He was willing but he couldn't—that was all. If they wanted to be damned fools, all right. Yet, that was what he wanted to be— really; abandoned.

Dearest Lou, how I love you.—But he decided still not to bother her but to let her sleep. The train was going at a rapid charge, charging down on the south. Vineyards, that's what they are. Vineyards. It was growing colder and colder, excessively cold. Looking out of the window just at dawn when he next wakened, Dev this time actually saw the mountains, great icy peaks not so very far off to the southwest. It was the Pyrenees! And beyond them Spain! There they were, covered with pure snow. Dev was amazed, he had not expected these simple wonders. They took him quite out of his doubting mood.

He dressed quietly not to awaken Lou but she turned over and smiled. He lay beside her for a moment, dressed as he was, kissing her tenderly upon her face and breasts. She petted his hair.

Have you seen the mountains? he said.

No, and she was awake in a moment.

Entranced, they looked out of the window while in the foreground the dim vineyards flew past them. The sun was just catching the tops of the Pyrenees. They were speechless with the beauty of it all.

Dev, she cried, Was ever anything so beautiful in this world?

Slowly the rosy tint of the mountains grew brighter. They sparkled, flashed.

What a country, what a country!

Lou had arisen from her bed to stand beside her lover to look out at the mountains. It was very cold. As Dev turned to look at her she shivered. Here, he said, throwing something about her. And he walked quickly out, smiling back and kissing his hand to her at her grateful smile.

See you later.

You bet, she said, laughingly.

Carcassonne, Carcassonne, Carcassonne. Dev was eager to arrive now that the strange character of the place had made itself known to him so powerfully. Lou was with him body and soul, as excited as he. They were like children awaiting a fulfillment of delight.

It was still early in the morning and cold, the sun having just risen, when the train deposited them, almost the only ones to descend from it, at the station of the new city of Carcassonne with its small irregular square, the park, the plane trees and, fortunately, a *fiacre* behind the station—out of the wind.

This they mounted and were soon jogging on their way a mile or so across the new bridge around the grassy outer defenses of the old fortress high above them, past the towers and crenelated walls, ascending by the old road to the barbican beside the Porte Narbonne. The drawbridge was down and the portcullis raised, rusted into place.

At the top of the steep ascent the *fiacre* had made a sharp turn and in a tiny graveled quadrangle before the principal gate, stopped—the inner city remaining inviolate to modern wheels.

A wind was whipping down from the tall battlements like arrows. It was February. There were no tourists.

In the barbican wall to the right, Dev saw the name "Blanche" cut in stone. "Blanche." Who was she? Blanche. He saw women—Blanche, all of them—moving in the streets, women violently contrasted with the stones.

The lovers had not yet breakfasted and they were cold—as it should be with beginning passion—in the narrow wind-swept channels of the old city streets, so that, gaining the rooms of the ancient castle, seat of the legendary counts, with their heraldry emblazoned all round the walls, they were glad for something to eat and to drink.

Carcassonne. They stood for a while looking out through the modern leaded windows over the new town across the river.—How can we imagine that old life, how rough, how inconvenient it must have been for them! In these stone chambers where they lived how the whiteness of women must have flamed against that coldness. With what a feeling of relief they must have welcomed Christianity, its softness—priceless by contrast. So different it is now to us—us whom it has wasted

—so that we look back on their crudeness with pleasure even—and admiration wishing for those virtues and that —flavor.

From the warm castle rooms sallying after a rest, by the tiny garden across the paved courtyard to the fortress church of St. Nazaire, the lovers felt very happy. No one else was there as they stood in the old church on its pagan stones contrasting the architectural styles—early and late, mixed, right and left before them.

Carcassonne, a rock ruined by tears. It had to be rock-rimmed to give it credence, rock-chapeled. It tapped the rock and sweet water flew out—a hidden gentleness which had no certain name, in them without excuse— but like rain on armor. A brief advantage for which they panted. Water! Christ. Water all within themselves. Themselves. Their defenses broken, out it comes. Tears. Which have now melted the rock which conserved it and caused it to run and disappear in the sand.

The chapel was cold. On the uneven floor they walked about whispering. Very old it seemed but full of a strange assurance, because, possibly, they were young and felt no part in it.

The garden was better, though best was to stand in the southwest wind that tore at their garments as they went to the western ramparts and looked out toward the snow mountains across the valley to the southwest, mounting the archers' galleries, peering through the slits of the *meurtrieres*.

Do you remember anything of the history?

Carcassonne

Not a word, never heard of it—

They looked long and silently, muffled from the past, at the far Pyrenees, hiding themselves as best they could from the invincible wind.

Boso and Irmingard, brothers of *Richard le Justicier*. The Arabs. Pippin the Short.

It cannot have been an important place or I should have come across it in my medieval history.

Hand in hand the two ran in the *lice* between the outer and inner fortifications and found tiny daisies pressed close to the ground, as earliest flowers always are, for warmth.

They saw much of the place but their minds became stiffened and their faces, too, with the force of the wind and the cold. They hid in sunny nooks of the walls, but sunless corners were desolate and they fled at last, up through a postern, out again oppressed by the stones and the death of the place—the cold—hating the obstinacy of the defenses—too strong—senseless.

God, I've seen enough of that to last me a lifetime.— They were weary too, with the early rising, the long climbing and the wind, so they decided that they would walk, walk back to the station—over the old bridge. At once they went fleeing away from the icy, towering walls and, if they had had to retrace their steps which an hour before they had taken with zeal, with excitement, they would have shuddered and violently pulled back.

Going down to the river, the Aude, they looked back once more with strange regret at the great northern face

75

of the inviolate walls, picked out with round slate-roofed towers—unpeopled, wholly lost—and a feeling of depression made them turn about again for the last time and run down the hill—by a tiny hovel where a woman was hanging out clothes. They seemed a thousand miles from the world, from Paris, from France—they were drawn together like children running together for shelter from the cold and from a nameless ague.

Behind them, the walls remained unseen, not to be looked at again until they were on the train bound for Marseilles when, covered by its warmth, they could spend their glances once more—in passing and in comfort—upon that forbidding masonry and its secrets—the image of a past they could not imagine: Blanche—Mother of Saint Louis.

But now at the old bridge they stopped, their faces tingling from the run and, looking over the breastworks, below them they saw women washing in the stream.

The water must be icy cold, Lou said. Look at their hands.—They felt that they had intruded upon some long-forgotten age.

At their feet the women had stoves to keep them warm as, kneeling in wooden stalls made of a box with one end knocked out, they pounded the twisted sheets on the flat rock each had before her with a wooden paddle.

The streets of the new town were desolate. The stores were dark, dead. The lovers looked down one narrow alleyway. It seemed an emanation from some impossible world.

People live here! Good God. And they are happy and they sent soldiers to the great war.

They went along the streets encountering scarcely a soul to observe them or for them to observe. The wind! A great tree leaned bending down over a wall. Two dogs they saw violently at their rut.

Spring, said Dev.

Lou was amused.

The driving wind which lifted the dust of the tiny deserted boulevard in a great cloud carried them also before it, until it drove them to the Café du Commerce by the station, behind whose plate-glass windows they sank at last tired to rest.

What lives they lived, what lives they must have lived, those old terrors of men up there—we are no more than their shadows. How must they have defended themselves, from the weather even?

Let us have an aperitif and eat later on the train—at noon.

There were but two or three old fellows motionlessly reading papers among the silent tables. It was not so warm in the café as one might believe on first entering. Cold currents from some corner assailed the feet. The street door kept opening slightly with every stronger wind blast.

God provide furs and brazier fires for the young countess in the castle to-day!

She will be thinking of her lover, and that will keep her warm. In the church it will be cold. The archbishop will have chillblains. War is a necessity when one is freezing and no help but an open fire.

What of the women washing in the stream?

Most likely they did not feel it, then as now.

Shall we stay over and visit the Cité again more at leisure to-morrow? It may be warmer.

Lou looked incredulously at him.

You said it, he replied. There is a train in forty minutes.

We'll take it. BRRR!—The twelve o'clock train to Marseilles.

Marseilles! I hope it's warm there.

VII

MARSEILLES

THE treeless plain about Carcassonne is covered with vine-yards; through these the train started at noon to the south. Sticking their tongues out at the old gray fortifications as they went by, Evans and Lou went immediately into the diner.

There is in this part of France, in the neck that connects the peninsula of Spain with the rest of Europe, a constant feeling of the sea, the Atlantic on one side—at some distance—and on the other, the Mediterranean, the ancient Oceanus. As the two sat at lunch they looked curiously at the endless brown of the bare vineyards, in February, itself a rolling sea spread off in waves about them on all sides. It was an earth ocean seeming to break upon the very walls of the little châteaux which occupied the hill crests here and there at varying distances from the railroad in the background.

Lou had on a dark traveling suit of some shaggy material Evans did not recognize, a small black hat in the fashion, flesh-colored stockings, and French shoes decorative in cut and boldly buckled.

At least he did not have to consider her a baby.

He liked her because she was strong—and brave. Here were bravery and desire, misty and unquenchable; and she had the wit to desire what he could give her. Not that she weighed it, but she knew—how to want, to feel and to get—as in a game. Of love how much was there in her? But what did he care, really? He felt that she would not break her heart over anyone. But he had to add that in spite of the constancy of types—none knows what will happen when the time comes. At least, they were on their way. He believed it and he was happy.

The train was running with few stops through the cold squally weather. There were miles and yet miles of grape vines, brown waves, colored like a satyr.—But the soil, Evans explained, is good for little else than these small bitter grapes, useless for eating and best where the soil is worst. In a rich soil the wine-flavor is nothing. It is where there is sun, a height and the salts which make for flavor that the best grapes are found. Here and there are rare soils, then a wine will be famous, and the years will bring special favors from the weather and again the grapes record it by their flavor and richer yield. So the secret of the waving soil gathers in the names of the great châteaux, gathers and is gathered and solicitously preserved. A race of wine men has grown up flavoring this country, by the soil, as the soil flavors the grapes: skillful, dextrous and solicitous.—This was not what he wanted to say, but everything was burning for him in his present mood.

Warm again, they sat at table for more than an hour after the meal had been cleared away and the other diners had gone back to their compartments.

Shall we talk?

No, no, not just now, dear.

They smoked instead. He had not believed she could be this way.—So much more credit to her then for the escape. From what? A fury always made Evans' head swell with blood when he thought of the U. S. Anyhow, the sudden anger cured him of his mooning. She was magnificent, her kiddishness would pass.

Thank God, we're here.

You said it, she replied, We're in no hurry, are we?

Comparatively not, he said, and she looked out of the window quickly.

He laughed a good laugh which made her frown.

Evans studied his companion carefully. She had a round instinctive head, a good complexion, firm chin and a large mouth—he had never quite so looked at her before. Her lips, however, were really sensitive and her eyes blue but somewhat shadowed by her brows so that they showed not brilliance but reserve. The whole face was laughing—best of all, it was young.

How old? Evans guessed twenty-eight. She had never told him. Too old to be beginning this sort of thing— perhaps she is much younger.

More of a child than I thought—and he felt a quick pang of regret. Perhaps she would welch. He looked at her and did not think so. He admired her.

You're a miracle, Lou, he said.

Her reply was that the secret of the Sphinx is that she is shy!

Then for an hour they talked of France, of the grapes, of wheat, and Lou wondered about the wine, as if the French were curious addicts to some rite which kept them idolatrous before the wine drinking, amazed, when if they would but plant their ground to oats or wheat—they would be wiser.

No, the wine is cash, answered Evans, and the cash brings more wheat than would the ground itself. It is the intoxicating savor of the soil itself that's gifted for these things.

Finally, feeling strange and too conscious of each other in the deserted dining car, they returned to their compartment.

Now the vines had ceased. There were swampy meadows to the left, great stretches reaching in the middle distance to the glint of water beside which were shining white mounds of salt—or so Evans judged them to be.

But when in a lift of the tracks they saw, they saw, to the right, a sail, over the edge of a dune and then the blue! a great exultation seized the two companions.

The sea!

Evans saw: Grecian galleys; Africa just there, imminent; the blue, blue water. Then over the dunes, looking out to sea—the granite changelessness of time.

The train is annihilated, what of the window or the

speed? It is the salt grass, it is the sand, it is the sea. There has been no change.

No change. The lovers were awed by the sea, giving up its history to the imagination. A richness, without loss, ran beside the train as if it had been a toy. It entered. on invisible waves that played about their temples full of pleasure: Greece, Rome, Barbary: to-day the same—the accumulation of all time—perfect.

Especially to Americans does the Mediterranean bring memories—to Americans cut off from its good.

It was a bright interval, for as night came nearer, the train turned north again and a cold rain came with the darkness. It was cold and black by five o'clock.

At six they passed Arles but the determination to descend and spend a day there had faded with the forbidding weather. Across the Rhone the lights were shining at Avignon:

No, let us go on at once to Marseilles.

Marseilles, the city of sailor love!

At the Hôtel de France the steam radiator was ardently hugged. Oh boy! A wash. Marseilles! And they dashed out famished, and down the *Cannebière*—thronged by Algerians, French, Spanish, English, Americans, down to the old harbor to the shipping, feeing one of the many beggars sitting there by the water. This was fine. At a table of the *Restaurant au Port,* they ordered a *bouillabaisse.* A cat, outside the glassed-in porch overlooking the harbor, walked up and down, confused by the glass, smelling the fish and trying to get in.

They talked long over their plates and a bottle of Meursault. Lou told him intimately of herself much that he could not have guessed and had not known before, talking in a low voice. He was interested and forgot himself completely in her.

After a while it began to penetrate to them that they were being watched: at a table nearby were four drunken Americans—or two American men and two French girls whom they had in tow. Lou was nervous, more scared than Evans had imagined possible. A product of Melrose High, enervated by a lifelong unprofitable contact with boys and men—without issue—she was not taking it as easily as he had believed she would.

He put it down to just nerves and hoped she would get over it later.

A noisy party in the next room, the four at their backs, the masts of all nations in the basin and the cat weaving up and down on the roof of the porch outside the glass— in front of the ships and the lights—before them, they continued to eat, toward the end without saying a word.

Lou was very ill at ease.

But it was only that she was eager to be alone with him away from the ears of the heterogeneous crowd. Back in the hotel, she felt serious, alert, alarmed. Her eyes were round and startled when he came to her after the bath, but she was tender and clung to him quite out of her usual temper, but, as she had been all that day, like a small child.

VIII

THE RIVIERA

THE next morning, windy, clear and still cold, but with a southern brightness of air. Ready for the trip eastward along the border of the sea, the two were in a mood of extreme exhilaration, more especially Lou whose constant warming glances and eager, simple questions, What's that? and Tell me, Tell me, soon had her companion nearly as alert and curious as was she herself. Oh look! It was her first mimosa tree in blossom.

Like your hair! smiled Dev. But she did not notice. Look, look!

All these things also will be discovered, said he half aloud but she did not hear; she was too busy looking from the train window—in this suddenly acquired south hitherto unsuspected.

Evans constructed a more conscious symbolism as they rode along by the sea.—So this is the new life, he said to himself. What would Bess think of me now?

Look, look, Lou kept saying, now darting to the sea side of the car—they were fortunate to have secured a compartment alone—now to the other. Olive trees and cactus and low palms; the sun caught in the protecting mountains; the pale blue sea—and Lou was all delight.

And still it was cold, but cold and sunny—a clear Mediterranean chill full of a crystallic light. So this is the Riviera! It was bare, as they edged along the sea. Scrub pine and oak clung to the towering gray rocks to the north. Now they would be running close by the sea with jagged gray promontories catching the low surges, then they would strike back into the coastal plain where some peninsula would jut out and near them at the left again they would see the low coastal range, the *Alpes Maritimes,* rugged, bare eminences of stratified gray rock, treeless for the most part—and then there at the peak of one, the tricolor of France. It capped a low concrete dome, the beginning of the fortifications about Toulon. Toulon whence Napoleon set sail for Egypt. Military roads zigzagged up the cliffs. A curious bare country into which the sun beat all day long.

Oh look, look, said Lou. It was an orange tree. How wonderful, and just the day before yesterday we were in Paris. It is miraculous.—At the stations men and women were going about in summer costumes and light top coats. In a little station garden there were flowers whose names they did not know. Tangerines were on the trees.

But again near the mountains a small brown village, startlingly apart from the new town, stood out to a peak on an isolated hill or there was one which clustered up the mountain side, reminiscent of the days of quick attack from the sea and the necessity for a mountain defense. Such was Cagnes—but the great town they first came to was Cannes. Should they get out and remain here for a few days?

At first Lou was for it. The tennis matches would be on, they could put up at some small place and see Lenglen and the rest. Tennis was Lou's great key with which, up to now, she had unlocked nearly every good which life had so far offered her. Through that means she had found her friends, formed her athletic opinions concerning life and built up her small talk. She played well.

Logically enough it was in a mood antithetic to her usual one, during a time of uncertainty, that she had fallen in with Evans. She wanted to stop and see the matches but as the train came to a standstill in the station of Cannes—the crowds waiting, the excitement, even the courts themselves to be seen from the window—she did not move.

Evans was already on his feet reaching for the luggage.

Well?

No.

Evans sat down. He put his arm about her waist and together they looked out at the jabbering mob rushing back and forth below them outside the car window: English faces, American faces, and the rest. It was easy to read in the compartment while the train was stopped; they picked up the map and located themselves, counting the stations before Villefranche where Dev had said they would get down. Another half hour.

Then they were in the station at Nice: Nice a smooth indentation of the coast line, the great hotels backing away from the town up on the hills, glass and bright towers. It was all a brilliant confirmation to Lou of her newly awakened insights into happiness. And then the mountains came close in and they were just at the sea's edge once more ducking through tunnels, with cliffs below them fringed by white foam.

In all crevices in the rocks were small gardens. In places high retaining walls had been constructed to hold the earth in place. These plots were planted especially with carnations against the time of the carnival approaching now. Few of the flowers were in bloom yet but here and there color would show.

Then after a moment they arrived at the lonesome little station on top of the high cliff, Villefranche, and there Dev bade her alight. Only a few others got down. The privacy, the light, the mountains, the sea, at once appealed to Lou; then as she turned she looked out over that narrow bay, far below her, with the wooded promontory behind which lay Beaulieu to the left and the old fishing port of Villefranche itself off to the right. Inaccessible, it seemed at first, approached, as she saw later, only by a footpath beside high walls stuck with cactus and overhung by flowering vines. It was a land of grave promise, gray rocks and the sea—but packed with brilliant light and a keen air.—No wonder they can play tennis in this country.

Three old men in blue blouses put their things into a small hand-cart and started off up the hill, over the bridge that crosses the railroad track and then up the path and down the path to the village. Lou and Dev came behind with their wraps and lighter grips.

To Lou it all continued an inexpressible joy. The old narrow streets by their quaintness seemed to be unlocking a long unused delight. She wanted to pat on the head the little boys whom they passed and who paid no attention to them. But she took tight hold of Dev's arm instead and kept looking into the small dark windows of shops down three steps below the street and below the natural level of the eye, with strings of onions and peppers—in the Italian style—hanging outside before them. The place was full of smells.

Evans explained that the city had belonged to Italy until modern times In places the streets were precipitous, paved with flat stones, narrow, with the gutter in the center, and went often down irregular flights of steps, dark and not always sweet smelling—yet it was a delight to Lou.

The men they met wore round blue caps. Many were dressed as sailors, though as the lovers found later this was an affectation—for the most part—since few of them had more concern with boats than with those in which they took tourists for a good price on short rowing trips about the bay in summer.

Following the old men with the luggage they passed the central fountain in a tiny square with a strong smell of wine barrels about it; there were all manner of tiny stores with small windows showing caps, dried figs, and other handy merchandise for sale, but all small, dark. Now it would be a smell of cheese, or they'd come to a baker's shop—or it would be cloth in bolts they'd pass, emerging at last into a diminutive plaza with steps leading up to the right to the church and down to the left again to the wharf and the Hotel Boston by the sea.

Before stopping their march, the two Americans, unused to such a February, walked to the edge of the stone wharf and looked down into the blue clear water, seeing the pebbles and rusty débris below them under the movement of quiet waves.

Oh Dev, how wonderful it is just to be here.—At the back of the hotel were two old men smoking. Boats were fastened to iron rings in the massive stones of the wharf. The two were ever filled anew with the charm of the place, its diminutive self-sufficiency, its antique streets and the near lovely sea.

They ate supper in the quiet, rather English hotel which pleased them—with its family air—not at all, and went off on a ramble in the dark looking for a better lodging.

Finding none at that hour, all the inhabitants it seemed having gone to rest bird-like with the setting sun, they went down beyond the hotel keeping beside the sea on the little dock and there lay back across the still warm stones where the sun had beat an hour before. Phosphorus flashed in the water but from a third story window someone emptied some slops near them. A little sobered, they turned back to the hotel for that night at least. The beacon on the point beyond Beaulieu kept flashing its circular flare across the face of the village every forty seconds. It flashed into their room.

IX

THE VILLA ST. DENIS

In the morning, waking refreshed after a good sleep which they had both badly needed, having breakfasted, they set out again determined to find a more congenial lodging. Unused to such a February the two Americans walked again to the edge of the stone wharf just back of the hotel to look down into the clear blue water, seeing once more the pebbles and rusty débris below them under the movement of quiet waves.

An old fellow, in a sailor suit, was leaning from the stern of a rowboat fastened to the wharf, slowly, carefully fishing for sea snails by means of a split stick. And in the sun, leaning their chairs back against the rear wall of the hotel were two men idly smoking. As on the evening before, the lovers were ever filled anew with the Idyllic charm of the place beside this lovely sea.

To Lou especially it seemed a promise fulfilled which she could not fathom. A light, it was, piercing a cloudy northern morning. She had not been at ease in the large city of Marseilles. Here she seemed to have come to rest. They intended to stay here a month at least.

The Villa St. Denis

It was a perfect day. They took a path south of the hotel through the square below the town and, keeping to the left on along the edge of the sea, they soon found themselves going close above the water by a narrow paved walk hanging to the face of a great wall. At its feet to the left the sea crashed in noisy rushes among the gray honeycombed rocks. They stopped by the handrail to watch the water brilliantly at play when they became aware of groups of soldiers sauntering toward them and passing to go into the town. Evans recognized the famous blue devils of France, officers and men, the *Chasseurs Alpins,* by their broad berets and dark blue coats, their hobnailed boots clacking and grinding on the creamy, smooth stones of the hanging walk.

At their feet the sea pounding in churned itself to whiteness in the gray honeycombed rocks.

Smell it, said Lou as they passed on above the beating surf. That's not the ocean smell.

No, it is less—less something. It is fresher perhaps. Perhaps it is because there is no tide here.

No tide? said Lou. Isn't that part of the ocean?

No tide. The tideless sea. So there is never any exposed sea bottom, as there would be every day at low tide on the Atlantic, and so, I suppose, that is the reason there is less smell.

Going round a bend of the old fortress wall, a hundred feet further ahead the hanging pathway terminated and the lovers came out upon a new vista—a modern extension of the old town, small villas and gardens, at the foot of the hill on which, higher up, lay the road to Nice.

And two hundred feet further on, close by the water, stood the entrance to the barracks of the *Chasseurs*.

Inside the gate there was a long parade ground at the edge of a deep blue basin formed to seaward by a breakwater with a small circular lighthouse at the near end.

To this they crossed on a footbridge and continued back along its top to the lighthouse, getting a fresh view of the basin, the barracks and the hill back of them over the water from that vantage. Outside, churning waves broke continuously against rough granite blocks buttressing the sea wall. It was a delightful ramble and one they would take many times under varying conditions thereafter. But now they did not delay but turned back in quest of a new lodging.

Emerging from the barracks entrance they found a broad wagon road leading up outside the old fortress, zigzag to the top of the steep hill. In the first elbow of this road lay a garden, all fenced in with a modern woven wire barrier. Inside there was a man in slippers and pajamas, beside small orange and lemon trees in fruit, leaning over some plant beds. Lou and Evans looked at each other and smiled, thinking of the man's pleasure.

The gardener, a stoutish fellow of forty, straightened himself and looked hard at them as they began to walk up the road which turned at the end of his garden and led back climbing toward the hilltop. The entrance to the house was upon this road a little further uphill. There was a ticket on the door. Rooms to rent! It was enough.

The rest of the day passed in transporting and arranging their things and there Dev undressed her when, supper done, they sat until after midnight, the two of them wrapped in a single quilt, the windows wide open, watching the darkness and the lights.

X

FIRST DAYS

NEXT morning, the second of February, at six, Dev was awakened by a great fanfare of trumpets. Jumping up he opened the jalousies and looked out on the narrow bay: the water was placid and blue. To the right in the parade ground of the *chasseurs* the band was marching up and down at drill, blowing by squads, *corps de chasse* carrying the tune at a great clip, then, at the proper moment, the rest would fling up their trumpets, twirl them high overhead with a flash in the sun and redouble the intensity of the clatter with their tara tara. Over and over again they played the same tune. It was stirring. From the narrow balcony Evans saw that it was lovely in the garden. A small tree with eight or ten tangerines among its brilliant green leaves was just beneath the window.

Turning about in the dimly-lit room he looked at Lou, still sleeping, with her arms thrown above her head on the pillow, the loveliest arms he had ever in his life beheld, he thought. She was breathing softly. He sat beside her watching her as she slept. He had never been quite so happy.

First Days

Breakfast was served to them in bed by the little Breton maid, coffee and rolls, with fresh butter which she fetched from town every day—walking along the sea wall to get it—and now and again, jam. She was very discreet, very solicitous and very prompt, was Gäite.

That first melting week the lovers were ravished merely by each other's presence. Everything they could think of that they wanted to do they did, repeatedly, lovingly under all the moods of day and night. And over all, before which they worshiped together at night, she full of growing certainty and he near her in everything, they discovered the parallel by day in the Mediterranean spring, caught by the gray mountains behind the edge of the sea—a clarity that picked out flowers and fruit and the faces of men—as if they had been preceded by Ariel or an eerie attendant who fulfilled all promises.

Sometimes they would stand talking for an hour at the rail of the hanging walk leading back to town, watching the waves as he watched her about the room, at first faintly diffident in posture—or was it the cold, for it was still cold most times.

There were nights when they lay hand in hand for hours while Dev spoke of—the things he would be doing. Her comments were foreign to the matter but to the point if one changed his perspective and this Dev could do quickly to enjoy her. She melted, melted, melted under his delighted warming love which was an extraordinary south to her—until she was nearly freed from everything that had been America.

Evans now set himself seriously to work writing. Lou did not interfere with this, she was rather glad of it. She walked, played tennis and read by his side. They walked together or she went with friends they soon encountered in the village to play on the courts at Beaulieu. He would wait on the balcony to see her returning down the garden path, which she invariably did, swinging along, head erect, eyes slightly raised as if in contemplation of a world bright and in fact visible. At such moments, he would be filled with the greatest admiration and love, waiting to receive her fresh from her athletic exertions and the bath.

At first her postures were staid. She would sit with her head a little bowed or lie curled up and smile at him. Often he watched her standing fixing her hair with arms raised in classic style.

He followed the smoothness of her back with the straightness of the hips or looked at her turned a third from him. Lou had had a great deal of petting—a strong taste of love in the American style as a girl—had been more or less engaged (as it is said) for a year to a boy of her own age.

They early found it necessary to have a fire burning in the hearth—a fire of oak roots, dug for the most part from stumps on the hills, stumps of trees long-felled. But the chief delight to Dev was in the mere presence of this kind of simple wonder, this curious variant of himself—moving about: A woman—lovely and young. Let me see, let me see! these were his constant words. He covered her with admiration all day long.

And, accompanying them always, outside, was the garden. Narrow paths bordered the little beds where, in a curious mixture, chrysanthemums, roses and potatoes grew. There was a grape trellis and chickens, two of them, in a little coop by the sago palm, and oranges and lemons and tangerines were in the small trees.

Each day it would be something new to be done or seen. There were several of the walks, however, they took nearly every day. The favorite was the one they had first enjoyed down to the parade ground then out by the tiny drydock to the breakwater's end where you could see a red light burning at night. Here, outside the breakwater, an old man would be fishing sometimes, while inside, in the basin, one could look down ten, twenty feet to the bottom and see small fish going about in the green water half way down playing follow the leader.

One day it was stormy—Lou was afraid. She had been indolent that night. There was no rain but gray waves filled the harbor. A small French cruiser squadron had come in and lay now rocking at anchor off to the left. It was beastly cold. Looking out over the gray sea, Evans saw the periscope of a submarine.

Dev, what is to become of us? said Lou at his side.

The submarine made straight in, rising slowly to the surface. Spray dashed from its prow. In the heavy sea, for some reason, it made a great turn, throwing up a white circle and headed out again. As it reached the heavier waves out ˙ le, it submerged once more till only the periscope could with difficulty be seen slicing the rough water.

It was the end of the first week,—the all-absorbing adoration of the white body was past now. Dev could close his eyes and see her standing, lying, walking, every shadow and movement familiar to his retentive eye.

XI

CERTAIN DAYS

I'VE got to go out.

Threatening as it was, they put on their things and
fled down to the walk before the old fortress. The waves
were pounding in now so that it was almost impossible
to pass. There were three bad places. They watched the
water as with a great roar it came in. Crash. The walk
was inundated. Milky white the recoil churned in the
hollow rocks. They passed and took the tram for Nice.
At the entrances to private grounds on the cliffs, blood-
red cactus flowers and mimosa and geraniums were blossoming; and in the commercial gardens were pinks and
daisies to their right. Restless and dissatisfied in Nice they
walked along the boulevard des Anglais—past the great
hotels. Wealth, English and French; a savor of undesir-
able sophistication chilled their mood completely. Over-
awed by the flood of inanity, or forbidding nonentity,
they scarcely knew where to turn.

A few dolled-up old women on the raised hotel em-
placements looked curiously at them. Now and then
someone would turn to stare at Lou. She was disturbed;

they walked rapidly from one end of the esplanade to the other.—Dev, take me out of this. I hate it. But turning into the city, through the public square, she felt somewhat easier. At a little dress shop facing the park Evans insisted on buying her a new blue dress.

Are we like these people? Dev, tell me.

No.

By chance they came upon a restaurant, which seemed to promise delight. It proved the find of their sojourn; to this they returned again and again,—for the Châteaubriand, the curiously crisp onions, the pears. Evans wanted to stay on and drink, but after an hour Lou would have no more of it. They hired a taxi, as it was beginning to rain, to take them back to Villefranche— as to a cloistered spot and, locking themselves in their rooms, Lou embraced her lover with greatest abandon. She sobbed. Dev undressed her in the dark as she lay relaxed unprotesting before him. Her body seemed to give off a soft light, lying there as if forgotten by her spirit of anguish.

From now on Lou was changed. She flew gayly about the rooms or went off for walks by herself while he was writing. She even came to Dev with her attentions, playing seriously, free—not noticing her own movements as she had done at first. She began to talk to the Madame in her broken French. On the sunny chairs under the arbor downstairs she would sit while Madame made her practice the words.

Not orange but *oránge*.

Citron. La mer. Un chien. They would laugh. Dev would hear them as he was typing his MSS. or reading or—he would find them there together when he would come back from an errand in the town.

One day they decided to climb the mountain back of the village. So they set out after breakfast through the old town and then the upper town and so up and up, to a path that redoubled on itself, a red dirt path, up, up zigzag until they seemed to be right above the roofs of the houses, with gardens of carnations near them and below them the mossy red-tiled church and far off beside the harbor their own home. The Mediterranean spread out its blue cloth, carrying tiny battleships, little tracings of waves and a V-shaped creeping line moving slowly where a small boat was coming to the shore.

Higher and they were in the midst of oak woods, oak and pine with gardens beside an old house by the wayside, the road passing the front and then crossing higher in the rear above. Old olive trees were there. Goats. A jackass. With a cry of pleasure Lou came upon her first violets. Up, until they were quite beyond the village and out in a rugged wilderness—with the sea shining, less marked by waves, over the tops of scrubby trees which seemed to start from the very rocks. They were exhilarated by the climb.

Still up they went with asphodel by the road and some pink daisies, daisies and violets again, until, quite unexpectedly, they were standing on a concrete road, with a roadhouse beside it and autos passing frequently by. It was the upper Corniche road. Winded and thirsty they went into the musty little inn there, where they drank some bottled beer and the old woman of the place presented Lou—as they were going out—with a bunch of narcissi she had picked in the garden. Dev wanted to pay her but the old woman turned quickly away into the house, bowing her head and smiling at them as they waved their hands and departed.

They decided not to take the auto road but instead crossed it and followed a narrow cartway which seemed to promise more pleasure. As they entered it, there was before them a half broken almond tree in blossom. To the left was Nice. But to the north they saw the pure white snowy caps of the Alps, range on range of jagged points, more and more misty as they disappeared into the distance. But the chief charm was that between the lovers and that mountainous snow field was a deep, deep valley right below them with green fields and a tiny silver river flowing through.

They walked now differently than ever they could have done in their lives before. They seemed to be alone. All that they could do, all that they could say to each other, had been done and said, for sheer necessity and delight. They walked and the movement of walking warmed them against the cutting wind.

Here, almost in fear lest a bandit should assault them, they wandered for two hours, resting and playing, picking almond blossoms, looking below into the valley, over at the snow mountains or up into the honeycombed rocks where asphodel grew thickly among the nameless stubble and low growth—up to the summit of bare rounded rock at the right.

Occasionally there would be diversion, rock-clefts that were dripping and dark, then to the left again a parapet where they would lean and look directly down—like gods—amused or merely curious at some farmhouse below.—Come, Dev, do not lean so far over.

But the fascination of the drop held them both and they would look.—So isolated. Alone. The two.

Then they came out on the main road again at Upper Ese.

It was noon now. Here they found a small outdoor restaurant with sunny tables, no company but a small pup and the proprietor, the most genial in the world. They were tired and flushed, hungry and parched, the food was good but the wine, a bottle of old Pommarc̓, cold perhaps as it should not have been, proved the final dot of perfection to their enjoyment.

After dinner, stiff, sore of foot, they didn't know whether to cut downhill to the sea and so turn back home or to go on. So they began walking, going round behind the inn where a very old man was knocking some kind of fruit from a vine covering a high arbor—and the road was peppered with over-ripe olives fallen from an old tree nearby.

Loosened in joint and in spirit they ended toward five o'clock by reaching the sea-rimmed botanical garden of the Prince of Monaco where in the caves below the museum they saw his delicate collection of submarine flora and small fishes—having covered about twenty miles in the day. Then by train they rode back dreamily along the sea to Villefranche.

Another day they spent the whole morning about the barracks, watching the soldiers at their work and at drill. A machine gun squad was charging down the parade ground under the eye of a superior officer. Each man carried a detached part of the mechanism heavy to carry. They would rush ahead, drop to the gravel at command, and assemble the parts in violent haste as the gunner, with his beret pulled down covering his face, took his position at the breech ready to fire.

Another day they walked out to the immaculate lighthouse at the point of Cap Ferat, footing the red walks of the former Emperor Franz Joseph of Austria.

Another day it was the chilly *Carneval* at Beaulieu, the first one of the season thereabouts. And it was for this the little round-faced men had been blowing all those weeks. There they were, assembled all, with bouquets in their coats, ready in the center of the court. Dev remembered with delight the efforts of the drill sergeant to make them perfect in their parts, how he had rushed up to one of them nigh apopleptic from his recent efforts and cried out: *Vous avez jouer de la salté aujourd'hui!* and how the man had taken it without the quiver of a muscle. Now the decorated carriages and autos were approaching. Small bunches of fresias, carnations, violets, stocks, mimosa, were flying through the air. One thrifty woman was picking up the best of the fallen missiles, carefully brushing and inspecting them to take them home, perhaps to sell them again in Nice later. It was very cold that day.

Many days, after the first week, Lou would be at Beaulieu playing tennis with an English lady she had met in the village. These visits to Beaulieu became more frequent as time went on.

But most days they would just bask in the sun, in the garden, on the balcony or the rocks, just soaking in the beneficent Riviera sunshine, an all-sufficient plenitude that ripened fruit and drew the sweet up in the trees and the alyssum to cover the rocks everywhere. The moat of the old fortress where the soldiers practiced rifle-fire was not far from the zigzag road to the top of the hill. Its edge was unguarded. The drop was forty feet at least—a sheer drop—to the trampled grass below. Another day they sat in the Casino at Nice, drinking cognac until two a. m. Walking to the beach, half drunk, a wave came up out of the dark and drenched them to the knees.

Another cold rainy day they sat by the oakroot fire in their rooms and Lou slept lying heavily half on the floor, half in his arms until he carried her into bed.

Another day he watched the old men, early in the morning from a boat in the harbor hauling in their net, laboriously, skillfully, dextrously, and catching nothing.

One evening they went to the tiny café just outside the barracks entrance with its bar stuccoed to represent a rock, a submarine picture, where the shrieking, squealing gramophone was playing interminably: Yes, we have no bananas—while the soldiers got up from dominos or cards to fox trot with each other in their heavy shoon. The drinks though were good. Now and then the daughter of the house would dance serious-faced, as if for the ten thousandth time, with one of the men, or more often, with one of the non-commissioned officers who fraternized with the others. It was a very small, very poor room with about eight tables in it, and situated twenty feet beyond the entrance to the barracks gates which were never closed.

In the town one day an agent—at the Credit Lyonnaise—wanted to sell them a place at Beaulieu for 500,000 francs. Evans smiled.

Then one day in the fourth week Lou came in from tennis, hot and uncommunicative, and waited to prepare herself for the bath. Dev went out to watch the waves.

When later he turned and saw her waving to him from the balcony he stood for a moment, watching her, unable to move—he could not tell why. Then he walked slowly back along the path.

Lou embraced him as usual in the room. Then she told him her story.

She became panicky once the excitement bred by the relation of the new adventure had passed.—Dev, dear Dev! What else could I do? You can't blame us, Dev, if we do marry rich men, can you?—He agreed with her that it was right. She had been proposed to by a man she had met at the courts,—an Englishman—and she had fallen.—He is rich, Dev, rich! Do you know what that means? What do I care, now?

That night he walked late and alone. Lou had gone to Beaulieu to a dance. In the little village of Villefranche whose streets even at this early hour were black, deserted, he stopped before a small inn. There was a great twanging of guitars inside and men's voices singing. He paused to listen. The laughter and the singing continued when suddenly the door burst open and a young man came out. Standing against the wall he let out a great hissing stream accompanied by a prolonged windblast, then suddenly seeing Dev, and laughing as if slightly embarrassed, he called out:

Ça fait du bien au corps, and went in again.

That she should go, he was prepared for that; but for this other—he was not prepared. That she would leave him he had sensed long since; but in this other, his sense had failed him. He had believed that he was going on. He had believed it, lived it for three months past, after all these years.—And nothing had happened.

· Now he must go back, he must go back like a beaten dog. But the sheer sense of Lou's loss rose keenest in him for the moment and he was crushed.

When he got back to the rooms, she was not there. He was wild with anger and jealousy. He lay watching the light of Cap Ferat; an evil eye it flashed back and forth across his window which he did not close. When Lou did come in, an hour later, he started up wildly to see her.

She flung herself into his arms.

XII

THE LAST NIGHT AT VILLEFRANCHE

Lou was speaking. Her voice was sure.—I'm not telling you everything I know and have felt, dear. You wouldn't want me to. You have made me know it would be ridiculous. Just say to yourself that I have decided to go it alone. You have been tender with me, you have sprinkled me with love as if I were some delicate flower. I love you for it but I didn't really need it. I shall never forget you. I love you, Dev, in the way I can, more than anything in this world. I'd marry you to-morrow if there would be any sense in it. I'll marry you to-morrow anyway if you want me.

He did not answer.

You see. You do not want me. You know that I could cling to you, if I wanted to. I could marry you, you know I could, I could return and live with you back there and life would be just hell for us both. Wouldn't it? And yet we have been happy as angels here. It is only that this is the end—for us. We have been happy and—that is all. Now I'm going on. So are you.

She did not know what the devil he was thinking.

You see, Dev, she continued; he did not answer but held her close to him; she pushed him gently away—Dev, I am not literary. I don't give a damn about all this talk of art and writing. It's all right for you and it may mean much—I don't know. Perhaps it does, but it's nothing to me. You have taught me enough to know that that doesn't make it good or bad or right or wrong either way—but it is not for me. I can't stand those people. They seem weak, inane, even the best of them seem to be putting on their pained lives—for what? I can't see it. I want to marry someone with more—I'm not afraid to say it. I want to marry a man who has a place. I have to have it. I want money—

Oh, Dev dear, perhaps I'm making excuses, but sometimes you seem—Dev, there's something the matter with you. You don't register. What in the world are you about? What does the world mean to you? You don't seem serious. You frighten me. Really, I don't understand you. I want someone I can understand. You are—You should protest more. You shouldn't lie there and take this. Why don't you do something about it? What is the matter with you?

He got up and looked out at the bay, quiet in the dark. —Blond break-up.

To be young, to be gay, to be clever, and not to know where one is going, nor why, nor how? Very well. Less intoxicating is to go differently.

But he felt lonesome and depressed. He was conscious of a lack of feeling—it was true. His design seemed frivolous beside the warm surge of Lou's realistic impulses.

By marriage you do not do a serious thing but a frivolous one—you shift responsibility back upon a crowd of instinctive, senseless—

Whoa! cautioned Lou.

Yes, you do, you lay off a burden—the necessity of invention.

The next day they left the place, together, for decency's sake.

There were two trains, going in opposite directions, due at the station within ten minutes of each other. No one was there to see them depart. Dev kissed Lou and put her on the train for Marseilles and Paris. She stood at the window looking at him with a wry face and half-laughing, half-tearful eyes. Then the train moved and was gone, only a whiff of sulphurous smoke coming back from the tunnel's mouth where Lou had disappeared. When she had said she would marry him anyway, he had been startled for a moment, thinking, My God! maybe it's going to happen now after all.

II

AT THE ANCIENT SPRINGS
OF PURITY AND OF PLENTY

XIII

THROUGH TO ITALY

As EVANS crossed to the other track to be ready for his own train, he had suddenly a luminous conviction that spring was definitely at hand. Lou! he called after the departing train, but it sounded hollow. She had gone and he was relieved, though he strongly suspected that under this lay something else which would make itself known later. He dared not think of certain days, passing backward forever and yet still close at hand.

He seemed to himself to be standing in the noon sun, waiting on the east bound gravel walk at Villefranche for a train that was to take him to Italy.—Well, so he was. What of it? He had not known he would be so utterly indifferent to his loss. Lou, he said again, and it meant—almost nothing. He looked down at the bay, rippling below the cliff, and unexpectedly wished to God he could drop through the air into it and never breathe again, yet the thought seemed pleasant.

But out of the tunnel burst with a great clatter the engine of his own train. In another few moments comfortably seated he was moving beside the same old road which they had taken several times during the weeks just past to Monte Carlo—but this time he was going through!

Good-by, Villefranche. He strained to look back to see if he could see the Villa St. Denis. When he succeeded, then truly he felt a hard stab of pain. But it merely made him set his jaw a little and turn away.

It is impossible to live, that is all. What could we have done more?

There for the last time he saw it, the same small red-roofed village at the bottom of the bay protected by the old fortress, tufted with straggly palm trees, and finally—as if they had broken through the confinements of the old town, as they had—the few modern villas stretching out at the foot of the rocky cliff beyond the fort by the blue, blue water. It was a swiftly fleeting view which disappeared rapidly as the train gained speed. Already they were at Beaulieu. A beautiful day. Three girls were walking slowly along a street leading from the station out toward the Cape. They did not even turn around as the train pulled in and came to a stop.

Impossible to live, impossible to live, impossible to live.—But impossible; therefore the arts have authenticity. All attempts at directness end in stupidity. Just to go, that's all—to turn into a steam engine with eyes. While, deeper down—Italy is there, where once men lived, not like me. What can I have done? Insane to lose her, insane to keep her. But the jog of the train was growing more and more restful, working a drugging power to take him from his mood into its own.

The train having passed Beaulieu ran close to the water with the fortified gray hills always to the north. Evans knew every foot of the way—and with happiest recollections to move him to emotion. But by now he had sallied out from his body where it sat slumped in the corner of the compartment, numbed to rest, while, in imagination at least, he enjoyed a freedom to come and go as he would, even in the running train, a sense split off from feeling.

Gardens came up to the tracks like wild deer in wonder of the passing train.

There was a hotel at B—with a blackish cliff behind it, hollowed out.

At the station at Monte Carlo there was fashion; English faces, long, assertive, bored, puerile, excited, demanding service; Americans, less noisy, more alert, getting to the right place at once without noise. There were French idlers in caps, porters looking up and down blandly or smiling at the foreigner—at Monte Carlo where they shoot captive doves over the sea, and old, brass-faced women and men like galvanized corpses sit by the gambling tables the night long. Exotic, fat-leaved plants grow in beds before the Casino.

Mentone! where Lou and he had gone one day with her delightful English lady friend and another. What a day! Snow up there. They had driven the whole way to Sospel in a taxi, stopping just a moment for a rest at the abandoned hilltop town of Castillon, a wild, inaccessible place, just grass and falling walls.

Sospel! Do you remember the cats under the tables right in broad daylight?

Then the hike back, the taxi following us, snow and asphodel again, and the old olive trees—marking the road with dropped fruit as if they had been old goats tethered there.

She gave Lou a great bunch of cornflowers, stopped the taxi in Mentone to buy them on the way back, a great armful of cornflowers.

That was a humane gesture; if one understood that fully, life would be pushed ahead two hundred years, no doubt. Two thousand more likely. Sospel, high up like a bell ringing in the mountains, holding time back, telling: stupidity breeds fast. We go ahead and leave the best back of us.—High up there, cold in the sun.

Impossible to live. From Sospel, we walked back to Castillon, we four, two by two, half a mile between us, alone on the road, the taxi following. That's sense, plain sense. We were tired. We talked. Impossible to make such things last. Only stupidity breeds. Sospel, like a bell, the bell of the asphodel, green, odorless—flower of Hades, flower of the dead.

So he heard himself talking pleasantly, without feeling, watching the words fall.

She was frightened the way that damned fool taxi guy took the upcurves cutting out near the edge of the precipice! Why in hell was she the one of us to be frightened? Lou just didn't notice it. Damned risky business though.

Hour after hour the train clicked on, hour after hour lulling him, wheedling him—away. The sea was always at his right all the afternoon, cold looking, flecked with light; the shore was pebbly and yellow.—The sunless sea gives up out of its body, fish.

He forgot the train; he himself slid forward—he alone, trainless—he, the train itself—alone. The sea, a fusion of metals, the zanthrochromic sea.—Now, never dropping back to feeling, he was all eyes. The world existed in his eyes, recognized itself ecstatically there. This then was real: all he saw—but not in man. Therefore never could he look long into the eyes of anyone: that, neither they nor he could stand. Elsewhere, everywhere he saw reality, split, creviced, multiplied. The brilliant hardness of the world, clear, full of color and outline, depth, shadow, reaffirming light, filled him with security and contentment. The seasons were to him like four fruits: one of glass, one of wood, one of the most luscious flesh and one of snow. He could see them clearly, plucked upon a board, in a dish—only one of them perhaps to be eaten and that incidentally, quite by accident. Toward them one did not extend the hand.

All along the shore the train ran looking at the sea out of one eye—and by the sea whole families of fishermen, French perhaps or Italians, were pulling in the red nets in the lowering sun, pulling them up, children,

women and men, all together, up upon the yellow peb·
bles, miles of pebbly coast about them. Why just here?

A presence there is, a thing that lives here always, al·
ways unaffected by man, always wild. A god be damned.
That was a Greek affectation because they were fools like
the rest of us—but a presence there is hears the waves
rattle upon the stones.

Ino. Who the devil was Ino? Ino weaving strands of
seaweed or something like that, on the polymorphic
pebbles.

Palemon, shaker of bright seastaff: like glass, a green
glassy spear with the sun shining through it, emerald
green—

He saw at Ventimiglia, the first stop over the border,
Italian troops entraining. He saw prominent among them
a stalwart and very much excited young man. His helmet
was circled with a garland of leaves and flowers. On
either side of him was a younger man, his brothers per·
haps. One was embracing him excitedly, kissing him
again and again, crying and hugging him and being
hugged in return. All about the station it was going on,
but this group was the cap of it all.

Leaving Ventimiglia, in Italy now, he saw on the gray
hills low hovels of gray stone. He could hear in his mind
the rasping voices of the old women, he could smell it,
tell it all, every detail known, the dirt in the wrinkles,
the pisswet nether clothes of the brats, the tan and grime
wrestling, the hair stuck together at the ends, growing
from the scaly scalps, from poor soil—

Through to Italy

Ç'est lui, l'homme qui ne tue pas les moustiques!
He fell asleep finally.

At Genoa it was near midnight when he awoke with a start to realize that the train was dead in the dark station. The people were leaving it, dragging all their belongings with them. He hurried and got out also.

XIV

NIGHT

GENOA. The name sounded hollow, depressing as the coldly sulphurous gallery through which he was passing, baggage in hand, to the wicket. He had not wanted to stop here. It annoyed him not to have foreseen this compulsory arrest. He felt stiff of limb, stripped of all pleasure, bewildered.

No, I do not want a hotel. I want to check this stuff.

He knew no Italian. The porter shrugged and walked away. Evans wandered around aimlessly until he found the check room. 12:05 to Florence. Thank God. Only two hours to kill.

The waiting room was gloomy, deserted. He walked out into the fresh air. Two drunks exaggerated in size by their shadows were doing a slow motion wrestling match among the heavy columns of the station portico. Evans began to stray off in the dark into the space of the great *piazza* before the station. The whole neighborhood seemed desolate. He had no idea in what direction he was going. He feared he might get lost if he went too far.

The harbor, he said to himself walking on. It was the

only thing about Genoa that stuck in his memory to attract him.

To the left the houses seemed to rise, one above the other in an endless embankment. He could not see the tops. They passed up into the murk. The stores near at hand were all shuttered. No one was in the streets. He wondered if he were going in the right direction. Didn't know how to ask. Gradually a nameless panic grew upon him. His heart beat fast. The sea can't lie this way. He turned back.

Behind him at the far end of the street whither he had been going a wild shouting burst out. Turning once more, he saw a small crowd passing under a street light, yelling and dancing. Boys, young men, they were. They were singing, hugging each other, running about, taking in the whole street, arm in arm. He caught the word— *Giovanessa,* many times repeated. For a moment they stopped, wavered, arguing loudly among themselves, then turned and hurried off whence they had come.

Evans resumed his way back to the station. Yes, one store was open, a shallow booth in the wall of dark houses. He smelled coffee and asked for a cup. Steam spouted with a roar from the nozzle,—he thought the machine had run dry: *Café expresso.* What a relief to get away from French coffee, the one thing he could not get used to in France. He swallowed the burning hot thimbleful of dark liquor gratefully.

His legs tingling now from the drink, he decided to strike in, to take one of the narrow streets leading among the tall houses, and climb the hill to see what he could see. Perhaps from there one might get a view of the lights of the harbor in the distance.

I'll never see the sun in Genoa.

Steps, hill upon hill, street lights at the bottoms of funnels. *Giovanessa*—arm in arm, drunk, *Giovanessa*—a mob shouting drunk—towers going up into night without top. No direction. No north, no south. Only the street to the railroad station; home. Lonely stairs, up, up—nowhere. Where is the sea Columbus sailed on?—He could see nothing but a very close darkness. He mounted. The way grew still. Two men in evening dress, one stout, the other smaller, passed down talking volubly. There was a desolate garden, empty benches, trees he did not know.

Alarmed lest he should miss his train, Evans sought to make certain his way out. Coming to a small open space at a certain level, with an electric bulb glowing above him at the far edge, he went to the edge which was a stone parapet, and looking down saw again the station sleeping below him. Up, up above were walls and lights. An overbearing weariness possessed him as if he were dead—and yet he must go on. He was dead yet his limbs, endlessly weary, would not lie down. They carried him—they would carry him now. He put his hand out as he had done at night to touch Lou's thigh and rest it there. His arm fell upon the stone.

Genoa! A city of nameless terror. From the parapet he looked down resting his breast against the stone, his heart pounding from the climb. The station! He leaned

124

against the edge of the stone wall and looked down upon its roof, the cyclopean clock's eye marking the advancing hour yellowly.

There he leaned alone for eight thousand years, inexpressible weariness having overtaken him. His legs would not move further since there was nowhere to go. He would not go on. There they should find him in the morning. At first they would not notice him but after, they would take him to the hospital; they would notify the American Consul. The Consul came. He was high-minded, intelligent and well off. He looked and ordered the patient to be towed to America by the heels at the end of a line—thrown from the stern of the ship. Evans accepted it; dead he accepted everything thus cast at him. He accepted it. There was no reason why he should fear anything for he was dead. This was a proof.

Waking, he sensed vividly with open eyes the formlessness which terrified him asleep.

Night. Not even an animal. The uselessness of all things froze his heart. All art is terror; one makes in the night. It is still. There is nothing. One is no more a Christian. One does not believe in a life that will be endlessly the same. One does not want anything that life can bring. Life is an insult, an injury thrust upon us. What could have done that?

All knowledge is at an end. Soon we shall have a wakening against the schools and knowledge will begin again. He saw all knowledge vanishing into the apex of a hollow cone—spinning off. Philosophic solitude—a dear delight. But that is philosophy. Alone is not philosophy; it is despair.

The terror of emptiness had come about him, the terror of no form, the poet's ache, and he pressed harder against the stone wall.

What, then, is art? It is a cathedral. No: a cathedral is terror, painted with the four points of the compass. The Egyptians made the pyramids so that by looking through a hole in the rock one could see a certain star; thus it began with a star. But whether you forbid the delineation of animals and men, like the Arabs, or whether it be the image of the devil or a saint—it is nothing but a form of the night. Out of this we make—they make: this is the mother stuff.

It begins at the finger nails—it is these we see and begin with in anguish, the fingers which annoy us, being always in our sight. We pick at them. Or we make, to extend their length.

This is Genoa, they say, because the train stops here and the train never leaves the track. No. It is not Genoa. It is night, upon which the light begins to build but it is night first.

Night is not damned. It is the only thing which is not damned. Because out of it we make what we please. The sun makes the trees and the grass and cows and ourselves by day. But we make of the night arabesques, paintings on cloth, stones cut into shapes. Darkness and despair: These are my home. Here I have always retreated when I was beaten, to lie and breed with myself.

Night

Their cathedrals and their chants are like buttercups to the night which puts them out or brings its stars to sing them to sleep—and adds its moon.

Night. It is the only thing that is sacred. It is ourselves.—And he felt that his body extended to the horizon. It is in the night that we love. It is the generative hour. Of this I am made.

He saw a desolate pantomime far up in the corner of his mind, a world empty and lost. It was not a Christian hell (this to which he had climbed) but one much older. And there sat Bess enthroned.

Weary, weary, weary, inhumanly, inexpressibly weary, he shook against the wall and waited for the train. More certainly now he began to take notice of his hands. He had forgotten that his arms were short. As when a child he woke terrified in his bed and strained to see, hating the dark, he would begin to think of definite things: a bird, a house—so now he looked at his fingers in the lamplight. They looked ghastly, as if dead. But he smiled knowingly and was satisfied. He felt his face.

The night is the body of someone else. Into which we have come.

Then he began to move. He found that leaning on the wall he had rested his legs. His elbows were stiff, aching but he walked down the hill to the station, checked out his baggage, found a compartment unoccupied (and warm) in the Florence train and stretched out. As the train began to glide forward, he fell asleep. Moving again, he slept—moving—slept without a dream.

127

XV

THE ARNO

By DAWN they were at Pisa. The train was still, in a freight yard. The stars were not yet gone. There was a moon in what Evans thought must have been the west. He got up and looked about, as the train began to move again softly, slowly in the gray light, thinking he might see the famous tower. Nothing. They left Pisa behind. So much for Pisa. Again he slept.

He woke greatly refreshed. The sun was up.

Leaning into the window he saw the world of form once more, vineyards, trees in rows to which wires were fastened supporting grape vines newly pruned, long reddish canes awaiting the sun of summer to grow new shoots and grapes. Peasants were coming into the fields. There were magpies, a bird he knew, in the young trees, magpies and crows in the furrows. Now there was grain and garden truck, and orchards pruned and ready. Fields of mustard flower there were and cows and goats, by the light of the early blinding sun. Italy! He did not think of an ancient splendor but of morning and fields and vines.

The Arno

Steadily the train took him into his delight.

The train which understands but a very few words and in the modern dialect only, was approaching that ancient Tuscan city of Florence—but without being impressed. Evans, however, was impressed and began to decorate his spirit with fitting clothes—saying to himself, They speak of these cities as if they were dusty or dead—or with scholarly abated voices.

The train was running beside a narrow winding rivulet.

It was the Arno flooding its banks, from whose liquorous bounty an army of sunbeams were drinking so that the air was luminous with mist and the grass and herbage everywhere was dripping. It was the Arno preparing to bring all its country charm to pass under the old bridge.

It was the Arno, before Florence, gathering tribute from the fields—a workaday river—countryman, maker, poet—poetic river. River, make new, always new—using rain, subterranean springs to make a great bounty.

Florence, city of makers.

To make, that's where we begin. Sooner or later, they call us in, to make up choir benches out of oak trees, make lace out of daisies, the circles out of roses, the white out of our despair—white as despair—totally colorless.

River, you make "the Arno" every day fresher than the greatest artists can make painted flowers: they may

come to you every day for a lesson remembering only
the sea that is greater.

Flow. Flow under the old bridge forever new and say
to it that only that which is made out of nothing at all
is forever new. Make new, make new.

And all the time he was watching the sun clearing the
mists over the wild Arno and seeing it up to the top of
its banks as if with ready fingers seeking to feel in among
the grass. I know that feeling, he said, to be full of
pleasure.

Flow new under the old bridge.

He was jealous of French painting and he was backing
the river against it.

Make new. (And the river meanwhile was getting
broader and going about its business.) One can put the
best painting beside you and judge it by the place where
the small stream joins your cool body. It is there! Nothing is more ordered, more certain nor more flexible, more
passionate, yet chaste.

And all the time he was going to Florence, Dante's
city, city of the old bridge, city of "the David," of
Raphael—and a faint pang of worn beauty struck him.
He wanted to say Giotto—Instead he called it: City of
the Arno, and the Arno before there was a city, teaching
from the fields of Proserpine, the fields of the Vernal
gods. Botticelli, Donatello—now it was nearer. But he
did not care for history. He knew only a river flowing
through March in the sun, making, making, inviting the
recreators—asking to be recreated.

It is the river god singing, that I hear, singing in the morning, asking if all making is ended. What to do?

He saw peasants leading animals, in the cold. Clickety click, clickety clack. People going into Florence began to get into his compartment. Be there by 8:30. They bowed to him, for the most part, with a momentary glance at his strangeness—perhaps; a foreigner. Then they looked out of the windows or talked, or read a paper.

If I were an agent come here to sell American shoes, or ploughs, that would be a common reason.

Idle as a river. Loafer.

I sing and loaf at my ease.

Loaf of bread. The Arno loafs and it is a loaf of which I drink. Pah.

It is drink nevertheless, the richest drink to me, in the morning this way. The natives of Bangkok drink the river and fish half-rotten drowned pigs out of it and roast them and eat them—and live.

Drink of the Arno like that; a kind of artist they are, the natives. Drink. A kind of cholera it is to be wanting to make. Loaf. Catch it from the river.

I caught a little silver fish: Pah.

Throw out both conceptions; reality, romance: it sums up, to make—that's all. Make, and that's the end of it, —if you can.

Fine careful fields, these *are,* their hands are all over them, making the soil, patting it, tying up the vines. Mostly that now. They left off there by that tree yesterday; you can see the willow withes they left there in a bundle last night. Just starting again now. Willow withes they are using, the same willow withes. That's why they cut the trees off pompadour, the willow trees. Get the withes for tying up grapes. Smart men those. Habit. Always do the same thing, year after year. That's work, work is worship.

I'm not in their class. I work home. Cure bellyaches. Come to Italy for something else.

Work home gives me an excuse to loaf now. Does it? If I were a peasant the river wouldn't look so poetic, but it would look more god-like, more real. Poetic it is just the same, even if they can't see it.

Just the same it is the prototype of art. Useless river— as far as itself is concerned. Gathers dewdrops from flower petals just the same. Carries them just the same. Nobody gives a damn. Goes under the old bridge.

The prototype of art just the same. Don't have to describe everything that's in a river any more than we have to say—like Quevedo, when the girls dropped a rose at his feet from the balcony (Mother told me that): That's not the only thing you drop, ladies.

Arno! maker. He was jealous of French painters. Make it. Giotto made colors out of flowers. What of it? No help in that. You must begin with nothing, like a river in the morning and make, make new. Arno! I want you to say this, I want you to take me into Florence from upstream and that is all I want you to say. I want you to say *this* and this *only* for I am making of it my procession.

I make my way out of nothing using what I find by chance: to make—new.

That's ALL I want it to say. I don't care what's in the river.—It was a fascinating view of a river from a train, a swift, bird's-eye view.

The presence of Florence so near now, exhilarated him, flowing in his mind like the Arno, forever recreating its own loveliness. Florence and the Arno and the newness of his despair, his lust to make—fused into an excitement of architecture, painting. By the time the train reached the station, he was filled with eagerness to look at the older things of the city, full of excellence for him to gather, if he would.

XVI

FLORENCE

Too excited, expectant of too much, Florence came to him when his enjoyment was already exhausted. He saw it coldly, through an aura of returning disillusionment which was really a good thing, a lens which sharpened his wit—not always sufficiently discriminating. But for the most part he was bored—after all.

At Cook's in the Via Tornabuoni, after breakfast, he had picked up a card from his sister in Montreux. It was the lake with a Moroccan looking sailboat upon it —laden with brick in all probability, he thought. It said, Hotel Asterial, February 15 (has been lying here two weeks): Shall be here for two weeks longer, Bess.—Bah. He stuffed it into his pocket and went out, stopping to look at the torch-brackets on the Palazzo Maximi. He looked up, Buenarotti's cornice overhung the street, and felt himself affected by the scale of the great windows, the roughness of the structural stone, the mass of the whole façade played upon so softly by the finely felt proportions of everything. This angered him.

He had always been somewhat irritated by the Renaissance anyhow. The crudeness of the material they used, the size, the coarseness even, he ate up with joy— but the touch of the delicate fingers bit into him like an acid.—God damn their impertinence, he cried aloud, to appease his own dullness and sorrow. It is too soft, *nouveau riche;* with their petty imitations of the Assyrian, the Egyptian and the Greek; soft and harsh, brutal and sweet. He found it lying, offensive, this unhappy American with nothing but the offense of New York in his mind to give him stability. Yet it was Florence he was seeing; the jewel of all Italian cities.

From Cook's he walked to the Duomo, with his eyes on the ground lifting them for a moment only at the flower market—But he went on from this as from a sickness.

With contradictory but rapidly mounting savagery his heart craved only that softness, if he must have softness, which might be in stones not flowers; stones cut, jointed —not haply irregular, like those of the Inca fortress walls, but not out of a machine either; made, each stone made. "I Matteo, made this column," he had once read. I'll accept that. So each stone had probably been made, selected first by some craftsman—some peasant, that's it. Some manual man, *that is* "the rock" and the neurasthenic Master puts his softness on it after.

But then he lifted his eyes to Giotto's tower of colored stone, "the shepherd's tower," that quadrangular thrust out of the bare ground, and his delight sprung at once to a brief release. Here it is! No Rome here. No

Greece. Pure Italy, tall, spare, severe, colored, flowerlike. He felt it powerfully—but from afar. It was too bare. too soon, he looked too hard and after all saw just the stones. At least it was hardly sentimental. Curious relic, he thought, finally. It seemed so obvious however that it fast became in his eyes like everything else, dulled.

Through all, he was conscious of the strange Christian influence in everything; he felt it with disgust, with despair. He tried to separate out Italy, the power itself, to tear it from this moss. The incense belonged to Apollo. They had copied their politics from Plato. It all worked so marvelously well, so smugly well. It had drawn in even the makers, warped them to its confounding delicacy.

Disturbed by his reflections, Evans wandered slowly back along the Via S. toward the Palazzo Vecchio on the way passing by chance Donatello's St. Michael, high in the Palazzo Medici east wall, quiet, in his shallow niche, holding his shield before him with womanly delicacy but good wrists; tall, fine of face—a face removed to heaven, contrasting rudely with his rested shield; a sensitive anguish whetting the taste for brutal combat. A wistful longing for contemplations beyond battle seemed just to burst from the moment of waiting. —Donatello has caught it, in his fashion. There it is, a moment, a balance, the time.—But the delicacy was strange to Dev's present mood. Through a mist he saw it and it angered him anew.

And so he came to the great marble David and stood beside that also. The false crudity of Angelo, the delicate

torment drove him wild again. That's Christian, big with
mental anguish, the genesis of which is the impossibility
of fusing the old power with the new weakness. The
pain, the weakening is the charm! Agh! He twisted the
Greek; put the anguish of the soul into it. The Christian
anguish. But why take *that* to torment; the Greek, the
quiet, the perfect, the lovely. No, no!

Evans could not frame it. He felt only the offense in
the David. The too big hand, the over-anxious Jewish
eyes. The neurasthenic size of the thing standing there
in the courtyard with the Judith not far off turning her
face away.

This is not Italy. The David meant nothing to him.
It is lying. It leans on the Greek, which it bastardizes, to
give it a kind of permission. Had to have something to
lean on—so it slimes the anguish over that, trying to unite
two impossible themes.

The next morning he found it to be election day in
Florence. Groups of working men were loafing about the
streets in their Sunday clothes. They seemed orderly and
more or less indifferent to the event; more a *festa* than
a day devoted to serious civic and national duty. Here
and there men stood before a voting place talking quietly:
a small election most likely.

But *carabiniere* and police with guns in hand could be
observed now and then in straw-paved carts going from
place to place about the town: and at the far end of the
Ponte Vecchio, where youths and girls clad in carnival
attire were returning from the old city, the police were

making them remove the masks and show their features before they could proceed further.

To this point Evans followed the crowd, stopping on the bridge half an hour to buy a green aquamarine for his sister at one of the booths. Then he came to the Pitti Palace whose simple fortress-like roughness delighted his mood. There and in the Boboli gardens he spent his time till noon.

In the afternoon he thought he'd take in the Santa Croce. Walking unexpectant across the bare piazza before it, he pushed upon the Cathedral's soiled red leather inner doors and letting them close behind him stood within, waiting for his eyes to penetrate the half light. And there he was overtaken by an emotional reaction, striking back upon him across that rolling floor, that lifted him into an enchantment he would never cease to recall thereafter as long as he should live—nor to enjoy.

He escaped wholly at that first moment the feeling of a church. A double row of widely spaced hexagonal columns held up the flat beamed middle ceiling painted with crude colors, a dark and intricate design of blue and red and gold, orange and green and red; it might have been the flat roof of an old temple. But the floor of worn mosaics, uneven, undulant, irregular, the tomb of saints over whose effigies in bronze and marble he walked; and in the side walls other famous tombs—of Dante, the Medicis; the Pantheon of Florence; it seemed all to him a savage, spacious present; direct, puissant—overwhelming, free, free somehow of all that which he hated.

But, looking toward the room's far end with ever-growing ardor, he stopped in amazement at that wall. It remained a wall, a decorated wall. In the center of it was the altar, a tall, shallow, vaulted alcove molded into the plaster of the place, the plaster painted with a fresco from the history. But on each side of this, standing up, one close beside the other, were the chapels: further, narrower bare alcoves, a rank to right and left, high and pin arched. And on the plaster, here also, figures from the history were painted.

He could not tell the Giotto from the Cimabue, he liked the unknown best—and there he stayed, disturbed in exultation—carried away by awe and antiquity—a presence nearer than the nearest day that he had ever known. It was close, close to him—its simplicity walked about in him, as if he were its garden and by its side he saw himself as he had known he was, but never could draw near enough.

It was a key. It was beauty. The colors of the dark floor, the smoky ceiling—into them he gazed. He sat, he watched a priest unshaven, sick, miserable—he watched him kneel and pray or seem to pray on the steps before one of the narrow painted altars.

Bare, columnar, plaster alcoves, sharp-edged, pointed and undecorated by construction or beading, molding or ledge—save only by the painting upon the plaster paneling, the back and sides; tall sentinels they were, of a strange deceptive holiness—whose fine aberrance from the Christian, Evans was feeling exultantly, a beauty that by its simplicity, not softened, reached back truly outside of church into a sunlight which he identified by his earliest uncaptured instincts—

To-day no resentment against the stucco of a church disturbed him; he drank as if the purity of the source could wash away all sins in fact—and he would come out clean, clean of the world: the bone-cracking, skin-muddying impacts of his life.

Clean! that was to him the purport of it all, a holiness will come out alone if we be clean.

Clean, stripped as were these chapels, colored with oranges and men from the streets—molded into figures—

It was with pain, as if leaving behind the best that was in his life, that he drew off at the warning of the sexton priest—it was dark. They were closing the church, he had been there all the afternoon.

But he had been purified past the walls of any church. Santa Croce held for him an unguessed holiness that had forever blessed him. Clean, the ugly tombs of the masters on the two lateral walls did not disturb him. *Clean, of all that!* It was none of theirs. Village worthys. Men of the place, sleeping. That was all. But a beauty had shone through their work, through it—through its Christian disguises. He, Evans, had been penetrated, he permitted it to penetrate him. A Greek beauty—a resurgent paganism, still untouched.

He went back to the hotel, exhausted, tired, neurasthenic, in no ecstasy but a pale, fragile mood. But the supper tickled him. He had Lacrima Christi which still amused him by its name, he drank much. He bought a Corona Corona—thinking of the Indians who mixed tea berry leaves with their tobacco, and smoked himself dizzy. To bed. To sleep. A marvelous bed.

XVII

TO ROME

Two days later he was on his way to Rome leaving the Arno and its vivid relics gladly behind. He had closed his eyes sharply to, at the height of his enjoyment, at the peak of his understanding. Enough. He had strengthened his understanding of what he had long since discerned. He carried his affirmation away in his pocket—with his time-table.

On his way he saw Cortona leaning upon its slanty rock like a bronzed god in rags, exiled from the centers, inconceivably ancient, yet living, living still of stone and snow with the railroad at its feet, the church its head, high, high in one corner as if ready to take flight, as the imagination does. This was the high point of his trip to Rome, a bare country, savage and untenanted save by drab mountain hamlets and rare names, Assizi, Perrugia and then, toward evening, Orvieto—he thought he would come back to them, but he never did—so eager was he now to get to Rome.

Rome! he could see St. Peter's in the distance. Rome! for an hour the fields had richened, farms, vineyards, orchards, planted fields—the servitors of that city they remained now as then. The Roman Campagna made him aware at once of how the ancient city lived, far from the rocks, surrounded by this great fertile oasis—yet limited. A taste of plenty these fields had offered them in this nook caught in a wild Apennine. River and field, grove and pool, and in the center, by the river, there was a rise in the ground, oaks, elms and a cave or two for shepherds or emperors; a house, a temple and the burning sun. All else came after.

Crossing from the Terminal at the *Piazza delle Therme,* he saw the ruins of Diocletian's baths and the brimming Fountain of the Mermaids squirting its stream of purity and plenty into the evening air. At once he felt the modern capital living upon the ancient like barnacles on rock, the old rock coming through,—and the wash of instinct over it all. Evans was possessed with Rome on the instant of landing there.

But the whole span of the middle centuries was lost for him at that moment, century upon century, and neglect, sleep, decay; followed by the second moody birth, the Popes, the Renaissance, linking old and new in a curious anomaly of beauty and ashes: renunciation, Venus standing as a nun, the head broken off and a cloud only in the cowl—

His room at the Pension Octavia was paved with red baked tiles. There were two iron beds in it; a table by the window with a red-figured cheap tablecloth on it. Outside, the new German Lutheran church shone in the finely grained Italian sun, its soft limestone neatly carved in the saltless modern public manner. Of the two beds he would use the one nearer the window. The door locked with an iron bolt. There was water in a white clay pitcher standing in its basin, a tabourette and chairs, and a wardrobe with weakly locking doors. Small rugs were on the floor. Across the hall he found the bathroom, a long narrow cell with the closet at the far end; this room too was paved with large tiles, but black and white. Its window looked into a little courtyard from which voices came hollowly—Italian voices, the voices of the concierge and his wife.

The host was a German, married to an Italian wife who had been recently delivered of her third infant and so was seldom to be seen. The man kept a decent table, fair wine and served broccoli—not too often. At breakfast next a. m. at the table back of Evans there was seated a German girl, too shy for talk but shining like some heavenly ornament. She had, when he looked at her, the brightest, fairest hair he had ever seen on a girl, and skin and eyes as if newly come into blossom, the inconceivable freshness of a spring flower still remembered in the clarity of her whole being. But he was sullen toward such things now. He saw her looking but he made no reply. He went out to walk.

It was nearly Easter. They had planted masses of variegated cineraria, purple and white and blue and velvet brown, in long beds between the sidewalk and the road approaching the Pincian Gate. As Evans stood watching by these, a youthful Italian army officer drove up to a house door near him in an open carriage. A girl was with him. They sat still, talking in the carriage when it had come to a stop, she with exaggerated interest, he with obvious devotion. She was in a fluffy light-colored summer dress and held an open parasol in her left hand. He seemed striving to detain her, to persuade her. No, she shook her head. She begged him to let her pass. He descended, took her to the door of the house, kissed her hand and she ran in. He paused to light a cigarette.

Evans walked through the Borghese gardens to the wall above the Piazza del Popolo at the foot of which, whither he had fled for safety, the self-wounded Nero was better stabbed by his enemies and died. Here on this hill blossomed once the pleasure gardens of Lucullus. Evans looked out over the city and again across the river he saw St. Peter's.

St. Peter's! The morning gone, he turned back for lunch through the fabulous gardens toward the Via Sicillia—to which, because he had said Cisilia instead of Sichilia, several passers-by had been at first unable to direct him—through the lost pleasure gardens of Lucullus.

At home, in the pension, sullen and lonely—beaten by his oppressive thoughts—he sat down and began to write. It was in Rome, in fact, during these days, that he most made a wife of his writing, his writing—that desire to free himself from his besetting reactions by transcribing them—thus driving off his torments and going often

145

quietly to sleep thereafter. But to-day all day into the night he was especially tormented. He wrote blindly, instinctively for several hours, a steady flow of incomprehensible words and phrases, until he was exhausted and stopped perforce.

He wrote what? that Rome filled him to overflowing with riotous emotions seeking intelligent expression one above the other. What is reality? He was too conscious of the old; to-day slipped too much from him or was too near. Or being alone, he had penetrated too far the veil of dust the gods had thrown up about their secrets to protect them. Thus Rome escaping him, he half sees it as a burning presence under the veneer of to-day. Panting with desire to possess it, he feels it slipping away nevertheless and calls it, strives to call it by a name, strives to fasten it in his sight—real among its everyday disguises.

He feels it real—strives to say this is so. There! There it runs! Or the fictive Rome is undoing him, seeming actual. Already he is too much alone. It is the old problem of reality: which and which? In his desire to be explicit he avoids no word, confuses his least important thrill of the moment with permanence, wants to omit no word, no small itch—in his desire to be explicit, to catch it— fleeting past (thus he writes in a fever of impatience). Reality he sees under the lacquer of to-day.

He was alone, in his room, on a bed. He saw the floor, the tablecloth. He saw it. Then he *saw!* Then he *did* see. Yes, then it is true, what he sees; or which is the reality?

No use to revise—for the presence is fleeting; revise and the thing escapes; only the footprints are left.

He would blink, at his table, and write, striving to cut between the show and the fact as sensible men must do. Rome, undeceiving, living—shedding fig leaves. Rome starting alive from the rock. He felt it, he could touch the fragments. There IS the Venus. There it *is*. Where? There, crouching at the top of the stairs. But that is a stone. No, it is Venus! It is she. No, it is a stone. It is she, I say. Venus! The presence is over the stone.

Evans was near mad with it. He felt himself possessed, bewitched, or else he saw the god.

XVIII

IN ROME

THE next day he changed his seat at the little table in the pension dining-room, where they had put dried figs and raisins wrapped in grape leaves on a flat dish for him; he changed his place so that he could more easily observe the little German girl whom the day before he had noticed. She also had changed her place, no doubt the better to see him, so that now they looked directly at each other over the two tables.

With wide blue eyes she looked full into his own as if amazed to recognize him, which she seemed to do; a curious wonder. Evans wished he might speak to her but instead kept rigid his unrecognizing face. Perhaps she knew English. His German was atrocious. French? He could not talk Italian. What did he care?. There was an older woman with her.

So he looked into her eyes. Clear pools they were certainly; the metaphor was never more apt. It was a Botticellian loveliness—it was *She* standing upon the shell; the hair, the eyes, the flesh that Botticelli had striven to imitate, though this thought did not occur thus

fully to Evans at that time. And she was attracted, beyond
a doubt by his darkness, his eyes—his age maybe. He
turned to his raisins, unwrapping them from the dried
leaves.

Later, it being Sunday, he went out for a walk, a long
walk, turning into the Via Veneto, to the Piazza Bor-
borini, past the dripping, green-stained fountain of the
Tritoni—as if raised newly from the sea—and so on and
on to the river and the Castel St. Angelo. Coming back,
he stopped on the bridge. The Tiber was swollen with
recent rains. The muddy water was whirling under the
bridge arches, great twists of it holding a constant shape
where the stone split the current so that the water seemed
unmoving, the bridge to be rushing upstream.

Wood of all sorts was coming down in the current;
roots, branches, bits of finished timbers, logs, boxes—all
that could float; and on the left bank, where a turn in
the river carried the stuff inshore, men were casting for
it, stray bits of fire-wood, with forked weighted sticks on
a line which they threw over the floating débris, snaring
the wood and bringing it to the shore—if they could.
It was a fine game requiring considerable skill.

Rome filled Evans with thought. It was to him a
public place to which all the people of the world would
come for an answer. All that his mind contained seemed
pressing for review upon this day especially. As he
walked, witnessing the streets, the trams, noting that
here the men kept their shoes always highly polished
and not dull as in Paris; feeling the vivacity, the carefree

youthfulness of the life against the ruins of a grandiose
antiquity; seeing the many horse-drawn cabs whose sure-
footed and well-driven animals were scampering about in
every street—it was like a stream loosening the very
dregs of his semi-northern dreaming. Rome! Over and
over again he said it. It seemed to him to be full of a
motion, a motion of crumbling monuments, himself
crumbling, loosened at the base, the motion of the sun
itself, a stream of light, insuppressible among the ruins.
He felt a quiet happiness beginning far off. He felt a
loosening throughout his own stalled sinews; his whole
body seemed to relax, as if it might fall apart. He thought
perhaps he might be going to be ill, and among flower
venders, dogs, the muddy back entrance to the Queen
Mother's palace, the Facisti boys, the wood in the river,—
through it all, he saw the Cyprian in her awkward German clothes and by her side the other, not her mother,
not her equal surely, no relative—an attendant she was,
but under her control. Evans had to confess, good or ill,
he had never fully admired a girl or woman yet, but
there was more or less of German in her.

It was still very early spring about the city.

He felt the old clarity overlaid, he felt that he wanted
to go on—to that. But that would be to return alone.
All the middle years were forcing him back. That was
what all the middle ages with their curious stirrings,
their religion, amounted to: to drive us back. So he
feared and hated them. She, the little Cyprian, was
poised against that. She was sending him away,

on to a clarity; on, not back. Greece is ahead of us, not back. The Middle Ages are back. He was disturbed.

Yet, breathless, he felt at moments as if he were about to live;—for the first time. The beauty was still there. And not there as a dying essence but nearly triumphant. Nearly! For a moment he saw the gilded Venus. The sullen, drunken modern days of denial, unworship; a barren clarity it was, all that. No clarity at all. The corroding truth. He could not, though, be deceived by romance. What is, is. If the maximum is despair, and all beauty is the flower of ignorance, in the geo-centric universe that Galileo killed, then all the core of his heart was indeed rotten. It is not rotten! Then he was soft—as Jack had said. But in his confusion, he felt—Rome, a hard denial of despair.

He sensed Rome as a trial that should cast him out with the refuse—or else it did live! and it would let him live. But he was not ready fully to face the ordeal just yet. He wanted postponement, he felt confused. The miraculous modern *must* be built upon a fine run, away ahead. Somewhere it must connect up. It cannot be that it is so graceless, nor can it be that this brittle, much praised skin—changed to dust at a touch, is to be loved in desperation only with a failing knowledge that it is only lovely since it is lost; that life is lovely when it's dying. Feverishly eat it and go.

Names came up as he walked back from the Tiber—old names of football players, school-boy friends dead and enucleated by their desperation, breath-taking daring which took life like a cherry from which it spit the stone laughing.

Yes, yes, that is life, a grass sandwich.—Eagerly he always listened to men who had lived that way, avidly, avidly without thought of anything. And always he had had the same feeling in himself. They eat so as to be blind. So it is with prime ministers.

They eat so as to be blind. And so they work, the great workers, the great scientists, even the great humanists, in the laboratory, the clinic. Science: to be blind, drunk with work. Science: the exhalation of a fever that has destroyed, eating too much away.—Let it go on. He, Evans, would not stop the least accuracy. He would drive it on. But with agony, against beauty. Beauty to him was to be going on, surely and not to turn back ever. When he would read of birds extinct, the wood pigeon, when he beheld manners decaying, when he saw the worn cheeks of the school girls oppressed by an insistent lack of peace—the wearing cheek, the darkening eye, the lips losing their outline and the seamy neck—for what? Against what? And religion, that childish horror of misapplication, the stewing and stewing of that stale sauce, into which the scraps of the last guest are thrown mechanically again each day and everything doused with the same dead flavor. That insult to death—that might be at least clean and not craven, staring upon dullness as if it were a jewel, staring and staring in the agonized choking moment. He knew all kinds of people intimately in their lesser phases. He longed through an iron mesh always—through which nobody broke. The same dregs of his old dreaming.

Some Americans, his friends in Paris, had escaped to no purpose. Just struck out desperately to have the filth off them. But they could not go home. What is home? They at least wanted to be clean.

Then he began to be aware of some of the gigantic old names—too dangerous to be well known by this craven generation. And we are scientists, ready to let wit and our minds go free—yet we have not the wit to read a truth in Heliogabalus, Caligula, Nero, relaxed upon the knees of nature—Saints—in essence—"Never returning." This was the kernel of his nut. This is what he always admired.

And the names of still other reckless Roman emperors came to his mind; their unchecked voluptuousness, headlong humor, which understood rightly, is the fullness of life, the obverse of that virtue among the saints which they fathered.—The same is the best of modern Paris. Eyes wide open will discover nothing till the man go on to the end as they do there. Frightened after the emperors the next age turned back to save what it could—and got into a maze of sophistry. Science should salute the Imperial Roman debauchés. We should adore their fullness of abandon. These then—who live desperately—are the salt of the world. The emperors, in manners, were one with the modern genius in chemistry, but larger, whose way with life, more mapped—falls down. Check not the children. The whole confused mass of modern thought oppressed him.

Rome! city of churches. Coming back along the Corso, Evans walked into that gloom. He did not know the name, it was near the Palazzo Strozzi. And there he saw "the church," created by excesses, calling the lambs, a shepherd with its shepherd's pipes, to come and drink of its pure spring. Pure! in view of all of life that it ignores.

Science! he thought again, coming once more into the street from the church. Anyone can bemuse himself with labor toward "discovery," but few can stay upon the point of the difficulty long. The difficulty is to keep on, not to stop. That was their honor, when they had it— the emperors. They exceed philosophy and science.— Evans had been berated in that he gave up hope of academic distinction as a boy, gave up a promising career in the city to go home to sit down at the place of his birth—to think and to see if there were any way—to do anything. Paris he could see, yes, for some it was a way. Not for him.

A man sitting at the table of his laboratory day after day inventing 606 or anti-meningiococcus serum, in what way is he different from the man sitting day after day sipping alcohol at the table of a café? None that Dev could see. Use?

Of what use had anything proved to stay the career of modern destructive thought and its attendant agony and impoverishment—save mulish instinct—not to know?

In Rome

But now he was in Rome, in Rome while passing back to the point of his departure, the place of his birth. What is the place of my birth? The place of my birth is the place where the word begins. Evans had not gotten further, nor had he detected any wise enough to instruct him. He laughed at his own egotism.—Which is at least well checked, and will destroy nothing—if it do not achieve clarity, if it do not create.

To create—it sounded hollow as his footsteps on the stones of the Via Pilotta into which he had turned. To create was no longer to be an emperor; this is futile. But to create is to shoot a clarity through the oppressing, obsessing murk of the world; *that* would be a reward. But not the church which lays waste nine parts of the light, the major part of morals, to have its penny's worth of clammy candle-promise of eternity. There must be in Rome a greater thing, inclusive of the world of love and of delight; unoppressive—loosing the mind so that men shall again occupy that center from which they have been avulsed by their own sordidness—and failure of imagination.

He felt somehow relieved, scarcely knowing how he had come around again. Mounting the Spanish steps, up to the Villa Medici, he came to the Pincio once more.

There he recalled those days twenty years before when with the rest of them as a kid he had gone up Monte Genaro—the pansies, the icy wind at the top, cyclamen in the hedges, the ass tethered under a cabin shed and the talk of Alba Longa.

Especially he remembered that clear air. In those days he had been going headlong ahead; that was it, dry and clear, on the mountain. The wind cut like a knife, but it was clear, crystal clear. That was it. That was what he really wanted.

And again, maimed, a stumbling cripple, the church was before him. He grew angry, but it left confusion in his mind. Restless, troubled, he began to walk again.

He thought of the beginning of Wilde's Salome, the imperishable beauty of Salome, the imperishable words of the prophet, the old prophet in the well—and the rest of it. He thought of it, smiling and wondering what place in Horace or Petronius would compare with it.

He failed to sense quietly the calm fields of criticism— how could he, and gather, actively, what he must—a free lance in the world. No use, he would not be that.

In the afternoon it came on to rain. Restless, hating the narrowness of his room, tired of writing, this would be the moment for the *Museo Nationale.* Thither he went and in under the great ruined dome of Diocletian's *tepididarium,* his heart fearfully throbbing, to face those ancient wonders gathered there.

Instantly his slightly held new peace had left him. His knees shook, he could not calmly breathe. For he knew that marble certainty which he must see and the defeat which he must somehow steel himself to suffer.

He went from piece to piece, not yielding easily but half surlily, looking the exhibits up and down. Yet he was afraid.

In Rome

It was that this reality that had once inspired these marbles, but now outside of experience, seemed more living than the living all about him, that unhorsed his wits. Before the two wings of the altar to Aphrodite, the seated figures of the women, he almost choked, between their beauty and anger at the world, so that he did not know where to rest, but depressed by the marble he had to go driven, driven—as before.

Between these feelings, the stonelike reality of ancient excellence and the pulpy worthlessness of every day, he wandered lost; or coming out of the worst of it, striving to find a footing and walking about from piece to piece, —about the old cloister built by the monks in the vast ruins of the ancient baths—he was bewildered, yet felt himself rescued at a turn in the wall by some new wonder of that old assertion—the Mercury's forward thrust leg of a fine dancer; and then he fell, it might be said, by chance, upon that white and perfect girl, the Venus Anadyomene of Cyrene—dug from that sea-loosened bank of Africa.

Coming alone into the narrow chamber where this solitary bit of marble stood, it seemed to him perfection, actually, which had survived the endless defamations of the world. Actually alive she seemed, that perfect girl, in quiet pose, pure white—her fringed robe hanging from a dolphin's sculptured flukes. He looked and looked at those perfections of the breasts, the torso, the thighs—forgetting the stone, seeing a woman—young and tranquil standing by the sea—and nothing of stone, just quietness and fulfiillment.

He felt in this no defeat,—he was amazed, filled up. In this shameful room he stood looking long and excitedly at the marble knees of Venus. Then he returned to the Pension for supper. Fräulein whatever-her-name was, was there as before. She glanced up at him. But his eyes filled with the Venus, he paid no heed.

Yet he was not wholly pacified. Rome frightened him. He could not sleep that night until he had made up his mind to get out of the city next day for a while at least.

So lying there in the dark after the first distracting glimpse of it, he decided to leave Rome for a southern tour—to be back again in a week. Having tested the character of the place, seen a few of the strong features, he would start south for Naples in the morning.

XIX

SOUTH TO NAPLES AND RETURN

EARLY in the morning Evans was on the train bound south. He saw again the Campagna, fertile, rich with farms, peasants everywhere tilling the fields, and tending the vineyards; then the mountain cities, brown with age, clinging to the rock near Frascati. First there were rich slopes, then later in the day the bare Apennines and up, up colder and colder, scrub and rock and snowy peaks upon all sides. On the way to the station that morning he had seen a young man strapping skiis to the running board of a car in the Via Sicilia.

Rome! in a few days he would return to do battle with it once more. He was going south now only for a respite. Rome! There it was, plastered with pale promises over the bones of its real grandeur that cannot have been a lie. There it is! It is there the same. But it had caught Dev armless. He would come back and go in. This was what made him such a poor conversationalist, as his friends discovered. He listened and then wanted to think. It was not all timidity. He despised (in himself) rash guessing, the sudden forgetting plunge (as he admired it

in others), the clever word. He would come back—
later.

This gave him a sense of security, almost of indifference to the country toward which he was bound, and
to Naples most of all. It was a small loop in his progress,
a mere decoration. It was pleasant to go there but it did
not matter. And yet it mattered more than anything else.
Neither was he going away nor coming back. He was
relaxed and so happy. This, then, was what it all meant
to him. This was himself at his best. He was glad to be
leaving Rome.

After climbing for several hours into a cold mountain
region up to the rocky height of the line, icy-cold and
bare, a railway station, water tanks, the train was running downhill again now, slipping silently upon the
tracks without effort. Off to the left as the train began
a long curve, he saw a sharp mountain late in the afternoon. Two American teachers in the next seat were
craning forward, a Baedeker open between them.

Vesuvius!

In Naples porters thronged at the station. A flame-
faced, gray-haired Englishman in a conspicuously checkered gray suit was the center of a grinning group of
them. His daughter was trying to drag him into a hotel
bus. But he was giving away fifteen-lira tips, and began
discoursing to Dev as soon as he came by on the danger
to the throat from the infectious dust of the Naples
streets.

In Naples a wind was blowing from the north out

over the bay. Early in the evening it began to rain; later
it turned to sleet. Evans walked out after dark to the
Galleria and promenaded with the other men; purchas-
ing there a bottle of good brandy which he needed.

Naples did not interest him. The second day he was
there he took the *fenicolare* up the hill back of the city
for a view of the bay. All he wanted of Naples was—
the bay, and yes, the Greek pieces in the museum, seen
once ten years before; wonders dug from Pompeii and
Herculaneum.

He paused only a moment before the frescoes, fauns,
satyrs—indifferent work, some of it. But the archaic
Athena he saw with delight, the fluted gown stretched
taut between her knees as she strode smiling forward,
the spear lifted to strike. Before such understanding, he
looked shamefacedly at the ground.

Aside from this he kept saying, Naples is not for me.
Should he go immediately back to Rome? No, not yet.
He decided to take the swing round by Pompeii, Amalfi,
Capri, instead; and then—back to Rome and settle it one
way or the other. Settle what?

And so the third day, he was up at six and off with
the mob of other sightseers, taking the early train between
Vesuvius and the sea. It was a day now cloudy, now
clear. You could see Capri in the distance over the blue
water—fabled fairyland of island peace. They passed
Pugliano, built over the land covering Herculaneum, still
unexcavated. Torre del Greco. Old fields of lava, like
slag from a smelter, stood where it had once, flowing,

stopped mid-field, at a graveyard wall, at a back door.

It was at Cava, arriving in the evening, that he began to feel his nerves definitely quieting under the soothing influence of country loveliness, the soft evening and the early spring weather. The son of the hotel proprietor, a fair English speaker, went with him for a walk to show him about the place before supper.

Softly the quiet evening entered Evans' disturbed mind. The young chap was hoarse from yelling at a soccer game that afternoon when Cava had beaten Torre del Greco, 2 to 1.

They started to walk back of the little hotel where there was a heap of willow withes lying ready for the vine-tying. They walked on down a narrow path between small fields where women were dropping potato-cuttings in rows being freshly opened by some men with mattocks going before them. They jumped a ditch with violets growing on its sides and came to the bed of a stream with a small sand bar in it and so on for an hour.

Evans peered into the doors of peasant cottages. Churns, tubs and the like lay about the back doors. The houses seemed wide open but deserted. It was growing late when they returned to the hotel for supper. The place was small, cold, and with but two or three guests in it. A solitary English woman of forty or more was sitting reading in the old-fashioned reading room of the place, unmindful of the cold.

That night in his sweetly musty bedroom of a small

162

country hotel, the window wide open, Evans could hear
the silence of the cold night as he lay quietly staring up
at the dark ceiling, faintly lit nevertheless by a light
from somewhere—from the night itself it seemed. Death
he thought might be sweetly like this, lying there forever.

Waking early in the morning he saw from his window
three peasants taking a gray bull down the highway to
the town.

The ride to Amalfi from Cava was not new to Evans.
He had gone that way in a carriage with three companions, the same year that he had climbed Genaro. *That*
had been a ride, especially coming after the morning
spent about the lonely ruin of the Doric temple to
Poseidon at Pæstum! That had been a ride Evans had
never forgotten—one of the most lyrical moments of his
existence; the urchins turning pinwheels alongside the
carriage even when the horses were at a run, the newness
of it all.

Pæstum! There it must be still, off there on that
promontory southward in the mist, temple ruins
in a weedy field, the marble turned golden by wind and
sun, the sea again below the sloping hill. He had never
forgotten it. To him, a stranger to Athens, it meant his
only actual touch with that ancient clarity of Greece.

Now in the auto with a chance companion who could
not speak his tongue, he looked south over the glinting
water where the road comes out high above the sea—and
thought again of Pæstum, as of a miraculous seed—full
of promise for the world. There it is, in spite of their

vindictive despoliations, perfect. And here am I, ruined. That's it, it exists still, it is as always, more than its stones, unless it should be torn apart and ground to sand, scattered and forgotten.

He thought of the antagonistic world.—The fruit is there but, missing the kernel, they think only to rip it, trying to get by tearing apart; sensing the beauty and their lack, they find a destructive energy to ruin what they fail to comprehend.

So, in this remembering mind, he continued sitting in the narrow seat of the car now tormented, and now full of an ease over which his moods played like sunlight and the shadows of clouds on the sea below him.

At Amalfi, after the long auto ride upon the cliff, he saw peasant girls bringing baskets of lemons down the precipitous mountain steps from the gardens above at Ravello. But he lingered most about the market place with the small cathedral above it. From this little haven Amalfi, a very ancient pirates' nest, he imagined Pæstum again which Amalfi (now sunk under the sea) the old Amalfi had sacked, despoiling the temple there to decorate its Christian shrine with columns and mosaics.

Then a guide in the church who knew a little English told him of St. Andrew embalmed in the cathedral crypt. —But can you see him?—No, the priests do that by the power of prayer. The body exudes a kind of grease. The peasants come each spring to know if it will be a prosperous year. They ask their questions of the priests. They look, the priests. If the body has exuded much grease,

the year will be a good one, and if not, the reverse.——
Dev listened. He noted the linking of the church with the
peasants and the growing fields. And there, sure enough,
was a priest, in his ceremonial dress of red cloth and lace,
a comic confirmation, jigging on the twin muscles of
his buttocks to the whine and groan of a chant and its
responses. Dev got a chill to see him, so degenerate was
it. But he laughed afterward: Not even modern or awake
as Paris is—but ahead of——.

He looked at the columns of the altar, bits here, bits
there; the loveliest of all from Greek Pæstum—and in
the niche outside, the colored columns stolen by the
church from the bare ruins of Neptune's Temple. Nothing in Amalfi pleased him more.

The ancient was his still Elysium, untorn by his wars.
It was the sensual world, the betrayer of his peace, as it
filled his delight; the thing he held and could not hold.
Lost in the getting, he pursued it and pursuing it he
failed to advance but turned back always in his delight.

And there at Amalfi, high up, where he had climbed
to be away from the few tourists who were about, above
the famous pergola of the Capuchin monastery, he sat
on a stone and began thinking again of his sister, a
woman of his own flesh.—God, I wish Bess were here.
We could see this with a single eye. Thus pleasure is
doubled, he said innocently to himself, looking out over
the sea wrinkled with tiny waves, patches of varying
color, great stretches of deep and shallow water.

From above he saw the monastery, the rotting oranges,

the steep hill slopes to the sea. But this, the thought of
Bess, somehow changed his mood. He felt alone, his
pleasure dimmed. Can't stay here forever; he thought he
had better be getting on. I must get back to Rome!

Summoning his car, he must go on. By evening he
had passed swiftly over that incomparable winding road
to Sorrento, witnessing the wild flowers along the road-
side, by prolific orange groves, the sea, across the ridge
of the peninsula and so out above Naples Bay, with
Naples far off over it to the west before him and Sorrento's little shops about him, inviting him to buy. He
bargained for and bought a few things, among them an
embroidered shawl for Bess. Pretty, pretty! That night
he went to bed in a great room at the Hotel Tremontana,
former summer lodge of Alexander III of Russia, and
there lay awake thinking, thinking—as he heard a
violent storm come up roaring in the orange trees.

In the morning he could not get to Capri. The boat
would not stop because of the heavy storm. No matter.
He was more anxious to get on now than to see. He
took the electric tram and then the train at Castellammare
back to Naples. He checked in at the hotel and within
half an hour more was in a train on his way back to
Rome. That's that.

From so much natural beauty, his spirit cured only to
be the more eager for its addictions, Evans arrived in
Rome again at midnight.

After some difficulty, he succeeded in getting into his

pension where he threw himself upon his bed, among his few familiar belongings, and slept.

He waked eagerly the next day, March 14, a Friday. The floor, the red tiles: he touched them with relief. He could not wait. Chuckling, he rang for coffee—eager to begin again. Rome! Begin what?

After his coffee in his room and the talk with the gaunt serving woman who wanted to go to America—speaks a moderately decent French—he went out for the day, following his plan—to see, to investigate his enthusiasm upon the spot, to make up his mind.

Five days continuously like a drunkard he would continue.

Passing through the hall to the door, always so solidly locked and bolted, he wondered if the little German Venus were still there. Then out into the misty morning down the Via Lucullo—they were still taking out carloads of dirt from the rear of the Queen Mother's palace—past the amusing lions of the Fountana Aqua Felice, to Cook's for his mail; then back to the Via del Tritone and on down past the fountain of the Tritons, one of his greatest minor joys in Rome.

Pagan wonder leaped up always in him at this souvenir of the sea with all its flash and hoary age upon it. The contorted gusto of the bronze figures all adrip! But when later in the morning he again beheld the Trevi water rush from its sculptured base, it seemed the ancients themselves had loosed once more the springs of purity and of plenty in the world. Out of the very house walls gushed its flooding stream, an amazing spectacle! With spirits profuse and dancing he went on.

He would search with instinct and with eyes. But slowly, certainly, his interest labored—more and more.

To the Forum! All that morning he walked in a clear light, back and forth slowly on that anonymous ground— to which history has added nothing but its irony of lost stone. Evans had the impression of being anywhere but in that place. There were but two or three others curious inside the enclosure. It might have been a rocky pasture in Vermont. It seemed more fit for rabbits and such small beasts than men.

No. No. The Forum left him cold. Not this—this wasn't it. It was not, then, the old, but something that goes on forever. A thing that goes on and never stops. Call it beauty. It is in the marble. It's not history—it's not stones. It goes on.

Surely Evans was a bit mad. For what was he searching? He himself felt it to-day a vain thing. What *could* he find? There was little of antiquity left for his labor, and of that no more than the few brittle relics—touched, it is true, by some undiscovered power—but nothing but stones for all that. Still it was that, to unravel it from the surface of a statue, to catch up the meaning, the meaning still alive, still operative. Not to be wonder-struck and to stand in awe, but to catch up the meaning that destroys banality. That is why conquerors must smash such things, it is because in things touched by genius lies a power to destroy stupidity—a column stolen from Neptune's temple. It goes on.

He began to realize that inside himself something must change, indeed had changed long since. He was struggling in a thicket which kept him back and he would come upon Venus at the head of the stair, Venus crouching by a pool. But after that? What?

And that figure of a naked fighter, wounded, fallen, dying; that man of barbaric features. The dying Gaul. He stopped once more. Clarity would not break in him. The position of the fallen fighter was too human, it was pathetic. Yes, he could see that dying country north of Rome, he could see G., the savage chieftain, mortally wounded, on the hill back of Dijon tricked out of his stronghold by his own traitorous tribesmen.

But that was not it. He wanted to come from behind the velvet into their reality, a reality of beauty. He hunted the rift in the curtain. It must be there. Only my modernity conceals it now. I am close to it, close to it. That which was, is.

Breathlessly near! He stood in the room of the athlete, the bronze boxer, the spearsman at ease holding the spear and looking aside, the boxer resting his elbow on his knee.—Like the water in the Trevi, brought from the hills, so beauty runs here and must splash over me if a breeze come.

Then in the Vatican one day he came up quite suddenly cured, sick of the city, of museums and that white disease which makes the gods stone.

He was weary now of being alone, weary and restless and ready to be going on once more. Should he speak to the little fräulein? No. He worked long that night at his notes.

XX

VENICE AND NORTHWARD

COMPARED to the rest of Italy, Venice was dead, softly beautiful—reflecting the East. St. Mark's was the epitome of this mood. But St. Paulo, with its stark reminders of battle, and the Carpaccios in the Museo, stringently drawn, the Colleone and the end wall of the Hall of the Great Seal, by Tintoretto, El Greco's master, all black crooks, these were beyond comparison—and from the west. But that was all.

Certainly this American wanderer never had had such a vision of the uselessness of beauty—and of how it transcends all else in the world. He walked many hours in the silly streets, he walked the length of the quai out to the park where in a hot sun he sat looking back over the water to the palace of the Doges and the shipping, modern seagoing vessels and launches with clusters of gondolas tied to the mooring stakes in the distance.

He went to the Lido, the fashionable modern watering place, now deserted, the season being too early, and lay upon the powdery white sand, picking up the paper-thin yellow and orange shells there and looking out over the

171

pale-green hardly stirring sea whose thin wavelets broke in long overlapping crescents beside him—widely, icily along the shore.

The whole world is a shell of past loveliness.

This mood of Venice, deserted by that second growth of modernity which in summer swarms where now only violets bloom in the gardens of the deserted villas, behind iron fences and locked gates; this mood of uselessness, of artificiality, took violent hold upon Evans so that he shook and was depressed, and wished he were home in the States drowning his mind in running about —to no end either surely, not even beauty—but it was an intoxication which this was not, even for him, any longer.

Too fragile even for that, too overrun with the vocabulary of prettiness, the East and West seemed to neutralize each other here—perhaps that was it. At any rate it is empty for me. Byron, Browning: In a gondola! that robust romanticism treading with its new paw among these flimsy paper palaces balanced on straws made him smile. Sleep in the wet dungeons! Why? all night as Byron did: to get the atmosphere. Good God!

Evans got the atmosphere quite well enough without that. He watched them in a scow dredging the black muck from the bottom of one of the ditches, grown too shallow with the sludge for a boat to pass in it.

No, it was deeper than that. Steamers start from here for Athens! All his friends who had been to Athens had written enthusiastically of their experiences.

But there—just there the delight of Venice got him. Venice is Venice. It has no antiquity, really; they were just swampy islands; and no future; just a middle greatness of ships. And now it lies like an artificial pearl in a modern shop window. Fragile, useless; used for international swimming lessons.

He dropped in at Florians on the way back, where he spent a lethargic hour in the shadow over his coffee. Venice with its circling pigeons, its swarming tourists, even at that season, was putting him to sleep. Actually he slept on the leather settee. He could not rouse himself but felt that he might stay on here indefinitely— not like that Englishman who had been schooled to be a gondolier and moved about native-fashion every day through the canals—but like an American—futile— dreaming of the damage done by the Civil War to the South; of Cambrai—or anything. Presently though he began to realize that on the morrow he would be leaving not Venice alone but Italy, and for good. He went to the water's edge and whistled for a gondolier. Climbing into the cabin of his craft he let the old fellow take him around for an hour—anywhere.

It was the thirtieth of March, three days later, when Evans stood on the steps facing the Grand Canal in the hubbub and confusion of gondolas before the railroad station on his way to catch the afternoon train for Vienna. It was the last train, the only train that day, no sleepers, no diner—Evans held a second class ticket—and when he, among the rest, clambered aboard, he found the compartments already packed, the racks filled with luggage and even the corridor clogged with traveling bags. Austrian tourists returning home from the Riviera, Americans, Germans, etc. He was annoyed; he did not fancy an afternoon and night spent under these circumstances.

But a fellow in uniform who spoke a little French tipped him off to a train from Milan through to Vienna, which would be waiting at the next small station on the way out. Here, after a wild dash across the tracks, the American fought his way to a seat in a compartment, the only one left, next to a fat old Jew and his blubber wife who had the window places, having previously jammed all the racks with their bundles and outer clothing.

Evans threw his grip upon the seat he had captured, then went out to bring up his other things with the aid of the porter. Everyone was looking for space in which to stow his belongings, seeing which the old Jew began slowly to make way for the other occupants of the coach, saying in his Yiddish German: "Take your time, take your time, keep smiling, everybody will be satisfied if we do not get angry at each other." And so finally the long journey began, the six travelers packed into the compartment with their luggage, like sardines in a box, and smelling not much different—from the presence of the greasy but good-natured pair by the window.

The train starts directly west from Venice to clear the swampy shoreline, so that one sees the wall of the distant Alps north on the right. But after a short run, the train sweeps northward, then turning through a bare country starts on its eastward journey paralleling the rapidly rising plateau and mountains now on the left. There was a thunderstorm going on among the peaks and slightly behind them as the train crept forward. The sea with the sun shining upon it lay off in the distance to the south. Venice and the sea. The scene was wintry.

In contrast to the usually well-appointed Italian coaches, this one was dilapidated, dirty and worn out as if it had never been cleaned, reflecting the impoverished state of Austria in its present distress. Besides the old Jewish couple and Evans, there were three other men in the compartment, all Austrians—or at least German speaking, one of whom Dev at first took to be a son of the old people. It was not long before they all began to talk with each other, urged on in the first place by the great curiosity of the two near the window. Only one youngish man in the corner nearest the door—which he kept open, seemed uninterested, though once or twice he said a few words in German, which Dev did not understand, to the boy next to him.

Within an hour they had reached the battleground of the Piave, the trenches almost gone before the grass, the towns newly built, the stream itself just a waste of pebbles and sand, almost no water in it.

At this point the man in the corner began to look about. He had served here in the Austrian Army during the war, a nervous, fidgety sort of fellow who, addressing himself to Evans in almost perfect English, asked him if he knew the place. Evans replied that he did not, that it was the first time he was making this particular journey. The rest listened attentively, especially the old Jew.

Without discovering his name or communicating his own, Evans learned that this man was a musical critic, had lived in New York, had been wounded on the Piave, had been resting in Nice for the winter and was now on his way back to Vienna for the return from New York of Jeritza, whom he professed to know extremely well.

But the old Jew quickly pounced upon Dev no sooner his competitor had finished, and what with his intense curiosity and Dev's satisfaction at finding his German working rather better than he had thought it would, the old man pumped him dry in thorough-going fashion on the present financial status of the United States—as far as Evans knew anything about it.

He and his wife had been in Nice for the winter. Now they were going home, armed with lunch baskets filled to capacity, sufficient to satisfy the appetite of a hippopotamus. Already they had begun to eat, fruit, sandwiches, pickles, bread, fish, cold cuts, cheese, etc., till the old fellow, seeing that the rest of the occupants of the compartment were watching them—explained with a laugh that his wife ate only one meal a day, adding with another laugh that it began when she awakened and ended when she went to sleep for the night. They offered no food to the others. The compartment was stuffy, so Dev went out into the corridor where he was joined by the musical critic, a drawn-faced, irritable fellow surely, who did not talk more than he needed to, for which Dev was grateful.

Hours slipped by in this way with the train striking upgrade into the rocks down which the Austrians had come in their modern attack upon Italy—and the evening was coming on. Also it grew colder in the compartment. The Austrian went in to take a snooze but Dev sat there on a seat hinged to the wall, peering out into the growing darkness for another hour, a wild, almost uninhabited mountain region it seemed, with peaks right above him at times, now in mist, now looming out like rock floating in the clouds.

He was alone save for a young woman in black who had come out of the compartment next ahead of his own and who stood leaning against the side of the train smoking—which apparently she had not been allowed to do inside. Dev looked at her once or twice, but since she paid no attention to him, he soon went on looking out again into these darkening wintry fields where patches of snow appeared next to the field walls in the fast deepening night. Now the train paralleled a madly rushing river, then a hedge, or a low house, and not a soul in sight.

At nine o'clock there was a halt at the border where the train crew was changed, the Austrians taking charge and the customs inspectors going through the luggage. It was very cold. A thin, tired-looking fellow in a brown overcoat, the collar turned up around his ears, said a few unintelligible words to Dev, penciled his stuff and went on.

At midnight there was the usual stop at A— for those who wished to stay there and sleep until the morning train. Dev hoped for the best, but not a soul budged from his compartment, so that when they were off again on the last leg of their journey, he was so dead tired and so nearly frozen that he went reluctantly back into the presence of the others. The place was black with the light out, one of the men was snoring and there were legs all over the floor. In spite of it all, he was himself also soon fast asleep, for it was warm there. He waked not even when the old Jew woman, having eaten too much, struggled over legs, flung open the door, and vomited full into the corridor—then came back, as she must have done, and slept again—perfectly unconcerned.

What a night! Dull, dirty, aching and disheveled, he woke finally, stifled by the bad air of the compartment and picking his way over the feet of his campanions walked once more into the corridor where the musical critic had gone before him and had had the floor cleaned by a train hand, disgusted with the stinking Jews—more cross and irritable than ever, sour and wrapped in his mood.

The girl was not there.

Cold and miserable as he was, wondering why he had ever decided to come to Vienna at this miserable time of the year, Evans was not encouraged by his campanion.— A rotten city in April, rain, wind, it is the windiest, dirtiest place in Europe. I wish to God I were back in my little apartment in Rapallo, and would be if I could afford to stay away from here so long.

But outside, the dawn was just coming up. Evans had always a childish delight in traveling on a train. It seemed to fit his very special and anonymous mood, his desire never to stay anywhere, to see but to be moving, to see swiftly, hidden from view, and to be gone—or never to move. The train was winding up great wooded valleys, the trees leafless, half-melted snow upon all sides, whole fields of it. At every turn almost, he could see great hotels, or sanatoriums built upon commanding prominences. Semmering, said his companion, the great Viennese winter resort. Here there is skiing, I have skiied here many times.

It was entrancing. It did not seem possible that the very afternoon before they had been in the Piazza San Marco. And Dev was thrilled besides with having come again upon snow, a fulfillment which all people who are used to it feel when they return north in winter after having spent a season in milder climates.

Cold as he was in that smelly corridor, yet he felt the thrill of winter in the mountains and the dawn coming up, casting a half light all across the valleys, with sparkling snow on the high slopes to the west.

By this Evans gained his first impression of Austria, the old world of pleasure, of fashion. The present winter season was over. Only toward the highest inaccessible peaks was the snow firm enough for sports. The valleys were bare: he could distinguish where the skii jumps had been, now blackish trodden leafmold, no more.

And so at last they came out, around six a.m. into the level farm land south of the great city, with wild hares, running about in it, here and there on all sides.—But don't they eat the crops? O yes, but in the fall there is a roundup each year and the carcasses are shipped frozen to market by the thousand. All the farmers join and drive them into coralles, then club them to death.—

By now, as they were approaching Vienna, many of the grizzly, cold, stiffened travelers were coming out, and among them the young lady in black who was talking plain American to an elderly English woman beside her. They were wondering when they would get into Vienna. Seven o'clock, said Evans. Oh, thank you, said the older woman. I shan't be sorry, she added to the girl—whom Evans was watching now furtively, from moment to moment, trying to see if she were very young, very beautiful, very intelligent, well shaped—all the things to be learned of a woman at the first glance; but he had seen her only in the half light. One thing certainly, her legs were straight, finely shaped, and she was not gushy. He liked her.

The arrival at Vienna was a miserable affair from every possible angle. It was early morning, it was cold, it was drizzling outside, the rain half freezing into slush as it fell. The station itself was barren, sad—neglected. A few porters moved laboriously about herding the people before them. What in the world is this? thought Evans.

He had no Austrian money, had to go to the window to have it exchanged for his Italian bills. Seventy thousand kronen it cost him to drive to his pension, the one Miss D. had recommended. The streets were deserted. When he arrived at the pension, there was no one to receive him. The front room would not be free for another week. He had his things thrown into a back room, clean but gloomy, facing a courtyard into which the rain fell dismally.—And to think I've come to this for a month.—Someone was playing piano exercises in the front of the house. The burly maid came in and put a handful of briquettes into the toy-like tile stove. So this is Vienna! He flung himself upon the bed—after bolting the door—covered himself with two blankets and his overcoat, and fell asleep.

III

THE RETURN

XXI

VIENNA

WHEN Evans arrived in the Austrian capital on the last day of March, 1924, six years after Versailles, he found Vienna still showing marked traces of a reduced condition. From being one of the world's greatest capitals, inhabited by a brilliant court, it had become no more than a socialist stronghold, chief city still, it is true, but of a small bankrupt nation, its richest provinces stripped from it to make up Czecko-Slovakia and the rest of them to the south. The public buildings looked neglected, smoke stained; the stone work on the Rathhouse had crumbled incredibly in the ten years since the war began—not a stroke of maintenance having been done upon it during that time. Just now workmen were beginning to repair cornices, ledges and window sills; blocks of new stone stood on the cobbles waiting to be hoisted into place, but very few laborers were on the job. Obviously there was no money.

But there was more than that of neglect about the city. Few motor cars were running, the stores were empty—the people themselves seemed subdued, impoverished. Taxis were scarce. Everyone rode upon the street cars and most who rode were of the laboring class. There was no flash, no aristocratic flash anywhere, no jauntiness. It was perhaps more the lack of this than anything else that impressed Evans so unfavorably.

Of course the Hofburg, the Imperial palace, looked like a tomb. People, very few of them, went haphazard across the great cobbled courts. There were no guards. Everything seemed let down. True, the grass was coming up and the trees were trimmed but that was all. There were blackbirds on the lawns.

Evans had never been in Vienna before, so that he could not estimate how much of the depression he saw was due to the cold spring weather and how much to national misfortune, but walking idly that morning on the Ring he was impressed by a feeling of desolation.

He looked at the people whom he passed, rather finely built people, heavy but with a good mien, even handsome, people of the office type and city laborers. Yes, he thought, Vienna is theirs all right.

On the inside of the Ring back of the Hoftheatre, he stopped a moment at the sound of bagpipes. A double file of men and women clad in peasant costume and led by a fellow who was doing a few dance steps now and then and playing vigorously on a bagpipe, was coming along the sidewalk opposite him. Nothing else happened. The little procession in costume, fifteen or twenty in all, walked solemnly on. A wedding, he concluded, as he watched them pass.

For himself he felt gloomy and alone. Perhaps it was the new Vienna. Seeking the *Algemeine Credit Anstalt* where he hoped to get some letters—perhaps one from his sister—and to cash a check, he cut in through the business streets striving to interest himself in what was going on about him. There he passed a delicatessen store, apparently a very prominent one, before which he saw more life than in any other place. The window was packed with foodstuffs among which he saw three whole roast chickens at 50,000 K. each. There were fish of several sorts pickeled in tubs, hams, roasts of beef and veal, cheeses, and all kinds of bread, dried fruit, preserves, sausages, and potted stuffs of many kinds.

People were standing looking in through the windows. Evans stood watching for a short time. Some simply looked. It was perfectly apparent that they were satisfying their appetites by the sight alone. It struck him at once that Vienna, even now, was not eating all it should. And of course it is not the laboring class who are suffering—but the people like myself, the artisans, the professional men, the schoolmen, the people of independent fortune. In front of this store their want was clearly written in their faces.

He paused again before an optical instrument shop and admired the array of photographic and laboratory material—at stupendous prices, but when converted into dollars, quite cheap. Book stores, he looked into, with formally bound volumes; he even saw a translation of Upton Sinclair's works. Good God, Socialism!

Old women were selling chestnuts on the corner of the Brühl and rising opposite was the Stephan Church. There was small business anywhere however. The only places that were surely packed were the pastry shops, marvels of their kind, the delicatessen places and the coffee houses.

Evans had heard of the Viennese coffee house, comparable to the Parisian café. Everywhere he went he saw these places, informal clubs with men and women—women sitting alone—reading the papers (free there) and sipping whatever it was they had before them. There they seemed to be sitting as if never intending to move.

There were no letters at Cook's.

He crossed the street and, through a transept door, entered the Stephan Church, Vienna's oldest place of worship. Inside it was at first as black as night so that nothing could be seen. It was cold too. They had laid boards upon the stones to protect the knees of the worshipers—that they might not die of rheumatism or pneumonia perhaps. After a few moments to accustom his eyes to the dark, Evans became conscious of the altar, guarded by a high iron fence; then, in the aisle quite close to him, he noticed a tiny shrine to the Virgin, covered with devout candles, before which many vague figures were kneeling. Passing closer he could hear them mumbling as they bowed low in the silence and induced night. This was terrifying to him. The gloom was excessive. He made his way quickly out of the old church and went with a hollow heart further upon his way, oppressed, out into the comparative brightness of the streets. The failure to get news from his sister or the few friends he might have heard from, Lou or Jack—coupled with the gloom of the city itself and the tomblike atmosphere of the old church—crushed him completely.

The bank, however, when he came to it, rather foot-sore from the rambling walk on the cobbles and pavements, was another matter. Here things were still alive. The building itself was modern, extensive, and seemed not quite so beaten as the rest of the city. It seemed to have had better days, as did everything in Vienna, but money moved in it, worthless as the money might be, moved and had thus a value. Dev sat on one of the great leather lounges in the alcove reserved for the tourist business, and looked about him trying to right himself, and to rest his feet, after the depressing hours just preceding.

To his inexpressible delight there was the girl from the train, sitting on the other end of the lounge, reading a letter. He still had his hat on. As he removed it, she glanced up. She looked at him for a moment and then went on with her letter.

I've got to say hello to you, Evans broke in smiling. Do you mind? We met on the train this morning.

She looked up.

Have you been in Vienna before? he continued.

Yes.

Speak the language?

Yes.

Seems a mighty depressing place to me.

Yes, in many ways.

But Evans felt desperate. No use batting the air any longer.—I wonder if you'd take lunch with me—somewhere, he said.

She looked at him for a moment, then smiled and said, Why, yes, if he wished, she would be pleased to do so.

Fine!

He hurried with his business at the cashier's window, while she waited. Then they went out together, boarded a tram car, at the lady's suggestion, and rode to the Opera Ring.

There she introduced him to an excellent eating place, *Am Weissen Hirsch,* a narrow room with freshly covered tables and expert service—the food being to Dev a surprise after his sense of the poverty of the city in general.

For a full hour they sat, eating in a leisurely manner, speaking politely of Vienna, of the war, of this and that, the trip up from Venice and then—with a few words of thanks—she bade him adieu.

As Evans had told his companion at table, he had come to Vienna, as do so many doctors from the States, to observe new methods, to check up on his diagnostic technique, and to prepare himself for new adventures in his profession, for time and cash and renewed interest in his work. He did not delay now.

Vienna

The great hospital of the Lazaret Gasse, with its cluster of buildings around the courtyard of the oldtime monastery and all the adjoining institutes of anatomy, pathology and the various specialties, formed the hub for many similar hospitals in the city, the external evidence of a high degree of scientific perfection and world renowned research in medical matters, which the world had had foremost in its mind for generations—great names which it had seen in textbooks and heard attached to various phenomena, discovered and catalogued in Vienna.

Toward this veritable city of the sick—rich in the knowledge of its chief men as it is overflowing with clinical material, Evans went after lunch, past the lower class coffee houses of the S. Strasse, the postage stamps advertised for sale in small shops, the surgical instrument houses, past the long low wall of the old hospital—having a vague idea of the location of the Kinderclinic where he hoped to see Von Knobloch and to get started at once on what he had planned as a month of concentrated scientific effort to be the apex of his tour. And then Switzerland—a flying trip—Paris again and back to the old grind once more.

The Children's Hospital was among a great modern brick group inside a formal entry with portals and a triple gateway that could be closed at night. Up a long walk, rather badly paved, Evans went, as he had been instructed to do at the entry, to the group of buildings on the right, decorative brick. He read the notices on the door and walked in. It was an empty tiled corridor where an old woman was going over the pavement with a moist mop.

There was no one else about; the immaculate hallways opening off the main corridor were empty. There seemed to be no reason why he should not look about a little so he asked the scrubwoman, Dr. Von Knobloch? to which she replied by pointing toward the doors at his left.

Evans walked through what seemed to be an outpatient department, with empty benches standing in rows upon the scrubbed tiles, and so into the passageway beyond. A young doctor in a white gown went by, but said nothing. Evans continued in the corridor, looking into the various wards, marvelously well kept and, strange to say, with few children in them. On certain doors he saw doctors' names until by chance he came upon the one he wanted. He knocked but there was no answer.

Then, greatly impressed by the quiet, the exquisite cleanliness, lack of bustle, the serenity of this world-renowned pavilion, he walked out again—back through those corridors, all unmolested. Here he would, for a brief month, touch again with wakening interest his profession—a profession which had begun to fade in his imagination through its money exigencies, till he hated it at times—he would touch again that sheer beauty cast upon it by the Teutonic mind; a spell which drew men and women from all parts of the world to worship.

Already he felt it, not an odor of food, of medicine—just clean.

Going out into the street again, Evans saw on a café entry the sign, *The American Medical Association of Vienna,* and stepped into this fifth class coffee house to see what he could see. There was a grimy door opening off the café proper into the suite of two rooms occupied by the Association. A few people were sitting around eating sandwiches or sipping cups of coffee brought from the public room next door. They were all doctors, women and men, regular American professional types. Evans wandered aimlessly among them until he came upon the bulletin boards where the courses offered were posted, and picked up a few pointers from a rather decent looking chap there.

Now he went back to his room. It was a cold evening. Rosa, the maid, lit the fire and brought in a few slices of meat, bread and some jelly. As he ate, Evans could hear a rattle of dishes outside and Rosa giggling—a man's voice—her husband's he found out later. But it made him angry as he lay thinking of—something else.

What a day! He undressed and went to bed. It was as dark as if it had been midnight. Watching the fire in the cracks of the tile stove he thought to lay out his course for the next few weeks, but hearing the giggles and talk in the closet, the clink of dishes and the rattle, once or twice, of a dumbwaiter, it was not long before he began to think of the girl, his companion of that morning. Decidedly he was attracted. What was it? Of course, the first thing was that she was young enough, straight enough, and willing enough. But the thing that caused him to recollect her with most serious interest was the inevitable one, that she was like no one else he had ever in his life seen before, yet he seemed always to have known her. There was not one flashy thing about her. Her conversation was extremely limited,—in fact, he was not a little startled to recollect how much he had told her of himself and how little he had learned of her in return.

She was reticent, then. Marvelous!

She had on another black dress, different from the one she wore in the train. But Dev could not remember the fashion of it to save his life. He remembered her arms, firm, well muscled, but slender; strong useful hands without the least affectation about them. One small ring she wore on her right hand; might have been an old one, a group of small dark stones.

Rather a small face she had. All he could say finally was that she was quiet, dark, reticent, about middle height for a woman, slightly but well built, with firmly rounded lips, an expression friendly enough by moments but, still, for the most part, rather definitely depressed. But her smile was extraordinary.

Several times she had looked up at him, when he was telling her of his life in the United States, with a smile that seemed to come from deep inside, long, slow and full, suffusing her whole face with understanding and interest. Then he could see it begin to fade and gradually disappear when the nervous depressed look would come again. Dev had never seen such an opening and closing, an opening to intense brilliance and a closing to absolute night.

Queer type.

So he grew sleepier—hearing her short replies to his conversation—seeing the deep flash in her dark eyes, looking at her neck, her arms, her shoulders, her breasts— when she would be glancing down and touching her plate with her fork.

Are you alone in Vienna, she had asked him.

Yes.

Dev told her then that he was here for the first time, that he was a physician interested in children—infants, nutrition.

You are here to study with Knobloch then.—She knew something.—I am here for the music—and because I enjoy Vienna.

She had been in Europe four years, in France, Italy, Austria—especially Austria.

Was she rich then?

Evans kicked himself, lying in bed, for his awkwardness at the end of the meal. At the restaurant door she had merely said, Good-by and thank you. It has been a pleasure. Then walked off. Left thus abruptly he remained standing stupidly for a moment watching her walk away, then he turned in the opposite direction, toward the left, around the Ring—Well, that's that, he had said—feeling a little irritated but—that was all. Damned good dinner. Must remember this place.

XXII

THE DOCTORS

He was up at six and out at seven next day. The rooms of
the Medical Association were rank with stale air and the
stench of cigarette stubs, and when he went to the toilet
in the rear, it was enough to knock one down. He turned
again to the main rooms and began to look over the
courses posted on the bulletin board. It was the Easter
recess at the University—something he had not bargained
for—so that several of the good lecturers were away.
Some courses were already half completed; some were
being made up; others were for him unattractive. But
Dev noted and got his name down tentatively for several
clinical lectures and demonstrations by Knobloch's assistants; differential diagnosis of diseases of the osseous system, with X-ray demonstrations; a course by Auchmuller
on diseases of the ear in infancy and childhood; practical
demonstrations, on the cadaver, of the pathology of childhood by Waldheim; skin by Hahn, etc., etc.,—coming at
different hours of the day, different days in the week—at
so much a course. He was absorbed in planning a possible
curriculum when a plump young Jew from Los Angeles,

Tieman by name, seeing him write down his name on the list of a certain course, accosted him.—Glad to see another children's man around, it's been hard to make up the courses, just about seven of us here, needs ten for most of the classes before they'll begin. What are you doing now?—Nothing. Waiting to see Knobloch.—Come on then with the bunch to Kern.—But—Oh that's all right, you are allowed to visit any of the lectures once without paying.

Tieman introduced Evans to three or four other fellows of the bunch, mostly under forty. All caught a tram-car and beat it out in a drizzle to the C. hospital on the outskirts of the town, a military-camp-like affair which had in fact served as hospital-barracks during the war.

Evans detested his profession in the herd; he had no intimates among its members. Enough that he had to be classed among them to do his work; when he was not working he never wished to see a doctor, barring one or two the mood and perfection of whose work he admired with singular enthusiasm. As for the political "lights" of the clan he had no use for them whatever—and so likewise for the rank and file who emulated their leaders. He had already seen the officious officers of the *American Medical Association of Vienna*—loud-mouthed about the rooms in Lazarette Gasse.—Come here to feed, to fill up in order to disgorge at a stiff price later; at their best, good only to acquire some skill which, as they turn it into cash, they do something of value with it, or at least keep themselves from doing harm. But which among

them is intent to be clear, to straighten out the muddles
of misapprehension which enfold them, to have it
straight, clean; to know, to have a light cast over the
whole? What is American medicine? A hodge-podge of
procedure, kindly enough but no head nor tail to it, no
wish to seek clarity in that mass—

What then was he himself here for? To perfect. He
moved away from the smoking, story-swapping crew beside him; blatant ignoramuses. What a life! To them cash
for cures. He remembered the agitant pathologist secretary of his own County Medical Society remarking,—
What, not a member! Why, Evans, don't you know that
no matter how fine a physician you may be, you have no
standing whatever in your profession unless you are a
member of your county and state societies?—He felt
nauseated at the thought. He remembered his name in
little print instead of heavy print in the Directory of the
American Medical Association. And he had seen the lack
—the pretense and the lack—which always gave him the
feeling of hopelessness that he felt before any successful
cult, the horrible emptiness—the impossibility of instil-
ling sense into men with piecemeal minds—gut minds—
without thought of the limits of knowledge.

Why, then, had he come here? to enlarge his view, as
an excuse for getting away from the grind for a year—to
forget.

It was wet, the hospital streets were slushy, it was about
as desolate a place as one could wish to see. Following the
bunch, picking his footing, swapping bits of information

—one of the men coughing and blowing his nose—they ducked out of the cold rain into one of the sheds where in a low room several chairs had been drawn up in a rough semi-circle. There was a nurse hanging around the room whom a couple of the fellows looked at and commented upon.—Wouldn't touch that bird with a ten foot pole.—A skinny young woman she was, puffing now and then on a cigarette and meanwhile eyeing the men with a disdainful half-defiant smile—which Dev could not help but admire, as much as to say: Some cheap bunch.—But she looked miserable just the same. Several of the men seemed to know her, mentioned syphilis—but she disappeared suddenly as soon as the professor came into the room.

At once, he impatiently called for cases—he was late —and began to lay them open in lucid German—but Dev was not particularly interested in the subject just then and began to look at the specimens more humanely as the nurses trotted them out. This must have been some poorer kind of hospital, for the people were the most miserable, the most dejected he had ever beheld.

Dirt, squalor, poverty, despair—the skin shows it all. Glibly Kern ran over the different features of the appearances, possibilities of this, that, and the other—and came at last inevitably as if by the pull of gravity, to a case of tuberculosis, which with dirt, neglect, lack of bath, was actually creeping over the surface of this woman like a fungus.

Hustling back with the same crowd Evans found him-

self drawn at nine into a steep lecture room with eight
or ten men of various curious descriptions waiting for a
demonstration of diseases of the nervous system by one
Gross—who, presently entering, they brought in two
cases, in ill-fitting hospital garb, which he began to lay
out for the students, two middle-aged men—the well
known picture of General Paresis—the slurring speech,
mixed ideas.

One poor fellow, an ex-delicatessen keeper, had suddenly conceived the idea that he would be a violin virtu-
oso: What is so foolish about that? he said. But you
are fifty-five, it takes time, money.—That's all right, he
said.

His wife had noticed he had begun to neglect his
business. She was distressed. He wanted to go to Chicago to study. A portly old Austrian he was. Very serious.

The other fellow was smiling, more used to the clinics
—and he was somewhat better off. Here Gross paused to
tell the treatment they were using: During the war when
they could not be too particular whom they drafted into
the ranks, they had drawn in some old syphilitics along
with the rest. A certain percentage of these developed
General Paresis; but living in the trenches, exposed as
they were to infection and disease of all sorts, some of
them had been seized with malaria; chill followed chill,
but, to the amazement of the doctors, as the malaria progressed, the symptoms of G. P. subsided, in some in-
stances, so that men hopelessly insane it seemed, were able

to resume their soldiering and even to return to useful occupations afterward.

Thus the treatment they had now instituted at the hospital was discovered: to give malaria to these patients, let them have four or five chills then administer quinine and cure them: the G. P. would be improved. This was spectacular and amusing, but Dev felt more than this the old lust he had had for following the complicated course of pathology of the nervous system—

From there he went to see von Knobloch. Coming out of the Gross clinic, Dev had just time to get across the courtyard of the hospital to the Children's Pavilion with his letter of introduction in his pocket when Knobloch arrived. Here he would learn to know this man whom in 1910 he had heard old Curschmann in Leipzig raving against in a jealous rage because of his—Knobloch's—discovery or invention of the simple skin test for tuberculosis known now the world over by his name.

This is Dr. Evans? Dev nodded. Knobloch read the letter. What do you want to do? A general survey, feeding, etc. Come along, then. I'll introduce you to my assistants, they can fix something up. Would you like to make rounds to-day? Yes.

They went upstairs rapidly, the tall Knobloch in the lead. Taking out a key, he opened the door of his office, went into the inner room a moment and, coming out in a white gown, started toward the end of the corridor where a small group was waiting.

There was a Jap, two men who spoke no German but

who looked like Turks, a big blather-mouthed fellow from Chicago or thereabouts, the various white-coated assistants and some others. As the group came into the wards, the children if not too sick, would call out in unison, *Grüss Gott,* very happily, or as happily as they could. Dr. K. moved rapidly on, commenting on the cases, looking at a chart here, a peculiar skin eruption there, asking questions.

But it was especially on the roof where they went last that Knobloch became most animated. Here were the cases of frank, outstanding consumption—children all, whom they were treating by air and food. The beds were in sheds and out before them the children able to be up were ready with their games for the good father of them all, Dr. K. Go on! he called out to the nurse in charge, and they began to play their simple games. He fondled two or three of the youngsters. Others stood beside him with respectful but tender looks in their eyes.

Tuberculosis, the Viennese disease. At once Dev began to get that sense of beauty in arrangement, that fervor which the continental scientific method, built upon their aristocratic thought, had engendered, to go far through the world. The children tested by the test Knobloch had invented, sorted right and left, every child in the hospital divided first into positive and negative groups by that test.

Light! these were the light bringers.

And all this demonstrated on the cadaver, in carefully preserved specimens—for the sake of beauty.

The Doctors

For beauty was the leader, he felt it at once, a clarity. Evans had always known that in the chaos of pedagogy the greatest genius of the future would be he who would give in ten words, ten illuminating words the limits of knowledge—permitting classification.

Knobloch here was great. Surely it was a great love that shone in his countenance. One could understand how he had wanted to leave Vienna at the offer in cash from the University of Michigan or whichever it was, and how being in the United States a few months he could not stand it but had to flee back to Vienna—and the children's hospital where he lived.—We do not keep them in bed for slight fevers, he told Dev, but let them get up and join the rest.

They looked at X-rays of some of the children, compared pictures taken months before, noted enormous gains in weight from the heavy milk diet and then looked at the child. One they were especially proud of, an unfortunate, butter tub of a girl of ten whose lungs were apparently in the last stages of destruction, and yet this was the one K. picked out as she who showed the best effect of what was being done in the hospital. It did not seem possible that she should live.

The rounds over, they went downstairs. There was a lame Englishman among them for whom K. was constantly halting his rapid, almost running gait.—Are you coming round to-morrow? said this fellow to Evans.

Why yes, aren't you?

You know you can't pay for this, and you can't get

much out of it unless you're right on top of him, and I think it makes an awful clatter in the wards for us all to be tagging on behind him this way. I understand K. has kept it going almost entirely out of his own pocket these years. They say they may have to close down any time for lack of funds, since the war.

Dev and the Englishman went back to the Association rooms, where after some backing and filling and talk with the harassed secretary (who had an awful cold) Dev made up his card for the month—more or less—and paid for it. As he had nothing to do for the rest of the day, he went back to his room—cutting in through the great Krankenhaus, the yard marked with convalescents, shielded by its walls, who were sitting on the benches resting. Especially interesting were two small boys in blue hospital wear running round with shaven heads bright yellow from what looked like iodine painted upon them.

XXIII

ROUTINE

AND the next morning he took his place in the little group of doctors with whom, more or less, he was to share his hours of instruction during the month to come—at one of Wagner's clinical demonstrations. There were Tieman; a middle-aged woman who had taken up medicine late in life to be with her cousin, a surgeon in Tacoma; a recent graduate from Chicago, a cadaverous young Jew; the Englishman and one or two others, one from Jamaica, Long Island, and another from the middle west.

So the week went by. There was Auchmuller handling his great *papier maché* models of the inner and middle ear, driving home the points—a world in which he lived. Never had Dev understood so clearly the ear in childhood. Never had he so lived in those spacious halls of pleasure, the coclea, the semicircular canals, the tympanic cavity—never so heard it magnified—into a life.

And now it was the criminal child, with a flat-faced stumpy doctor at the head—curious perversions, suicidal, homicidal manias.

And always the little group of Americans were being conducted in this inferno by these devoted men: It got on Dev's emotions. Never had he seen anything like it. Kern, a fat butcher-like man transformed into a thing of beauty by his talk.

There was a strong sense of the priest in all these men, a priest presiding over a world of the maimed, living in the hospital, pondering and dreaming—a great sense of beauty over this sordid world.

Tuberculosis again. A bang on the elbow, a stroke on the back of the hand—the disease gets in. Lupus, scrofula—carefully Kern would take up the thread and unwind the same beauty of discourse, dwelling on every detail with care.

The patients became devotees of a great cult—and as the week went on, more and more it grew certain why men came to Vienna, to Europe to study—and what it was they came for.

There was no feeling but the presence of the truth. It hurt an American. Old, deformed, or young and unfortunate, they came there and were stripped to be inspected. The gross nose of Cyrano, the girl with the warty face, the peasant with deep ringworm of his beard. One especially Evans was fascinated to see—a girl, barely fifteen—with the pock. Poor child, she was brought in cowering, the tears streaming down her face from anguish and shame, her body marked all over with recent syphilis. Kern patted her, but there she stood and was turned and inspected—studied while she cried and bit her lips. It seemed pitiless, but there it was. She was taken out to be cured.

Tongues were projected, men were turned upside down, women were exposed in minutest detail to the last recess, eyes, nose, mouth, fingers, toes; ulcerated, blistered and stained. Pocked and eaten, swollen and bleeding—nothing remained that was not seen, described and —a clarity put upon it.

Nothing remained. In spite of himself Dev was caught by this wonder of abandon to the pursuit of knowledge. The beauty of it took him again and again.

Sometimes the strange inhuman art of curing which possessed these men, so differently from Americans, seemed to reflect too harshly the difference between them and his own soft western kind. Service, use—for what?

Here was the answer. For beauty.

In America we save men, without too much curiosity. Here they are lustful for knowledge, for completeness of living. These priests of beauty save men, but keep aloof. That was it. Dev remembered in Philadelphia when Trendelenburg had given a clinic at the University he had been invited to operate on a gall-bladder case. T. was one of the world's greatest and he had made an incision Z-shaped, from the pubis to the edge of the ribs, till the very surgeons gasped and commented afterward —on living autopsies.

Once Auchmuller had asked the class to wait if they wanted to see a mastoid operation, downstairs in the old Policlinic. It was cold, no heat—since the war. The patient was an oldish laborer, who was standing around cowed by the doctors, joking and elbowing him as they swapped lies in the dressing room: Dev had never seen anything so crude, so informal—so heartless. Finally the fellow was stripped, in front of everyone, who paid not the least attention. They let the old man lie on a cold metal table for nearly half an hour, covered only by a sheet. Finally fat old A. was ready. The assistant socked the chloroform to the patient. He turned nearly black. After a while, however, he breathed again and A. standing over the ear, nonchantly took up a chisel and a mallet and with one mighty whang was in the middle of the bone soon gnawing away with his rongeur like a beaver.

Evans gasped thinking of the nice, timid, immaculate methods at home. He had never seen anything like it.—Never again, said the woman from Tacoma. My God, what are these people made of? Why, my cousin says she sees one hundred and fifty cases of tuberculosis of the larynx in one morning—something we do not see ten of in a year at home.

"An American experiment," these men would say of some of our tentative prematurely advertised work at home, and smile.

These things filled Evans with admiration, wonder, amazement. The clarity and thoroughness of the teaching filtered into his mind and his emotions. What American will understand this? Not surely the washed-out soul of his own country.

But nowhere was he so overcome by this overwhelming

mood of science as in the course on pathology of children —by Waldheim, that tall kindly man, curious god of flesh, carefully, carefully taking apart the unhappy bodies of dead children and unwinding out of them the secret stories of rickets, of tuberculosis, of syphilis and the gland deficiencies.

Dev's nerves had never permitted him to get fully past the smells, the unsightly acts of pathology, the great science of unhappy flesh. He shuddered now and would have turned back, had he not been so eager to know more, as he entered this building, inevitably foul, though never so scrubbed and clean, with the flesh of generations of the hospital dead—over whom the great spirit of W. and his confreres had presided so many years.

At the very beginning, the trays of specimens, passing in the hall made Dev turn away. He was not a pathologist—he could not overcome his aversion. But when, seated around the autopsy table with the professor speaking his perfect German, carefully, lucidly demonstrating point by point, everything else was forgotten.

Fascinated, Dev saw the intricacies of tuberculosis disclosed, the lung invasion, the scattering, the tiny gray points all over the body. Each part W. would take in his hands like the maker taking apart his model that had failed. This day he had been searching through the miserable remains of some child whom they had seen alive in the wards just the day before,—until the fascination of that clarity was so great everyone in the group had forgotten when the hour was ended.

They arose to go. The boy from Chicago, lean-faced and despondent, was beside Dev. He, to Dev's amazement began to speak of the pleasure of it all.—I must go home and write to my sister about this, he said. It is amazing. I hardly take a breath from the moment the man begins until he finishes, so beautiful are his demonstrations. I would as soon think of taking notes at a symphony concert.

So the first week had gone. One day in the Association rooms Dev ran into an Austrian who spoke English and who was selling instruments to a group of fellows. The discussion turned to morality. The lady doctor from Tacoma was there, it was among doctors and it was a frank talk.

The Austrian was maintaining that if it were true, as the American said, that fifty per cent of American young men grew to manhood virtuous, then fifty per cent of American young men were little better than perverts.

That raised a row. He said that every Austrian male who reached the age of twenty-one and had not known that, had something the matter with him. He maintained that if you wanted to do something and didn't do it that such a stand was perverse and in the end pathologic. When you want to go to sleep you do, don't you? If you want to eat, you eat. Well, then it is the same with that.

Hold on, hold on, cried an American, If you are in a company at midnight, and you want to go to sleep of course you don't go to sleep. You take a couple of good cups of coffee and stay up.

Routine

There is no such thing as anything natural. We do what we want to do.

Nonsense, cried the Austrian—But it was lunch and Dev walked on with the lady doctor who said she had been court examiner for a year in Tacoma examining delinquent girls who had been brought to justice for various social offenses in that district. And very few indeed of them, she said, had a venereal disease. But her dentist in Nice had told her that thirty-three per cent of the girls of France were syphilitic. What are we coming to? Dev did not know.—We've *got* to be restrained. I think American men are so far to be praised for their abstinence that I wouldn't look at an Austrian knowing what I know now. It is horrible. Why in Tacoma mind you, these were all court cases, not five per cent of them were infected. But unless we guard ourselves by some kind of abstinence, we'll be not better than these people in another twenty years.—

The problem was too much for Dev. America. He shuddered at the sickening recollection of his own morbid youth.

And the women! But the terrible ravages of disease in Vienna made him recollect his *Measure for Measure*—Better to geld the youths of Vienna.—It was all tied up. He thought of his favorite theme: the abandon of life and the—check; what it does to life in America to ruin it. *Ils deraillent,* Brancusi had said. America never will do anything. Raw, not primitive. Afraid.

Syphilis or none, he could not see but that Europe was in the van—

It seemed a beastly morbid problem. The syphilitic right on one side, and a caponized athlete on the other. It seemed hopeless. He left the lady doctor at her door and went home. Saturday.

XXIV

FIRST WEEK

DURING the week he was certain he had seen Miss Black
—and that she had seen him—when he had gone to the
Opera Cassa Tuesday morning. As he was coming down
the M. Gasse she was just leaving in the opposite direction, but she failed to stop. He watched her go down the
street as he stood at the door to see if she would by
chance turn, but she kept right on. All right, lady, if
you don't want to, I should worry.

Sunday morning he decided to walk out to the
Danube, to see if it were blue. A few people were about.
It was cold, windy—as usual. He turned to the left about
the Ring and gradually, walking briskly, came out on
the canal in which lay the market fishboats, their tanks
clamped down. He was leaning over the wall looking
down at them listlessly when someone came beside him.
It was she.

They walked together toward the Danube.

She said: I shall never return to the United States.
Here, little as there is for me, there, there is nothing.
Here it is terrible: but there it is empty. Democracy, she

shuddered. It takes away from the top to feed the—maggots. Here it is sick, but it *is*. I shall never go back to that. But I am an American.

Dev said merely that he was going back.

America, or the United States, we should say, not Mexico or the English to the north, casts a veil, a pallor rather, on everything. Music, how shall they understand it? Jazz! That *is* their music. But the quality of music, what it *is*, not what it sounds like, what it *is*, they do not understand.

Music was one thing Dev never said very much about. He pricked up his ears now.

They do not need music or poetry.—But poetry, again, he knew.

Their dreadful, dreadful colleges with no inkling of where knowledge begins nor where it ends, actually teaching, thinking they can teach the young—the hopeless young, deceived as to history, their own history, misled as to their governors—never an inkling of actuality, but to gather up a hod of small facts of "general information"—looking for day with a candle. All they know is to wall off, to stop—to injure. The stultification of youth, that is all it is, and not of youth alone, of men, dragging their lives out to escape leisure—to escape the horrible fact that they are alive and ugly and maimed and helpless. Never will they wake up save in a company, *gedüldige schäfe:* frightened—or forced.

And women—but it is no worse than life anywhere—except that here they have an inkling that it is not to be a hog or a dog kept for the bench—or—to think you are right because you are packed in a case with one hundred million others.

The surface is all they see there. Can't they see why the negro is the only product of the country that is anything? Can't they see that they can't be—that their silly salvations are puerile, their prohibitions sordid, their minds blank? That sick as it is here, a culture exists among a few who can smile at the gross absurdities of life and who can at least have art, or your science.—That one can exist and *something* of it flow over into the common effigies even in such a place as England, in Germany, in France.

But in America they are stupid, they only know how to maim, there where truly one rich man or woman with intelligence might finance a useful purpose in the world, even in America, not to fetter us to the crawling inanities which they think is education, that dreadful myth, to inflict on us their amputations which they think is morality but to break through that surface to—show us the childishness of our hopes; humanity, beauty—

What damage is being done by our laziness, our hysteria to all that is penetrant, deep. Instead they give us airplanes, radio, and philosophies to accompany them, instead of to show the pettiness of our politics or religions—just so many things, puffed up with wind, just small playthings, useful as rattles for children—and the fury about them: just disheartening, cruel, sordid—distracting mistakes. Can't they see, just to open the eyes and to look is enough. Every child can see. But he gets to the point where he knows and falls upon a dreadful initiation, barbaric, maddening, defiling—like Fabre; late in life dragging themselves out of the slime, out of the pitch. American young! Slimed down into a flashy happiness. All smeared over with success, with athletics— and hysteria to oppose it. Olympic champions, they do not know what it means to see, even. But, to see!

They come over here. I hate the sight of them. How can they know Europe? Yes, it is sordid—well. How can they know? Or if there is a class of them that knows anything where are they? Americans tell me I am wrong. I am a fanatic. That there are Americans who know that all the political flimflam they believe in as a horde is baseless, without foundation.—But they never emerge. I have never seen one.

Dev did not answer. He did not feel himself a hero. He thought she was a little excited. Maybe insane.

They walked on in silence, out the long uninteresting street to the bridge. The wind by now had come up in great violence and was exceedingly cold. But they kept on.

So that is the Danube. The water was a dull river-water-green. Toward the city there were docks with river craft tied to them, coal barges and the like. But on the other side the bank was just a great greening meadow.

America, she continued, the only hope they have is to give up their democracy, if they can, their primitive pact to bind them up like cattle all together to keep the wolves out; to forget their fear and to generate, not by consent but by any means, an aristocracy, a small haven not of brains but of understanding, some few who understand, who do not postpone and hope.

Then they can have music—

An anachronistic government, pretty enough to paste up a kind of union when every Tom, Dick and Harry had to be flattered into thinking he was the head—but used up.

But what? Dev was about to say when she interrupted. Can't they see the perfectly plain truth that it doesn't matter in the least one way or the other all this turmoil of belief or no belief, their democracy, royalty, fascism, soviet, anarchy—that it is just a great kindergarten diversion—useful enough, serious enough when it is ringed (the object of understanding) and that it must be seen and abandoned.—Some few, some gist, must be able to be quiet above it and to live—be, conscious and ruling somehow—ruling enough to get a minimum of sense into the situations which concern us, and powerful enough, devoted enough, to see to it that some light continues from antiquity. And they mustn't slip, and that in America there is nothing of this—that all this claptrap of seriousness is just the buffoonery of nitwits. Just by opening the eyes—She weakened off and gradually stopped talking; morose a moment, looking at her feet, then gradually brightening she turned and smiled.

Along the eastern grassy bank of the river were anchored at intervals of fifty yards or so, ten or more flat scows one behind the other stretching off into the distance, round a bend upstream. Dev and the lady stood on the bridge watching the river rushing by with a tremendous tide when he became conscious of these scows. At the back of each was a long pole pivoted near its middle on an upright piece, the far end projecting over the stern downstream. As he looked at the boat nearest them, he saw this pole being drawn down inboard, forcing a great square net rapidly up out of the water astern. The bagging net hung poised there a moment dripping and was then lowered again into the river. Come on, he said, I want to see that.

They trotted amused to the far side of the bridge where they discovered a winding stair in the eastern stanchion which led down, in a lot of filth, to the flats below. It had begun to drizzle lightly but Miss Black was game. Not a soul but they was on this great stretch of what seemed to be filled-in land along the river bank. Evans was elated, after the travel and the winter and his tourist life, to be setting foot once more on unhedged green turf; he sprinted forward to catch Miss Black who had gone ahead for a moment, then he shouted a bar of some tune, he did not himself know what, but it turned out to be the first eight notes of the clown's song from Pagliacci. Miss Black turned and snickered insolently at him, then laughed outright.

What's the matter? he cried a little out of breath.

Look, she cried, in response catching his arm to hold him. There comes the net.

Sure enough, the men in the tiny cabin of the second boat were plying a windlass, Dev and his companion could hear the squeak and grind, while swiftly—slowly the quadrangular net came up and was scanned. Empty it was released and sank again into the water. Almost at once the net from the first boat was coming up again. Again they watched. Something was flapping in the water. Both started to run. Yes, shouted Dev.

It was a big eel which a man, coming from the little caboose on the scow, scooped up with a long handnet. The cable was then released and once more the great net dropped into the water.

From far up the flats came two girls crying out at intervals as if they had lost a child or a dog. Seeing the man and woman, the children made a detour around them through the wet grass and continued calling out but giggling and whispering together as they looked at the two standing there in that great meadow.

Now the walkers went slowly back to the bridge, the same fine drizzle still falling. Back to the city with the wet wind behind them, they walked. There Evans asked her if she would lunch with him.

Thank you. I have promised my friends. Won't you join us, though, at one o'clock in the Rathskeller. I'm sure you'll be interested.

XXV

OLD VIENNA

It was strange that Evans could be in Vienna a week and not have discovered the Rathskeller which was in fact no more than two blocks from his room. To be sure, he had seen the entrance to the place on the north side of the Rathaus but it looked so unattractive, so few seemed to frequent it that he—feeling disinclined to drink those days—had passed it up.

Now, having gone home to change and wash up a bit, he found himself going down the broad stairs leading under the Rathaus foundations to this cellarway. It amused him to be there on Sunday, in the City Hall, going down to a drinking place. Superhuman intelligence these people have, he said, while he tried to read the legends painted on the walls, wine, wine, wine, and man, ill off for the lack of it, raised to exultation by its magic. There were the usual frescoes in the German style, vine stems and grape clusters, with figures caught in them, monks straddling hogsheads, cavaliers and buxom girls with glasses and steins; while in the panels so entwined, were legends, in colored German script—from

Goethe, from the Bible and common legend—praising
the virtues of drink and the wisdom of the drinker. Dev
paused here and there on the steps to read but a delicious odor of cooking came up to meet him—and he
was ravenously hungry after the morning's walk.

What an idea to keep the wine in such a place—but he
had not realized, until Miss Black had intimated such a
thing that there was a restaurant there. High prices?
Good? Bad? He wondered as he pushed upon the swinging door at the bottom of the steps and looked around.

Waiters were going by in rapid succession but in the
room into which he had come no one was being served.
It was a large room spaced for generous boardtop tables,
by columns like those in the dungeon of the Château de
Chillon. At the tables men, women and children were
sitting eating bread and cheese, drinking wine or beer
or doing whatever they pleased. The simple wine list was
posted on cards hung about upon the stone work, wine
of the country sold by the glass, white and red.

The mood of the place was decidedly familial, informal and inviting. It might have been in the mountains
at a village tavern. Dev liked it well with its stone walls,
floor and arched gothic ceiling. A couple of waiters
walked around in a leisurely manner with tall glasses of
the favorite greenish white wine on trays; or mopped up
the wooden tables as a party would get up and go.

But there was another room. Into it the waiters with
laden trays were passing through glass doors. Evans
looked in. This room was high, columnless, and filled

221

with tables, with white cloths on them, at which perhaps two hundred people were noisily at dinner.

Hardly had Evans seen than he heard Miss Black beside him and he was meeting her elderly companions. Her immediate friend Frau Von Linden was a small, nervous woman with a fine, intelligent, narrow face, who spoke English beautifully; while with her was another woman, older, much more vivacious, a face of true humor and full of spirit, the Baroness De Groff who spoke French and German only. But Evans saw at once that these were people of the world—whom the war had injured. He held open the door for the delightful Baroness who went in first, followed immediately by the others. A table had been reserved for them far over in one corner.

All the tables were close packed and everyone was taken. There were people waiting at the doors. As they were being seated, Dev took a quick look around. The usual restaurant crowd, it was. In the middle of the room was a large group of fat men, fat and skinny, just finishing their repast, the table was littered with plates, bottles and the miscellaneous débris of a heavy meal finished. There were the usual quiet couples at the wall tables, young people leaning over and talking intimately to each other; the usual vicious-looking cyanotic men of fifty, each with a young woman companion; and the family groups—children lolling about and their parents talking bloatedly. The guests were of all classes, serious men, middle-aged, impressive faces, eating alone, seeming to be in the confidence of the waiters, scanning the bill of fare; while quite near them was another family group, apparently Americans, two small kids, with the character of their bright young country written all over them, in free confidence making a good-natured waiter show them how he held a paper bill between two fingers at the same time flipping it with a third so that it gave forth a loud smack.

But from that time on Evans was absorbed in his own immediate friends. The meal was delicious. None of the ladies drank wine so Dev abstained also. To begin with, they had an excellent omelette with greens, cooked to a lightness and fluffy texture such as he had not seen bettered. So it progressed. Everything they had was good and the bill was extremely moderate. Frau Von Linden who was the hostess would not permit Evans to take her bill. It was she who suggested that they go to her apartment after, for coffee and cigarettes.

So there they went—the Baroness and Miss Black in the lead and Dev and Frau Von Linden coming behind. The conversation had been animated, Dev had explained his mission in Vienna. They had apologized lightly for their city—wherein Dev could read their pride and their sorrow in the present condition.

At dinner it had come out. The war. Frau Von Linden, a widow, had been wealthy. An assured income from English gold bonds had allowed her to partake of the life about her: Italy, Semmering, Salzburg and the rest of it. She had her apartment, all furnished with finest appurtenances, three servants, in fact a woman who knew the best people in the city; while her friend, the Baroness, a member of the outer court circles, had lived in her modestly fashionable house surrounded, quickened, enlivened by the heat of the great court, for to her its affairs, its gossips, its fashions, its manners, were the bread of life.

And now—the little party arrived at the entrance to the apartment with its formal, broad corridors and took the lift to the fourth floor. They were admitted by the simple-minded old serving maid who still kept up the appearance of old times there—though Frau Von Linden admitted that she was more a care than a help. She had to have her, however, to keep the Socialist City Council from requisitioning half her rooms to house—anybody in.

She had had a battle to prevent it, the requisitioning of her rooms, a heart-breaking battle but by acquaintance, persistence, and in the face of insults and doubt to the end, she had managed to keep her great dark chambers for herself—stripped of their richness it is true—but still unbreached by the new order.

Here the little company sat down to coffee, Miss Black taking charge for her friend.

Inevitably the conversation drifted off again to the old Vienna, the war and the havoc left after it. Dev started it by telling how, the day before, he had gone looking for the Museum where he had heard there was an exhibition of pictures by Brüghel, and that in passing a large building on the Ring and seeing a man sitting in a chair at a small side entrance beside the great formal one he had asked him, *Dies ist der Museum?*

Nein, said the man, This is no museum, this is the Parliament!

Thereat, the old Baroness on her corner of the sofa rocked herself back and forth in her glee, holding her napkin to her face to hide the gap in her teeth, laughing, laughing, uncontrolledly.

That's right, she said, that's right. It *is* the Museum, with all those socialist nincompoops there. Yes, yes, it *is* the museum, and she was mightily pleased.

The conversation was in French.

Coffee was served with brandy from a decorated flask, each of the older ladies putting her dram into the dark fluid and sugar too.

It is terrible, terrible, said Frau Von Linden what has happened to poor Vienna. It was not so before. The people on the street cars, the peasants, the common people elbow you aside, they push, they take everything to themselves. It was not so before. There were good manners in everyone. Now all that is past.

In the opera! said the Baroness whom Dev liked immensely for her half-closed wrinkly eyes and enormous amusement at the tragedy that had befallen her and her people. There it is wonderful! The *shiebers* took all the boxes. You could not hear the music for their talking, they had to imitate everything without knowing anything. They brought their supper and ate it in the boxes; beer steins they sat on the railing and food was all over the floor until the place was so full of rats you could not go there any more. But they are better now, the newspapers made so much fun of them.

It was awful during the revolution. It was not safe. An American, a friend of ours, was in the streets, in afternoon dress you know, with gloves on. A mob gathered around him. They knocked him down, they smashed his hat. I tell you we were frightened. We did not have enough food but we dared not leave the house. You could hear the firing all at once. Some American friends came to bring us enough to eat. One Englishman was wise. They broke into the hotel. He had much money and jewelry so he rushed out into the hall, without shirt, just his pants, and yelled to the mob, Here, here! and he burst into his own room and began to steal his own things, as much as he could get, leading the others, so that he got almost all. If he had fought them, they would have taken it away from him, but he joined them.

But the funniest is a delicatessen dealer I know, said the Baroness—who confessed to making a fair living teaching *hoi polloi* a few rudiments of good manners. I had not seen her for three years. Once some years ago, just after the war, her daughter had come to me for piano lessons. So now she asked me if I would come to her house, she would send her carriage. No, I could not do that. What! ride in the carriage of a delicatessen dealer.—The old baroness here laughed so she could not speak. What do you think? The house was magnificent! Furnished with everything, everything and, in

the hall, armor! What is that? I said to her. Oh we
have to have that, we bought it at the store. Think of it!
Armor! and they bought it at the store! and the old
Baroness was again convulsed with laughter.

But to me, said Frau Von Linden one of the saddest,
most maddening things I know was when after Charles
was beaten and the Empress had to leave the city, we
had to give her, the Empress, imagine, enough clothes,
a few things we could get together, for her to travel in.
Nothing would they let her take. And all that priceless
linen, the laces, the bedclothes of the palace, the finest,
most beautiful—one of the socialist deputies had it
given to his daughter when she was married, all of it.
—It was terrible; stolen, and given to nobody, gone—
ruined.

Yes, that was very hard, said the Baroness, but it was
worse in those times of war. We had no fat and no meat.
We all got sick, we did not know we were sick at
first but it was terrible.—When I began to eat meat after
we could get some, said Frau Von M., I was made ill.

But the lack of fat was worst of all. The people at the
delicatessen stores were pitiful. But I was lucky, said the
Baroness. One day a little Jew, a boy from Budapest,
came to me to buy furniture, so smart were they. I
told him no. But he came and he came and he was a
nice boy. So he asked me if I could tell him some friend
who had furniture to sell. I told him of a lady, Princess
J., who I knew was in very great trouble and would
sell some things. The little Jew went to her and bought

many things. He came back to thank me and said he
would send me some wine from Budapest. He did too.
He brought me a bottle and, when I opened it, it was full
of goose-grease. It saved me and when it was eaten very
slowly, he brought me another bottle. Now he has the
finest store of old furniture in the city just near the
Stephan Church.

It was the better classes who suffered most and the
people in the city, said Frau Von Linden. The peasants
were not so badly off. It is strange how the peasants are
wise in these things. Why when the war began, I was
in the country with my niece. *That very day* when we
heard there was a war and everybody was saying it would
be quickly over, I went with my niece to a peasant to
buy some things to take back to Vienna. Do you think
he would take paper money? Not at all, so wise they
are; but the very day the war began. Coin, that was all.
Or later, when there was none, they would take a piece
of linen, or jewelry or what we had in exchange for
butter or eggs or a cabbage.

And then Baroness de Groff who was working on some
embroidery, told of the decay of manners. Imagine. Love!
she said. What it is now. Why when we were girls—but I
heard of a young woman, like Grace—and she looked at
Grace,—about her age. She was alone and would walk in
the park sometimes and so she gradually became acquainted with a man, a very nice fellow it seems who
fell in love with her. She liked him too and they would
meet in the park in the evening and sit there. But then

one day he told her he was in love. But, he says, I am
a poor man—Imagine that! at such a time, to say, I
am a poor man—and would she come with him to his
aunt's house—and the old Baroness rocked with mirth
once more—And that is love! I am a poor man! what
is that? To talk of love and to say, I am a poor man
and would she go with him to his aunt's house!

Dev was amazed at this old fire. She had few teeth and
as she spoke, she could not control her spittle well. But
her vitality was brilliant. There was no money for a
dentist so that was that. She lived as she could, embroidery, lessons in etiquette, etc.

At the door Dev asked Miss Black if he might see her
again soon.—They are singing Bach's *Mattäuspassion* on
Thursday, said she. Let's have supper together and go
after. But they start early you know, at six. All right, see
you later, said Evans and he ran down the stairs.

XXVI

BACH

Dev wrote regularly these days: every evening not other-
wise engaged, he would spend in writing. It was his
diversion. He made notes. Auchmuller at 7:30. Waldheim
at 10:00.

Dark spring days they were—full of rain. He bought
tickets at the Opera Cassa, walked, and went to this
place and that—the Hoffburg's sad relic. But in his
mind, like a somber flower, stuck Thursday and Miss
Black. Occasionally he would drop in at the rooms of
the Medical Association. Fräulein M. at the desk still
had her terrible cold. She accepted his money for the
lectures. One day especially she was exasperated. Some
American was quarreling with her, on principle, about
a half cent's worth of American change. She was angry
and down-hearted.—You'd think men who come all the
way from America for this would not be so small. Yes?
Dev answered.—They borrow and do not pay back.—
Cheer up, said Dev, the money isn't worth much, but
he felt sorry for her.

When he called that night, Miss Black was dressed as

usual in dark colors; she was moody and had at first little
to say.

The Baroness is a wonder, isn't she? Dev volunteered
after they had been walking for several minutes toward
the Rathause Park.

Poor soul, what a life she leads. I don't think you realize, even now, what these people have been through, the
better classes, I mean. Frau Von Linden has had her
English bonds taken away by the Socialists and worthless
Austrian ones of a similar value substituted, while
they steal her interest as fast as it is made, and no
redress if you don't want worse. Is your sister here in
Vienna?

No.

Tell me about her.

Shall we not have a bite first?

No let us walk.—So they turned back along the Ring
making their way on foot toward the concert house. Do
you enjoy music?

Yes, but it is a mystery to me, replied Evans. I enjoy it,
sometimes, though I do not know why. It escapes me
entirely.

You are bored sometimes?

Yes, even with what they tell me is good music.

That is good. What do you enjoy?

I have not heard much. I have enjoyed certain perform-
ers, Pablo Casals, some harpist whose name I cannot
remember—I remember once, in Leipzig, it was not a
very great ensemble, but they had for a visitor a singer

called Sohmer, who sang the part of Wotan in Götter-
dammerung. That I enjoyed.

Yes, but what sort of music?

Music where I can follow the design a little, the older
men.

Handel?

Yes, when it is something I can understand. I think I
am more swallowed by Bach than any other—but I have
never heard enough, it is too hard—

Yes, one must live in it. That is my life.—Dev wanted
to ask her about her life but she did not seem to invite
the question.

I never know exactly what to think about music, he
continued. Sometimes it seems the most perfect escape
for—

Not that please, not escape.

Sometimes the most perfect, the most designed and
sometimes the vaguest of all the arts. Literature seems to
have firmer values, more thought; it is less primitive, less
instinctive, less a matter of feeling, but it gains by its
solidity.

. Nothing could be more lucid nor more firm in thought
than the statements of music, beginning with the earlier
melodies and coming down through César Franck, let us
say, to the crudities of Stravinsky. To me literature is
bare, skeletal even at its best, compared to the refinements
of musical statement which sensitively enters where literature is wholly barred by its lumpy words which cannot be made to flow but always seem either frozen or

sticky. I think that the moderns are improving the medium, however,—I have seen some recent work of James Joyce that resembles music most intimately.

What, said Dev, do you know about the modern writers?

I know them very well, for one not literary.—Evans did not press the point just then.

Music, he said, then changed and finished the sentence —Bach has been my greatest curiosity in music for many years.

Fortunate, and here you will perhaps hear him for the first time. Music is a presence which you feel occasionally during the playing. A whole season of opera, of symphonies, of concerts, may go by and there be no music. It occurs here more frequently than elsewhere that I know of. Therefore, I come here.

Evans was thrilled by her statement and did not answer but kept repeating it that he might not forget her exact words: Music is a presence which you feel occasionally during the playing.

Music is—

But I am extremely interested in the modern phases also. The only place that is hopeless is America. Jazz is very amusing. It makes me laugh. That is good. The percussive element in it is the most interesting; that and the newer voices quite as much as the syncopation, the street sounds—but they are very silly if they think they can ignore a complete mastery of musical form. They copy the phrases of excellence, a bit of

Schubert, a phrase from Rimsky-Korsakof, but not yet with the ability to advance them further.

But it is anchored, said Dev eagerly. It is extremely local.

Yes, you mean like peasant themes in European music.

Somewhat that, but——

No, all of it is pure trash. Music is something else. Percussion is too limited, syncopation is much livelier in Brahms. Yet, jazz is extremely interesting if for no other reason than that it paralyzes the modern sentimentalists: it kills off the great mass of drivel and shows some reason for the masters. Music is the youngest of the arts—

No, the oldest, Dev interposed.

The oldest instinct and the youngest art.

Are you a performer?

No, she said, I play enough to work out the details of that which I wish to understand, but that is all.

You compose?

Yes, nothing of moment.

And they were at the Concert Hall. At the same moment it began to rain. A regular downpour.

To Evans, inside the Concert Hall, the great chorus, male and female, the choir boys way up in the loft back of the proscenium arch, raising hell, far off, leaning over their balcony, it all seemed a little exotic. Below and in front sat the grave Philharmonic Orchestra with the soloists, three men, Christ, Peter, Judas, and the woman Mary, in their chairs before them; while the early audience, gathering around, was reading, staring, eating sand-

234

wiches—and there was one woman in front of them in whose disheveled hair there were head lice.

Miss Black was extremely serious and silent, absorbed, probably recollecting the themes, practicing the listening, Evans thought. But he, knowing nothing of what was about to happen, was curious in his usual way, wanting to see everything about him.

Not that Dev was not acquainted with Bach—but, that was all; the interest was purely inspirational, pure music-æsthetic. He hated the word.

And now the show was on, the chorus was beginning. Evans knew no more until with eyes almost popping out, his heart wrung, and his mind flooded with the presentation, he was walking out after that black fleeting figure, through the crowds in the lobby.

Never before had an opera affected him with this sense of its reality. He had heard Christ speaking, he had heard the wail of the voice. His hair stood up; the crowd, the insistence of the voices—Crucify him! The tragedy, blowing like a wind into his very blood, had been fused with an art never before nor since equaled; the very monotony; the piping children! No scenery, no strutting!

Miss Black said nothing; nor did he, except to remark, No performance has ever affected me so deeply.—None ever will, was her reply.

They walked back on the Ring toward the Rathause, slowly, without succeeding in starting any conversation of interest. Dev was sure he had heard the Christ speaking, but not repeating a rôle. It was present, the agony and the compassion, the whole range of the feeling was there, invented by the little organist from Leipzig who almost didn't get the job for lack of Latin.

Must have had a servant to pump, or did they have a mechanical arrangement—springs, weights, his spirit rocking and soaring perilously. No, must have had a man up there. Forget him. I'll bet he sweated sometimes. Just press on the keys and hold them down—fill the church with a roar. Never knew what it would be to us—scarcely an element was there which we see to-day— not even his organ, all different now.

Let's see who were alive then? The Empress Maria Theresa, yes, we remember her. The mayor, the bosses, the vestrymen—Mammas of the boys in the Choir, all dead, forgotten. In United States—China—prime ministers. All dead, forgotten. Professors, princes—But this fellow gets himself remembered. What is it to remember? Good to nobody but the fellow who remembers. It pulls us up together, old and new, together.

Bach eating.

So that is music, he said. He had seen it, felt it, passed through that experience; so that is music. I saw him, my God! He wasn't there; just those singers. The music didn't chase him away. It made him come right there, in power, and say—not sing, there was no singing. He was *there* suffering and we heard him.

What kind of an experience is that?—

It had stopped raining. Evans took Miss Black's arm

at a crossing. The pavement was full of shallow puddles. The street was glistening with splotches of velvet black and streaks of crooked yellow light. They crossed the Ring and continued walking together without a word.

Bach! Dev began to call to mind the few things he knew about the composer. Strange to bring up the sight of a man against his music.—He recalled the statues and the lithographs.—Lived across the street from the church, middle class. Back and forth. Sat in the loft, must have been cold sometimes. Lamps, tapers; maybe no light at all, teaching them to sing. Damned choir brats. All dead. He was a singer himself, violin, organ, had to make it up, had to make up something or other, so he did. Had a time getting the job. Rival had Latin—he didn't have much.

Two wives, about twenty children, taught them music too, made 'em sing in his choir I bet, maybe whaled hell out of them if they didn't know their lessons. Christ, there letting them put him up on the wood.

Art's a funny thing, doesn't seem to have any connection with our lives, just gets itself made—and when it is good there's no time in it at all. Kills time, that's art. Brings up a lot of old ideas we though were dead. Not dead at all. Time can't kill anything, says art. Art kills time.

Funny old figure he must have been going across the street having generated another child in the night. Over to the old organ loft. Something uncanny about it.—Dev was concerned. A light—coming, I saw him, I heard him and not like a man on the street. I heard him agonizing. I saw him *inside,* not cold but he *lived* and I was possessed by his passion.

XXVII

A NEW PLACE TO MEET

THE classes at the University were fascinating, fascinating. Waldheim especially continued to absorb Dev's interest and attention. His studies were all of children. Pitiful and patient, he saw and analytically dissected these sad bits of humanity in all stages of illness, recovery and dissolution. Meanwhile, he looked into street windows; the bookshops interested him marvelously. *Das Buch des Kussens*—with poorly drawn figures on the cover. *Jenseits des Lust-prinzips* and a list of Freud's pamphlets, an amazing list, and all perhaps soon to be refuted, he said to himself uninterestedly.

He wandered much—and alone.

But at last in his walks up and down he began to realize what he was looking for. It was a coffee house, of the right class, secluded, warm and light—not filled with cigarette smoking mobs—not like the Europæische Hof, or any of the ones he had so far visited, but—one where he could sit and talk with Miss Black as he wanted to.

And such a one he found, not far from the flower market on the N. Strasse in a triangular court back of the Scotch Gymnasium. It was not late enough in the season for them to have the tables in the open air, the space was there and the chairs upside down were more or less in place, but the business of the café was conducted in a kind of pastry shop to the south. When he found this place, he rested, went to writing his notes again.

Sparrows were singing on the window sill when he awoke one morning after a restless, dreaming night thinking of money and poetry, and wishing for he knew not what. He looked out of the window and saw a hawk flying over the city. He was restless, though it was but six, and unable to stay in bed. This was the day on which they had planned to take a trip into the country. His mouth was dry, he felt weary without reason.

She was at the tram station waiting.

It was early in the year, few were out, but the day was exquisite. At the end of the tram line they began to climb the worn paths at once, noting with mounting spirits the advancing season. Hepaticas! Violets! as if it had been a novel creation—with petals made after an original design of their mood—growing brighter with the day. They grew hot with the ascent, delightedly treading the grass again, with its springy resilience.

Hardly a thought passed through their minds. They were all among the flowers that day, for no sooner had they reached the summit of the first ascent—overlooking the city from the north—than they ran into a profusion of flowers such as Dev had not expected here.

Oh, look at those violets, and she ran off to lie flat on

her belly, fondling the thick white clusters beside a thicket and under it.

You could not walk for violets white and blue on the bright grass under the chestnut trees. Children were about plucking and flinging down the flowers. The two went farther, Grace insisting on gathering a fistful of the blossoms to take back to the city.

Dev took several photographs of her and she of him, then they went up into the woods—quite alone and away from the rest—where the ground under the beech trees was starred on every side with pale lilac hepaticas, thick, thick up the steep banks—millions and millions of flower-lets, in the midst of impassable thickets, edging the paths or rolling up the clear spaces under the trees.

In America the hepatica is a shy flower. But look at this—What can be the meaning of such a difference. .

But Grace did not know.

Yellow cuckoo flowers and purple bethany.—A strained day for Dev, full of foreboding in which he had seen Grace as a disembodied spirit flying before him, while he had gone alone walking through flowers—alone.

They were home by one p.m., where she left him. After an hour he met her again when they walked around the Ring, a beautiful day, to his new coffee house.

She liked it. The coffee was excellent. They felt deliciously tired of limb.

It was now that Evans definitely acknowledged to himself that Grace might do as she pleased with him. When he looked at her now his glance came definitely to a point for the first time in the center of her eye. For a moment she looked down smiling. When she looked up again, he was not certain. At least, she had not rebuffed him.

There she told him that her mother was partly French and partly Indian, a Canadian, who had come to live in Maine, on the upper Kennebec, and so forth, and so forth.

Here Evans would meet her afternoons after his work in the hospital. She would tell him of the music, plan their concerts; they would sip their coffee and cream, read, talk of Vienna, of the frowsy, at-home-looking people about them, watch for the papers and magazines and so grew to know each other, and to be indispensable one to the other until the acquaintanceship seemed to be settling down into a still pool of talk—one thing only continuing to strike a flame whenever mention would be made of it: America—and all that word so differently signified for them.

From now on they saw each other more and more, music together and a habit of meeting at the café at about four or five, and sitting for long talks about America and—their lives. They went to concerts. Piccaver. Schelling. A Brückner Symphony.

But Grace relaxed in this mood. She grew careless and sweet in the warmth of Dev's devoted attendance. A bitterness, which had become habitual and which she no longer thought of as anything but the gray walls of life itself, melted in his subtle sun of endless devices for living which was working its way in through every crevice of her uncertainty, prying apart the stones like a lawyer's tongue between the sentences of the law—till she felt on these days, in this hot baker's room, actually happy. She would run there as fast as he. They waited for each other, one as eagerly as the other. Grace was changed, and Dev, sensing that here was a rich ground, a profound rootage, had strange thoughts come into his head,—they were like children playing around the back ·steps.

Here she told him more of her mother.

A deformity of the legs and hands—those lovely hands shrunken, twisted—Arthritis—you doctors don't seem to be able to do anything about it.

Oh, Father, he's breaking his heart over me—perhaps—I guess not.

But I can't stand him—that is all—I have what I need separately. .

Here they stumbled on the *Querschnitt* in which he read of the *Spanische Reitschule*. He mentioned to Grace that they must get admissions. Strange to say, she had heard of it but with no great interest. And they secured tickets for the *Meistersinger* the week following.

But if they would talk of America—instantly the new quietness would disappear and she was stirred to a viciousness which Dev would sometimes incite with malicious amusement—

But she was too quick for him. It's not America. What do I care for that? It's life itself. How tempting it is to men to be spiritualists—as if more life could solve anything when life itself—any kind, anywhere—"that scintillating inheritance which we share with the animals, the insects and the plants." . . . What is Europe, a little more tolerable—that is all.

There is not another country on the face of the earth whose best spirits have run from it as do its artists from the United States of America.

And so they talked—they went to the museum together, to *Grafin Maritza*—etc.

One day, after a long week in which Dev had grown more and more silent, amazed at his distress—not daring to say what he was thinking—he had made up his mind definitely to ask Grace to be his wife—But the nearer he came to speaking of it the more panic seized him, and the more he desired her to be his wife and go back with him, back to—

XXVIII

SCHÖNBRUN

AND so one morning, it was Good Friday, April the
18th, Evans noted with alarm on turning the page of
his diary that the month was past the middle and beginning to wane. On this day they had planned to go to
Schönbrun, the former half-wild royal estate of the Haps-
burgs, situated about three miles outside the city to the
southwest.

It was a clear, hard spring morning, but still somewhat
cold. Two women were talking French volubly in loud
coarse voices toward the front of the tram about a man
who had offended one of them.

At Schönbrun the two Americans walked with scarcely
a word uttered, on along the smooth paths under the bare
trees of this great park, thinking. The place was lovely,
but the sense of departed royalty was everywhere over
the ground.

On they went at random over the rolling parkland of
the approach, coming out of the woods finally upon the
more formal portions of the great estate near the palace.
The day did not grow warmer. The spring seemed reluc-

tant. There was still the hard wind blowing—even more chilly there in the open than in the forest.

Men on tall ladders thirty feet high or more were trimming the old plane trees, clipping them into formal twiggy walls that would be leaves later.

Glad they were, the two strollers, because of the wind, to enter the glassed-in Gloriette on the high ground above the palace where Maria Theresa would sit with her famous Frenchman and, talking earnestly, look out over Vienna and the country to the right, to the left, and beyond.

As the two came out again into the cold wind, there were four brightly colored swallows sitting on a low wire near the path, huddled quite close together and swaying back and forth, with the wire's swing. Two small boys and a man were staring up open-mouthed at them.

Crocuses and large dark-colored anemones were coming up on the parterres.

Grace especially was in a still, though friendly, mood. —How quietly beauty goes to sleep, this garden. It is illuminating to be here alone in the garden of the Empress, now before the summer mobs have come, and to be enjoying, because of her, that which she seldom looked at we suppose.

But it's cold, answered Evans, the trees are only half out; that's what one gets, mostly, for being too early.

From the hill back of the palace they saw Vienna and the hills at its back and the plain with the Danube in it to eastward. Unfortunately the palace was stuccoed a dirty yellow.

They passed several hours in walking, sitting in the glass pavilion and watching the birds. Some old men were cleaning about under the bushes, their backs and legs, feet and heads, moving here and there beside great wicker leaf-baskets.

Returning to Vienna at noon, Grace and Evans sat in the Rathaus Park half an hour before separating to go home. The same saturnine anemones they had noticed at Schönbrun, too dark for flowers, soiled, empurpled— made a curious impression on Evans, startling and stirring him savagely, the unwashed half of him seeming at their sight to stifle him with a mad insistence.

Shall we meet at the coffee house later?

No.

She looked at him, surprised at his rough voice.

We'll have supper together in the Rathskeller.

Very well.

He did not reply nor look up to see her going. Presently he began to walk.

In the evening he met her, having made up his mind. They went to their old table. Grace was still in the dreamy mood of the morning. But still as she had been, she had clung to him this day as if he had been a buffer between herself and the world.

They ate quietly, Grace placid, contented, Dev stewing and sullen, unable to say what was in his mind.

And so he began. They had finished their slight meal

and were sitting waiting—for what?—It is past the middle of the month. In another week, I shall be preparing to go—

Grace seemed suddenly to awaken, startled. She grasped his hand as it lay on the table. But letting go again, she gathered her coat about her shoulders. Then she got up. When Dev had paid the waiter, he followed and found her already in the street. She was violently disturbed.—Oh, what stupidity it is, she said. We do not even know each other when we are face to face.—And she turned from him as if to walk away.

What is it dear? Let us sit down in the park awhile.

No. You must take me with you. It is too stupid to stop any longer.

Let us be married. Come back with me to America.— He had not understood her.

Don't talk of that now, but take me somewhere, at once; take me to your room, can't you? or anywhere.

He kissed her hands and they walked back around the Rathaus where he let himself in at his pension without being observed. Grace followed him quietly. Through sheer folly they had gone direct to his room, and by merest chance reached it without an eye being wasted upon them.

But—there were no buts at all.—Do not think of me, I am satisfied, ecstatically so—more than I ever imagined I should be. It is you. Go on.

She had a faintly coppery body, excellently moulded,

the breasts small and firm—unusually so for a modern woman of her age.

After, they went out as quietly as they had come in. She would not stay. They walked about the Ring seeing the street cars, the people mounting and alighting, the façade of the Parliament beyond the globular balls of light flanking its grandiose staircase, and sculptured groups of men mastering wild horses. It was a dark spring night. They could sit a short while in the park without feeling cold. They talked.

We must—you must find a new room, dearest, she had said. Somewhere for us to be together without question, at ease.

Let us go to a hotel—

No. You must find a room of our own, at once, tomorrow morning. In the evening I will come to you again.

In the morning—

No. In the morning you will find our place. Some pleasant corner facing to the south so that the sun will come in. Not too far away from this quarter. Good night —she kissed him—dear. Please let me go alone.

He remained sitting a while, letting her go, as was his custom. Later he waked the old concierge who grumbled at the door as usual, letting him in. Evans doubled the usual fee.

In his room he seemed to be sinking back through imprisoning circles of dark light as through the center of a flower, back to some dimly remembered past, Indian

249

games—mad escapades. Back, back to a lost grace—his own early instincts, perfect and beautiful. Scale after scale dropped from him—more than he had known it to happen under any previous condition in his life before. He never felt less voluptuous, but clarified through and through, not the mind, not the spirit—but the whole body—clear, clear, clear as if he were made of some fine material strong yet permeable to every sense—opening, loosening, letting in the light.

XXIX

THE NEW ROOM

IN THE morning it was a wild scramble. Frau D. was surprised at Dr. Evans' sudden departure. Rosa was disturbed. She insisted on talking.

Dev had to wait for them to make up the bill; he offered to pay the full time. Rosa had a bad cold. He decided he might as well drink his coffee and eat his rolls there.

He talked to Rosa (his German was improving). She was feeling quite ill. Go to the Clinic? Never, she said. I never went there but once. Treat you like a *"Tier"*—an animal. *"Kein Wunder Oesterreich zum grunde geht."* She went on to say she wanted *"weisse Zähne,"* porcelain teeth, not gold ones. The dentist wants 1,500,000 krone for four.—Evans went over his accounts. Not much left.

Then he rushed out and began his search, looking for a pleasant street, then scanning the windows for signs of a room to rent—and finally, just before noon, he located the very place he wanted, a southern window, no hindrances, a clean chamber in an old house not three blocks from the Rathaus. There he went, leaving his traveling case, his books—slinging them on the floor, anywhere. Then he ran from this strangeness, failing to connect it with Grace as yet anywhere. In fact, he began now to doubt that—

Having retained the taxi, he motored over to the city to return the typewriter he had rented. No use for that now.

Now the afternoon lay before him, seeming a year. He could eat little, he could not rest. He walked the streets and began to distrust his own senses.

Now he knew he would never see Grace again. Why else had she thrown him off? Why had she not come with him to find the room?

He doubted everything, while the cold hours seemed like stones which he was pushing aside that he might go on.

Fool. You should have clung to her. Now he began to reënact the whole scene of the night before. He saw her from the first moment, when she had entered his room and looked about wonderingly, surprised to have come upon these walls and the bed—the bed, the chairs so familiar to him, so strange to her. He saw her half nude. He could feel her mind, subdued by her desire. There was no modesty, no hesitation—no amusement. They had been very still. Every sensation, every word he recalled. He felt again the startled wonder he had experienced at finding her body so perfect. He had not, somehow, expected that. It did something to him which

he recognized but found rare in his mind—like a note
struck fairly and true, like a bell ringing perfectly in
tune and time. He had sought a defect, he could remember none. Now he sought a weakness to it all in his
mind and still he could find none. The whole episode
had passed as if it had been the rolling of a glass sphere.
Perfect. Never before in his life had he known anything
perfect.

With dread he reinspected his own bearing. Strange
that he had not been strained, self-conscious, slow. His
whole being had moved like the body of a performer,
a perfectly trained artist for the thousandth time repeating the plotted gesture. But he had been alive, going
forward for the first time into a virgin continent and
he had behaved—perfectly. What had become of his
usual distress?

Now he was sure he had lost her. Damned fool, not
to have held on. He was certain that it was an impulse,
that she had thrown herself away. What?

She had given way to a flood of emotion. To-day she
will regret. She will not come.

Several times he found himself looking into windows,
the old familiar optical instrument shop on the Brühl.
Walking, he would awake and see things in the windows and wonder where he was. Then he would rouse.
He felt cold. He walked on among the people in the
street.

To-morrow will be Easter. He bought some roasted
chestnuts from an old woman and ate one or two of

them, keeping them in his pocket to warm one of his hands. It was cold. Only three o'clock.

Why should she come?

Get a room. Not at a hotel. Some place with a sunny window. A home for us. Our own. I will come to you in the evening.

Then he began again to rehearse everything that had been said and done the night before, hunting for a clew to what would happen to-day. From that he began again to see her nude, after; standing with her arms thrown above her head a moment as if she were about to sing— there in the darkened room. He strove to recall the features of her face.

Walking so, Evans wakened to find himself in a dense crowd before Cook's offices across from the Stephan Church. People were lined along the curb, while behind them the crowd was pushing slowly ahead toward the cathedral doors.

He went along with the rest, wondering, and making the turn at the bottom of the blind way which approached the nave on the south side he stopped at the door of the cathedral. Pushing forward, he made a place for himself on the curb between two women. There he waited with the rest.

The great cobbled square before the church as well as the narrow part of it at the side where he stood was walled off by the crowds around it. A few police were walking back and forth in the cleared space keeping the onlookers in position. A dog ran out and looked self-consciously about. Time passed. The situation was an exposed one. Evans' feet were cold, his heart was like lead. He waited with the rest, he did not know for what. Overhead three aeroplanes hummed by in formation.

Then after an hour, an hour, another hour gone by! he felt a stir about him. Over to his left, he did not see whence they had come, but presumably it was from the great portals of the church, around the other side, the poor procession had started. There were boys in ordinary dark street dress, singing to the blowing of a few horns. This past, there came men in silk hats, repeating a response at a slow walk, just a few. Then behind them walked a fat old man, the archbishop, old and gray and bareheaded, under a canopy held by four boys; an old man, walking on the cobbles, dirty-looking in his white laces and crimson tunic, bareheaded in that biting air. He was unconscious of the crowd which kneeled on the stones at his approach—some of them. His hands were held in the attitude of prayer and his fat lips were mumbling while his bleared eyes seemed those of a man half dead.

Evans stared and wondered. The significance of the ceremony escaped him completely. Poor old gink! And before ever he was by, Evans' mind began to wander to the evening; the nude figure of Grace was in his mind once more.

Furious jealousies overcame him. But what in the world have *I* to be jealous of, from her?

Sore of foot, he must have sat down soon, even upon

the curb, to prevent fainting if he should have continued longer in his obstinate wandering, waiting for the evening. After a rest and a cup of coffee at their rendezvous, he sat about for two hours longer—realizing what a Viennese coffee house is for—since no one so much as noticed his presence and there were several there who had come in before himself and who were still there when Grace arrived.

To him her arrival was like the rising of the sun. Fresh, even gay, she came hurrying in through the door. But in a moment he had her out into the street again, hustling along, kissing her hand until she laughed, protesting, a little out of breath, and stood stock still for a moment.—Wait a minute!

Oh, come, dear, he cried, to our room.

They took a taxi.

From then on, they spent all the time they could together in their new home. She came to him when she was able, which was every day, for as much of the time as it was possible for her to spend there. He would return from his classes to find her reading, putting neatness in his few belongings, even sewing a little.

—I am like a bird that has built a nest, she said. Already I have almost forgotten how to fly. It is beyond belief.

They had planned some time before to take a country trip to Neuwaldegg when the weather should be warmer, but now Dev wanted to spend all day in their new room, to talk and to play. No, Grace remonstrated, we shall do everything just as before planned. To-morrow the walk; Sunday, the *Reitschüle*.

Her mouth was like honey to him. He had never realized the fact of such a statement till this time.

XXX

REITSCHÜLE

SUNDAY: the day of the *Spanische Reitschüle*, four days before he would be leaving and Grace had not yet permitted him to speak his mind to her concerning marriage. A weak idiot he called himself from time to time. She must. It was uncomfortably cold this day with wind and a little dash of rain now and then darkening the streets.

He went to her friend's to fetch her. At 11 a.m. they were taking their places in the gallery at the south end of the late Imperial Riding Academy, the famous *Spanische Reitschüle*, among the other guests, leaning forward over the broad railing above the tanbark arena to witness this most aristocratic spectacle of horses, one of the chiefest pieces of living beauty left in the world, the exercising of the Imperial Arabs trained in the Spanish manner, for which even "the Museum" still granted funds sufficient to maintain it.

As the fanfare of horns sounded outside and as with the swinging back of the doors directly under them the eager Arabs bounded forward four abreast down the

center of the tanbark, tears of happiness sprang into the
eyes of the two Americans. They clutched each other's
hands like little children, holding their breaths with
admiration, knowing that here was the thing, the great
impossible perfection of the world, without let or hin-
drance, "without fault," without sin, that had drawn
them together, the one reason for their love, a parade of
horses by grace of the Arabs—inventors of mathematics
—and trained in the Spanish mode.

Grace's nails were dug deep into the back of Dev's
left hand, so generously did she squeeze him. All they
could say was, Look, Oh look.

At the first glance, Evans realized the gross subversion
of the circus to a cruder taste, lovely as he had always
thought it; the crowd, bred of vulgarity; the blatant
claptrap; the untruth of it to the finest traits of the
animals.

All the first horses were white, abreast they marched
forward and abreast faced the Imperial box, saluting the
Emperor—in memory. Then, to a fanfare of trumpets,
the riding began. First, they went through their paces
gently, composedly, each animal an individual, each distinguished in the perfection of neck and fetlock.

Neither of the lovers was a rider. It was not necessary
in them for a rapt appreciation of the scene.

The grooms in hunting dress, blue and buff, carried
frail natural birch twigs which they brushed from time
to time against the beasts' sides. Right and left went the
horses, walk, trot, canter, gallop; gracefully, restrainedly,

passing each other without confusion at the sides of the arena.

As the horses left the oval to a great round of applause, Dev and Grace relaxed the stare of their watching and sat back exaggerating their limpness. A feeling of futility, of the passage of greatness, the end of desire, passed over them.

Then again the beasts, a great chestnut stallion this time among them, were in the ring, waltzing now, now turning, now clipping the ring through the middle, side-stepping, momently breaking pace to catch it again instantly. And one, the name was on the program, hitched between two posts in the center, did her steps unmounted, at a word.

During the intermission, wishing it might never end, Grace who had been leaning with her head on the railing, on her crossed arms, looked up at Evans. He saw that she was about to say something of importance. No one was just near them at the time.

We are leaving each other the day after to-morrow.

He made as if to answer but said nothing.

Is it not miraculous that everything that we have felt for each other, animal, perfect, aristocratic, so strange to our country and training; that thing that makes us indispensable to each other, that no one but an American can understand as we understand it, with that same longing that we have had, you and I, what we call "love," has been evoked here before us now, by these glorious beasts; everything that we are not, that I hate.—She smiled.

And we shall always have it, when we think of this perfect, untarnished, foreign master, the horn blasts, the stallions and mares. I think few people have had their happiness pictured so perfectly to their eye as we have had it done for us to-day. Here we have reached the climax of our minute. Now it ends. Good-by.

Evans did not at once grasp her meaning.

Dearest, she continued, there is a thing that I want to tell you. It is that you are a thousand times more worthy than you have ever dared to give yourself credit for being. It is amazing to me.

How—?

You understand perfectly, everything, but you will not let it enter your mind. You know; I see it in you but you refuse to accept it. You keep off the bare truths. I shall probably never see you again after to-morrow.

So it would not be to-day; he clung to the hope.

It is perfect that it should be so—but you still fight it though you know better. You see, do you not, how futile it would be for us to marry?

He was straining to keep from accepting her words.

Good, she cried, squeezing his hand, it is your honesty and your fear to accept the truth that makes me love you, dearest; you are as timid as a horse. Accept it, like the aristocrat you are at heart, beaten by that despicable country, our country, dragged in the dirt, hated.—But she shook herself away from that by an effort of the will. Accept it, right or wrong, and stop.

He wanted to, but he could not. He looked at her and

he wanted to kill her—to take her. For a moment something evil flashed in his eyes—soon dimmed.

But she was like lightning.

No good, Dev, it's always the savage that is too civ-
ilized by civilization. Dearest! And she looked at him
with drooping, morbid eyes, a look that he had never
before seen in her—as if she were narcotized for the flash
of a second.

Now the horses were out once more, but his mind
could not follow them, yet he looked, studying each
feature of the exquisite beasts. The spectators had been
cleared from the Imperial box; the Emperor defers to the
animal. Dev wondered if the Emperor actually came
down, allowing the horses precedence. How magnificent!
He did not believe that anyone on earth had the understanding to do that. The horses walked in through the
box over the wooden floor which resounded with their
hoofs to accustom them to treading on hollow bottoms,
and out again into the soft arena.

But now he turned deliberately to fill himself with
Grace's firm profile, the nose, the round chin, the eyes,
fastened with unusual brilliance and sharp attention upon
the scene before her. But the sudden change from hardness almost to appeal in her eyes brought him back with
a start. She rested her hand above his knee, idly. He did
not place his own upon hers but remained leaning on
the rail.

The quadrille. Then the curvet, the capriole, the four
jumps taken standing on the hind legs alone. Then all

the horses at once performed to the maximum of their bent, the high notes of their cultured accomplishment— so that Dev saw them in his fancy caparisoned before a great assemblage—and their riders riding them proudly.

At noon the company filed out into the wet court-yard, how changed since that first day when he had walked by it—now wringing his heart, almost as it must have done the imperiled owners to leave it—Grace had her arm in his. Neither mentioned their conversation of the morning. Neither spoke.

Grace left him, inside the portico of her aunt's apart-ment, with a kiss, patted his cheek, made him smile— said she must rest. He did not want her to go but looked suspiciously at her—almost a stranger already in his eyes.

Think of your gods, she bantered. It is written.

XXXI

WALKÜRE

Evans spent the afternoon miserably; slept. Thought he might go out to see the Carpentier-Townley boxing match. But it drizzled. He began to write to his sister but had not the heart. For several days, as a fact, he had been carrying a letter from her unopened in his pocket. Now he found and opened it, just a note:

> *Dearest boy: Will meet you Hotel du Lac,*
> *Geneva, May 9. Room reserved. Don't fail.*
> BESS.

Dashed into the middle of his intense preoccupation with Miss Black, it came like water in the face, leaving him startled, ill at ease. For a moment Grace was pushed far away, a stranger, the companion of a month, and Bess, old Bess, came up close—for a moment; then she was gone again in the intensity of his reaction, quickened by fear of loss, toward the newer attachment.

By mid-afternoon he could not bear to remain in the room longer but walked out to drive his uneasiness from him, going to their rendezvous behind the Scotch Gymnasium where he knew she would be coming to join him presently. They had tickets that night for *Die Walküre*.

He had jammed Bess' letter back into his pocket. Very little had he ever said to Grace of his sister.

After a restless hour Grace came. Dull as he had been, Evans was quickened instantly as always by her presence. She, too, seemed content to have found him again. So they were going to begin once more. For a moment he thought all his fears were groundless.

Putting his hand into his pocket he felt the letter and drawing it out placed it on the table.

Grace took it in her hand.

Read it, he said.

She turned the paper over curiously, then read what was written. She seemed to be studying the writing. Having turned the page over and back two or three times she laid it on the table once more without a word. Evans took it, folded it and put in into his breast pocket. Grace was looking down at her own hands resting on the table.

What time is it?

They went out. As they walked along, side by side toward the opera, they said scarcely a word. It was Jeritza's homecoming from New York. They had good seats in the center of the first balcony. As they took their places and looked around at the gradually filling auditorium, Evans felt singularly cold to his companion. Bess' letter had opened the world to him again. The fiddle strings were being scraped discordantly in the orchestra pit.

Tell me about your sister, Grace turned to him.

Oh, Bess is a good kid.

Is she young?

Yes, about your age.

Pretty?

Yes, he said.

Tall?

He nodded his head. About medium.

Do you know Walküre, she went on.

No, barely.

It is a brother and sister against the world.

Really. Damn her, he added to himself, what's she up to? I'd like a libretto.

What for?

I'd like to read it.

He left his seat and went into the foyer where he managed to pick up what he wanted.

He came back, took his seat and began to read the libretto.

After a moment he saw she had turned and was looking at him.

Do you know the music? Foolish to ask, I suppose.

No, just the Brünhilda bit where the War Maidens came in. Though the pumping of the horns has always seemed to me ridiculously heavy—or no one knows how to make them seem less so—at any rate.

She laughed. Why in the world do you go to Grand Opera?

He saw she was irritated and thought he'd give her more if she wanted it.—I go for the show I suppose, like any other, to see the story played and hear it set to a tune.

She turned her head away without smiling.

Why shouldn't I? Isn't it interesting, or shouldn't it be so to a musical ignoramus like myself? It's a show, isn't it? I want to know what's going on, what the meaning of it is anyway. What good is it if you can't understand what they're saying?

It's music, music. Nothing else.

All right. But I want to know what it is about.—He felt rotten.

Do you know enough German?

To hell with the music, if I want it to be that way, but he didn't say this aloud.

He had not read far in the first act when the lights began to go out. He had arrived at the place where the brother and sister were become definitely lovers in the forest lodge and Sigmund was about to attempt the sword—to draw it from the tree. Then the overture started.

Evans dimly knew the story, but for once he felt that he would like to get the thing well in mind before the singing began. He was excited and determined. The orchestra was now in full career.

Unable to read further in the dim light, he reached

instinctively for his physician's pocket flash which he carried always in his vest pocket. The sudden flash of the light on the page startled Grace who had been intently absorbed listening.

She turned and gave him a quick look curiously in the eye.

To hell with her.

It was Jeritza's homecoming from New York, Siglinda, that great, nightgowned woman, amorous, tragic, eager to please her people.

Still Evans kept the libretto in his hand but now he was following the music. Sigmund had come from the woods entering the heavy door of the great forest abode. In the center stood the huge oak with the haft of the sword sticking from one side of it. The two, Sigmund and Siglinda, unrecognizing, filled the foreboding scene. All around, Evans felt the depth of the forest wilderness. Before Rome, he said to himself.

The music rose and fell in unctious waves about him— as his mind wandered to Bess—then back to the story he had just been reading. Once or twice he glanced quickly at the page of the libretto to see where they were. He had heard Walküre before but idly—not with the words in his mind as this time. They increased his enchantment. The music seemed to him to be enforcing the speech.

He could see it now, a prehistoric passion, destiny drawing up the inevitable misfortune; love like a glowing metal now invisibly—of the gods—drawing the brother

Walküre

and sister from their own breasts and making of them one—the husks to lie discarded presently.

The music was enormous, too big; one could pass by that. That was Wagner's idea of it. Bess. What the hell, I don't know.

The music raised the words, Which are after all, very bad, he said, the music piles up the feeling on the words, a feeling which isn't there in them.

On the stage, Jeritza was lying with her head in her brother's lap. Now the music had gone over completely. Couldn't put that into words. Words just a blank outline. They'd suppress that if it were in words. Think it's fine, hearing the music. Because it's just excited sound; clear, in words, that would have to be good writing to get by. It ought to be said clear though. The music says it with too much excitement; ought to be clear. Maybe we couldn't stand it. Proust, I suppose that would be. Music is sloppy. Can't write Wagner any more. Music should be clear now. That explains perennial interest in Mozart—Handel. Most music is always muzzy.

But he was carried away by the great surges of sound, and by the story in his mind, when the music would again fade.

Music! a kind of stupidity it requires, a kind of German thickness—light through trees, misty. No good to get all excited this way. I suppose there's a clear logic though, she gets.—He looked a little at Grace who was leaning over absorbed as was her manner when music was being played.

Now, in the face of destiny, the brother and his sister had been united in each other's arms, the sword was drawn, and the first act had come to a close.

For a while the two waited for the aura of the music to fade. Both had been absorbed by the perfection of Weingartner's performance—here in Vienna, a technical perfection which in itself Evans had never seen equaled.

Is it not superb? ventured Grace more to herself than to Evans—in sheer generosity of spirit after the exaltation of her mood.

Yes, I have never realized the full meaning of great conducting before. The *piano* passages, the wonderfully managed crescendos, and the lack of offense in the matter of time and the clarity of the orchestra and other voices.

Grace was pleased that he spoke as he did. She was still absorbed in her pleasure with listening. Now she had forgotten all else in her admiration for the great beauty of the work that she had just heard. But with the lights in the auditorium lit once more, Evans wanted to get on with his reading.

An amazing story, this is, when you think of it, this brother and sister. Do you remember the scene in Sanine where he sees his sister coming through the garden and he admires her breasts—of course you couldn't write a libretto to an opera and have it mean anything. The music saps the sense out of the words.

Yes, of course.

And without improving them. That is, good writing

270

seems to me far superior to good music; a much finer instrument.

It depends on your ability to listen.

But you *can't* put into music the brother and the sister of this. You don't hear it at all, it isn't there. They're just lovers.

That's why we can listen to it.

All right.—He wanted to read.

Lovers are all brothers and sisters—like you and your little Bess, she added.

Evans wanted to read the second act. So he went on, realizing a little as he read, some of the meanings of Grace's last remark.

Before other words between them, the second act had begun—a colloquy of the gods over the fate of the lovers, then the ride of the Walküre, the battle of Sigmund and his sister's husband, and the magic sword, no good at all, just a sell! struck up by Wotan, and Sigmund wounded, —left to die in his sister's arms.

Sigmund, Siglinda; *Brüder, Schwester.*

In the excitement Evans wanted to see the words. Out came his light as he began thumbing the pages.

In the midst of the music, his mind taken up with what he was doing, he seemed to hear Grace's voice, say-ing distinctly: If you persist in turning this performance into a personal debauch,—he lost the rest.

Going more carefully he found his place, saw what he wanted and turned his attention back upon the stage.

Jeritza was sitting with her dying brother's head in her lap.

Evans began now to forget the stage and to think of Grace. He was surprised at her sudden ill nature, and yet.—Had he not himself felt several times far from in love with her to-day? To-day. That's it, to-day.

What kind of a woman is this? I have started her on a new track—where will she end? He felt mean, cowardly. She was just beginning while he was going back. Back! A shudder went over him. Back to work. To work. She probably did not love him. Already he was feeling the cost of her loss. He had been inundated. What am I? She will go on. Then he began in his mind to cling to her again

Brüder! Schwester! he had the libretto in his hand.

Before the third act he was ready to say again, You must come back to America with me.

She replied, Shall I not ask you rather to remain here?

Wotan was giving way to his wife. Brünhilda must be punished for her interference on behalf of the lovers. The orchestra was perfect. After the fire music with its flickering, eternal rising and falling of the magic flame, they started home.

Come fully out of her mood, once the music was behind, Grace seized Evans' arm again in the old impulsive fashion, hurrying him along on the half dark Ring by the trees and empty benches—and all his depression went off like cigarette smoke disappearing—

Only, for God's sake, sweetheart, don't ask me to go

to America. Don't act so tragic, she continued, we are young, dear, yes, we are young. That's what the machines have done for us—you especially, you'll live fifty years yet, maybe. Forgive me, dear, you'll go hurrying back to your sweet sister. Forgive me, I'm a jealous fool, I could murder the little cat. I wish I could see her. I'd strangle her, I know.

Come, said Dev, dancing with the spell she could cast about him now at will.

No, not yet. I will later, as long as you like. Let us go over to see the Johann Strauss monument. There is nothing more fantastic in the world.

They walked and talked for two hours as happy as they had ever been in their lives.

XXXII

PRATER

In the morning, two days before his departure, Dev went to the steamship office to secure his tickets for America. Then lectures, a snack of lunch—and, impatient, he awaited Grace—who came eagerly, direct to him, looking happily into his eyes with such unabashed delight that he felt a fresh pang of misery at the thought of losing her. I shall lose her in only two days.—He caressed her cheeks, kissing his own hand by mistake in his unseeing earnestness, which made him laugh and her also when he told her of it.

No, she said, not now, it is too wonderful a day, come out with me for a walk first.

Will you come back?

Yes, and stay all night.—Come on.

They went by tram to the Prater, the great holiday promenade of the Viennese: There they walked all the afternoon for three and a half hours strolling along always in a straight line southward on the great central promenade to the end near the river by the willows—talking, resting. It was most beautiful weather. The vio-

lets were thick under the trees and many were picking
them. They lay on the grass in the hot sun listening to
birds, the frogs, and seeing boys playing by the reedy
shore of a little inlet. Toward evening they returned
up the drive stopping at dusk in a summer garden
where to good music they had good beer and an
ausschintz.

Lights, sundown: an evening forever memorable coming at the end of a day full of their love together when
every speck of the meadow grass was felt equally between
them and their talk was too trivial, not to mar its weight,
to bear repeating.

Returning home to the room, their legs tingling with
fatigue, they lay in each other's arms a long time talking,
Dev not daring to mention his alarms at their approaching separation, which stabbed him so that he had forcibly
to push it away, burying his face in her breast to drive
it from him.

They slept for a long time, Evans dreamlessly but
Grace troubled, crying into her pillow. When they wakened it was nearly two a.m. Both wakened at the same
time at some loud noise in the street. They turned to
each other instinctively in the dark a while without a
word, and then began to talk. The dark was hard like a
crystal, faceted and shiny to them now.

I want you to marry me. I want you to be my wife—
and come back with me to New York.

I don't want to and I will not do it.

Grace, dear—

No, I will get up and go out into the street if you continue.

Grace, dear—

She got up from the bed and stood in the dark room.

Come back, he pleaded. I will not speak of it again. He was on his feet beside her, wrapping her in a blanket against the chill.

Now she lay beside him once more, she was crying. He kissed her tears away.

After a time they were quiet again and began once more to talk. She was now again as he had always known her, self-possessed and inflexible.

Your sister will satisfy you. You are that kind. Forgive me. This is not romance, Dev. This is reality, wake up! We are caught. Cannot even we keep one thing clean? What are our lives made up of, tell me: bitterness, disappointment—not with each other, nothing to do with any of us—it is inevitable. But not one thing clean. I hate America simply because it is my own slough—but we have found something clean, one small clean spot. And so it must remain: clean, a place to rest our heads on. We are leaving each other. Face it. There is no other way. Marriage is sordid, it is nothing that either of us wants.

That's all right, dear, but I don't give a damn about your reasons.

Neither do I. The fact is much harder and more certain. Go to sleep. We both need it. Kiss me and go to sleep.

But he was desperate and continued to plead.

No, dear, it's no good, she answered him. Let me talk to you then if you won't sleep. You are a curious mixture, Dev. There are two parts: that hard clearness which is your inner core and makes you go, and the tenderness of a woman. Dearest, I love you sometimes when I am alone so that I don't know what to do with myself. I am rock. I know myself. I am cold save when the sun is on me. But you are alive, a thing of the earth. Can you feel it in yourself? I want to tell you how I admire you, how I debase myself before you. How I understand your difficulties, how I want to liberate you—to fling you in the face of the world. But I can't do that, Dev, and besides you don't need me. That's the terrible thing to a woman, you don't need me. You will go on just the same. You are alive, you are a part of the earth. But not as a peasant. There's a good deal of peasant in you, as in all true aristocrats who are attached to the land. But back of that, what a peasant does not have is your mind, your spirit, that true hardness which sparkles like a diamond and which you—part of you—dreads to trust. You are right, too. I don't want you to be like me. You know better than I, down inside you, what is right. But, Dev, it doesn't come up in you—pardon me, dear, it is jealousy of your powers in part—it doesn't come up in you save by moments and with dread; you are afraid. Your tenderness makes you so. You are you. You must be as you are. But it maddens me; do not mistake me. No two human beings can live together. Your softness maddens me. I despise it. I am hard inside, that's why I can never do anything with music. I know all these things. I am hard and I like it. It lets me go about Europe this way. I am hard—and I have been madly in love. Even I. I tell you I was never so surprised in my life. No one but you could do it and no one will do it again. I am married to you, dearest, as few people are married. But I cannot live with you nor you with me. Get some one else. I tell you—your sister. I cannot tell you—I never want to see that woman. She is good for you—Oh, I don't know. It doesn't make any difference. I wanted just to tell you that I see how you are. There is moss and green stuff on your rocks, you are warm, too, all alone. I am cold. You are alive—You belong to the earth, you are hopeful. I am hopeless—I would kill you, make a senseless infatuated lover of you if I wanted to. And suppose some day I should take it into my head to deceive you. I'd do it; do not doubt. I love you, dearest, but I would do it, if—oh to keep you, to torment you, to make myself feel again what I should know I was not feeling. You are you. I am I till the end of time but there is no end to anything. Maybe we shall meet again.—

Dev was lit with excitement by this speech and the strict attention he gave to it, his mind picking up each word as a magnet picks up needles. Now he was overcome with admiration. Still.

A while they slept, close in each other's arms. When they waked it was just before dawn. There was a faint light. The sparrows had not even begun to twitter. They were not tired. They could just see each other as they smiled.

The conversation began of itself nearly where they had left it.

You like America, thoughtless Polacks, Italians, Wops, not too much of them—because they do not matter to you, they do not cause you any serious concern. But fine people should not cause you any strain; they do though, they make you irritable—wanting to run. You are not at ease with them as an aristocrat should be. Forgive me. That is why you want to run now to America, to America where there are no really fine people—or they are buried, voiceless, lost—which amounts to the same thing, lost to sense, to understanding—and cut off from the ground; stemless unless stupid stock like some Marylanders—or worse—silent, ashamed. They are neither aware like the best of continentals nor even the English with that temporal effectiveness, neither fish nor flesh.—

It is not even so much the place but that such a place exists at all—the terrible, unattackable, sphinxlike stupidity, so hard a riddle. It must be somewhere in our first principles, that error—with which we are surrounded—that our best efforts—intensities are lost; the confusion must have arisen by failure at the beginning, somewhere near the start. A false premise which the further we go by it, do our best works, the further we go astray. So that the utmost we can do is to stand still, to keep something clean. You see, I, too, am tainted with a fatal altruism—but something clean, it is the maximum.

No, he said seriously, answering what she had said before, I do not run from fineness, but small doses of it suffice. I soon tire. I feel a real need for the vulgar. I have been accused before of running away. Well, I want to plant it, IT; to see if it grows. Fineness, too much of it, narcotizes me. It drives me wild. I do not want that.

Yes, Dev, you are right. You really *do* thrive on the ground. You are alive. It amazes me. You are growing— like anything—like a burdock. I remember burdocks by the old barn because they grew there back of the house where we lived once when I was about five years old.

When it was seven o'clock they got up and began to wash and dress in the little room. Grace found a few things to make up for breakfast. Dressed and the daylight come, Evans began to speak to her of his writing —perforce, not knowing what else to say.

Yes, I have suspected something of the sort, of course.

Once before she had mentioned it! You are not just a doctor, Dev, what else do you do? Probably you write, since I see no evidence of paint—it would be impossible to be a bachelor of your age, not morose, theoretical, not stupid, lazy, opinionated, defensive, not unbridled, not inanely sensuous, not rich, not a gentleman, not an inheritor, not spoiled—but alive. What is it, writing?—But he had not told her more than that he kept a careful diary—as an excuse for the typewriter, the constant secret application.

I publish nothing of any value, he said now, very little, at any rate. I'm not interested in money or getting known. I write, that's almost all. I do try to get things published. It's all I can say. Meanwhile, infants, he added.

Why infants?

Because I don't have to hear them talk, I guess.

But they do talk, they cry. But that's not it, of course. They do not tax your mature wit; that's why you like them.

He gave her for a keepsake a copy of a book he had once published upon some characters from the American History. She was delighted.—Free from the collegiate taste, she wagered, pressing it with a real pleasure.

After breakfast she asked to be let go alone as usual.

When shall I see you again?

When do you leave?

To-morrow at six a. m.

To-morrow. I'll come here late. Good-by, dear.—She kissed him and went out.

XXXIII

GOOD-BY VIENNA

The day of turning homeward, back once more! Raining again. Good-by Vienna. What a difference now, grown a' part of me. Every stick familiar. Must go back and see it all again, a quick rush around. Fool. All that was familiar is grown already strange. Like going back to old familiar haunts. Wonder if she has really left the city. Grace. My God, what a fool! Grace! dearest, where are you? *Wo bist Du?* Where art thou? Unreal. Did she really love me? Here? He looked but saw no trace. A dog could scent it. Helpless. Did she veritably say it? The room is a strange room, a going away room. The room looked sleepy, he felt burning, the legs shaky, unlocked at the knees. He could see Switzerland stretching out behind the west wall of the room. There, too! no dream. If someone should say, stay here! If God should poke his head through the ceiling and say, I will bring you Grace back again, stay. Would you stay? No. Never. Under no circumstances; she knew that. Must go, must get on my way. What for? I don't know. Get on your way, it says, *Mene, mene, tekel, upharsin.* Maybe not, though. Worse things

than to get what you want. No sense in it, just go. Go
BACK. Oh you blackguardly, snivelling craven. Back.
Back and for no reason at all except that it is back, just to
go back. Glad of it just the same. Good-by Vienna.
Clothes pressed neatly. Tip her. Here, Elsa. Good luck.
Ganz gebügelt—what in hell's she laughing at?

All the preceding day closing his affairs he had had a
little relief in the detail, selling the tail ends of his courses
of lectures, etc., clearing up his elastic mind—thinking
even of Switzerland which he had not really seen since
boyhood days at school when he used to collect birds' eggs
there, finches', black-birds', swallows'; even a magpie's
egg from some impossibly high twig in the school
grounds, pursued the while by Madame Harson aided
though and abetted by Pont the stealthy, so that often they,
outwitted the old lady. But then the sense of anguish and
of loss closed down again "vice-like" upon him. How shall
I leave it? Home? Vienna is my home now, forever.
Come back! He smiled at his own simplicity. For
what?

Having settled his affairs at the Medical Society head-
quarters he went back to his deserted, desolate room—
where she had often come. And she was there! Tears
came into his eyes in the amazement of his delight. He
kneeled and buried his face in her lap. Baby, she crooned
and stroked his head. Then he looked up into her face,
into her eyes to see if she had relented. She had not.
What then?

You are kind, he said, getting to his feet.

She did not answer, but he felt he had spoken like a fool, and said no more.

When are you leaving?

In two hours.

I had to come again,—I could not bear it.

Dearest! He kissed her with an empty tenderness.

She stayed an hour. Asked about his sister. Wished him a pleasant trip through Switzerland. Hoped he would find his sister well. Told him to take care of himself, not to be foolish (what does she mean?). Kissed him again in tender fashion and departed. He opened the door and let her go.

Rushing to say good-by to her aunt, he was told that she had left Vienna.—She left Vienna three days ago. Did she not tell you?

Toward noon he phoned for a taxi and in a heavy rain got to the West Bahnhof not looking out, but looking down at the dirty floor of the carriage, counting his pieces of luggage, fifth time I've counted them. Fool. Grace! Dearest—Oh, you fool, you fool, you eternal, everlasting, god-damned slobbering fool. Why else did she refuse to stay with you than that? A weak-kneed, diffuse, aimless, senseless, instinctive, slippery fool—running away from what? to what? to save your dirty hide. From what?

God, but it *is* raining. It was pouring down in plenteous rivers. He ducked for the shelter of the station portico, umbrellaless. Then suddenly he remembered the letter, Elizabeth Evans, Hotel du Lac, Genève, Suisse. Leaving his luggage with the porter (Dull excitement of going away, people not all so overwrought, indifferent smokers, ticket agent frowning behind his wicket, looking out at the rain, tapping fingers) he ran across in the rain to drop the letter in the slot in the wall of the Post Office, *Hotel du Lac,* he read it again. Stamp first. Last Austrian stamp I'll buy in my life, maybe. New money too, soon.

Back in the station in the middle of the waiting room there was a bird in a large wire cage wrapped in paper, the bird inside piping shrilly; couldn't see what kind. In the rush, when the gate was opened, he had been able to be in the lead. He got a good forward-facing seat next to a window.

The train jerked and started.—First move in many movements that will end only when I am in my consulting chair in my office at home. The first move. The train slipped and with effort got under way. Good-by, Vienna. What a fool, what a—If I could go back and have her now again. If I could go back. Go BACK! What a fool—

A Jew of the usual objectionable type made himself objectionable by closing the door to the compartment and smoking copiously, a vile smell. Dev by the window opened the ventilator, froze out the other, who took to the corridor. Fresh air! For this relief much thanks. He felt irritable and sick. Vienna was going by in the rain.

Heavy eastward clouds were to the north filling the sky in painters' masses, low and heavy (glowering) lowering. Rain was still falling mightily. Vienna was passing, rapidly now, a dull curtain hanging under the clouds, a dull curtain of wet roofs and window-gaps.

West, westward. Just the same it was a relief. Gone. The city was left behind. At the same time the sun shone through a cloud loop making the wet grass gleam before a back drop of smoke-gray hills. In a cut, the embankment rattled by; in the open again the ground was puddled with the brown wet; still it dripped and ran in the gully beside the track. But in the country lay the Danube. Is it the Danube? The river was even with the fields, ovals of sheet water with grass sticking through and shrubs and trees. But steadily the sun came forth with ever a steadier shine, and so for hours the train marched, or rolled or rattled or flew or crept through the smiling dripping farmland, and pastures and low hills, the streams everywhere flooding their banks. The fields were sometimes in flower; God has sent all the colors there. Yellow bunches of cowslips Evans saw with his mind, deep orange buttercups, purple stems that seemed hyacinths, and a blue of gentians, intense cobalt as if instructing a recalcitrant sky. He saw heavy woods where some logging was going on, the red spruce logs lay numbered systematically on the butt ends, in even piles. And in the evening, having eaten well on the diner, he came to Salzburg, Mozart's cradle, gateway to the Tyrol, feudal castle, playground of the emperors —in a heavy rain, which lulling him, he walked to the nearest hotel and had baked carp for supper—a great hotel almost empty by reason of the too early season.

From his room he could see the *Festung* and the snow

mountains to the west behind it, west—and behind them
Switzerland, and beyond that—what?

In the evening after supper he went to his room. Music,
he heard. Down he ran again to the salon. A few were
dancing. An old titled Austrian lady, very old, smiling,
sat on the sidelines, brittle, holding herself firmly together, a hat balanced upon her head, a shawl about
her shoulders, "Baroness," wattled and alert. Her fixed
smile did not relax before an old man, dozing by her
side, his head drooping. To waken him, she ventured:
Sie haben nicht ihr buch, sonst lesen sie? An old pleas-
antry, so old Dev shuddered. He did not waken.

Evans slept that night thinking of—another place,
another place in which to be.

Waking next morning it was May day! The chestnut
trees by the station were in blossom but the cobbled
streets were still. He went out and began to walk toward
the *Festung.* From the town came a slow procession,
working women and men, with signs—Bread! Red flags
but no music, no sound—they came on over the bridge,
walking. Whither and for what? Women and men and
children. Dev, walking, went on, stumbling by chance,
among April showers, into the Dom where someone
was about to perform upon the gigantic organ high up
in the gloom, in the cold, in the hushed spicy air. He
sat upon one of the cold oak seats and looked around
at the vacant spaces of the medieval edifice. Very few
had come to hear the organ in the cold damp church—
far off from the world. The organist was playing a

confused fuge. The air shook before a sound was heard, so low were the heavy tones. The notes seemed blurred but never had Dev heard so powerful a roar, so deep toned. He looked, absolutely cold, and heard and went away.

He climbed the *Festung,* winding up the leaning causeway, past the portcullis, now eternally raised, by the weedy ramparts, wet with rain and lack of sun where the weed stems were loaded with snails large and small. But entering the fortress, the sun shone in the little court. There were the archbishops' rooms, handsomely ornate; the ancient stove of tiles,——1509 (was it Huntington wanted it for $150,000? Thank God they wouldn't sell), yellow tiles, built by one man who knew the art, five years it took him. He saw the two-man organ on the open east porch under the eaves, the spiked drum that plays nine tunes. At an open window at Vespers it plays its hymns over the town. He saw the decorated doorways and the cruel dungeon, a deep pit, and the implements of torture, made of wood; the well they drank of in a siege; the twisted columns strong enough to have deflected a cannon ball without deep injury—and from the topmost tower he saw the view!

Returning slowly to the town, at Peter's Keller in the rocks, he drank his beer and had two shirred eggs with a slice of toast. He looked at a tart; a fat stolid thing she was who should be working in a factory somewhere in New York, he said to himself. She made him ill, so still she was, to look at her. He came then into the

Peter's Kirche whose columns had been raised and raised into the narrow nave, up and up until they seemed three times as thin and long as actually they should have been, holding up the roof, taller than any other columns he had ever seen—much the same as those of the double nave at Toulouse—save that these seemed monoliths. So tall and gray they were it was one of the most beautiful things that he came upon in Salzburg, these slender columns with their square capitals so plainly cut.

XXXIV

THE MOUNTAINS

THE train next morning was at five. He got to the station in the half dark. This compartment. Two men were in it; the midnight train from Vienna. Two men were in it sleeping under overcoats, windows closed; the place was stinking, smoke filled. They were much peeved at the American who walked in and flung open the window. *"Furchtbar kalt."* Hell, it stinks in here.—Mr. and Mrs. Aleck Johnson of Virginia, Pinky Pank River, 1627 on his mother's side, it was who had come in just before Evans. They were charming, talking all morning: told him all about their farm, the pangs they felt at selling it. At six the sun came out, a superb day. The country was half green, half forested, now. Chalets on high hills, isolated; a few people. At one station stood a woman with glittering head dress, gold or brass, stiff lacy frills, medals and metal earrings. The Smiths got out at Innsbruck. Must visit Innsbruck some day.

Now indeed, after leaving Innsbruck, the real mountains began, the train was winding and laboring to avoid them and slip in. Now on the right Evans saw the jagged edge of the great cliffs. As if coming from a shell he saw the cold, withered mountains cut out on the blue sky, snowcapped and with wind making a play of the snow on the high glissades.

He saw slanting ledges where his mind walked at ease aloof from the crawling world; V-shaped gorges he saw and inverted fans of fallen rock and sand by the cliff's face. Into his spirit he drew, along with his breaths, the stillness and the cold which his body could not have reached. Or he saw a great knob of even granite, shaped like a rock to hold smoothly in the hand and to stroke. Rocks precipitous, perpendicular, measured only by a few thousand feet but straight up, to man most difficult. Now he saw the pine, the evergreen woods starting up the slopes and stopping, or from the recent rains, finger-like spouts of water fell from the tops of the visible mountain walls, speaking of cliffs higher and melting snow. Or on flat rocks, black stains of running water spread out lacquerlike on the rock's face. To the north with the sun on them were great pinnacles, sparkling, snapping, cut out with its sharp knife on the lakes of hard blue. The minute features of the rock drew Dev from point to point; the particular conformation of some slowly turning pinnacle. Eagerly he watched it turn revealing its person. So arose the personalities of the gods, aloof, particular, visible, deathlike, near but far, nothing between us and them but air, space—frozen. Or from behind a running wall of rocks he saw a thing emerging, rising, growing in dimensions and he thought: taking his breath!—If these cliffs were *He,* what of that? The *Doner slag!* a great saddle, ten, twenty, thirty miles away, a bay of whiteness, inhospitable, but soft as feathers.— But there is an agony. One might pass through it if one were strong and skillful enough. Something MUST live there, that's imperative. Then what? The *Saeter girls* are nearest.

So he sat for an hour, two hours, his face pressed upon the windowpane absorbed in the mountains, while the train labored, and wound and stopped and started again at the little hamlet stations. To the south side of the car he shifted and saw a more gradual rise across pastures, green and flowery. But to the north a stream ran by the railway, tributary to the Rhine,—Its headwaters; I don't know. Rhine and Danube, headwaters hereabouts, about the same parentage. One goes to Budapest; the other to Holland. Parting of the ways.

He went back to the mountains, once more rock ledges where no snow clings, a great snow field, then up, up to the forbidding summit, sunlight painting it orange, purple, black—A hawk there, a hawk!

Fish, trout—chamois too and ibex there must be up there. On the railroad folder there was a scene, an Alpine hunter with an ibex over the nape of his neck. In the center of culture there is a wild park—Switzerland.— He looked to see if he could see any wild life on the crags. No. Almost all shot off for meat during the war. Fish gone too, mostly; fished out while the game laws were in abeyance.—I'd like to see a chamois, said Dev.—

There used to be a pair at Interlaken in the park.—I'm going there.

The gods began to appear to him again, as mountains and small flowers. Both he could see from his isolation in the shell of the moving train and he knew the details of the flowers, from within the train, the minute perfection of spot and fibril, the cold details of the mountains; though he could see but the gross contours—yet the details came to him. In the bark crevices of the trees, he could detect with his mind ants running, their slight antennæ working nervously in and out—running perpendicularly.

Far off he recognized the aching sense of a woman, far off, a woman whom he had known, outside, far outside, going, not inside anywhere any more. A memory. Memory is the affirmation of genius; a fast-fading memory. Once he thought he saw her in the car, a pair of green satin slippers, and back he came with a start out of memory. She is in this train! Who? Should I know her if I saw her now?—He tried to remember her features and remembering he had been trying, he found himself looking at the ridge of a frost-cold, distant peak—having forgotten what he was trying to recall.

What have I forgotten? Just to recall it would slaughter me certainly. I have learned painfully to forget: from the first moment, remember and forget. The weight of the stabs, one on the other—forgotten. Every painful wound carries away, forgotten, a share of memory. To forget the pain, we lose memory itself until there is nothing more. Nothing should be forgotten, yet we must forget.—He tried to remember hours of agony and moments of pain—I have felt too quickly and too much. The hooks of memory are worn smooth with the weight of pain that has slipped from them. I remember nothing. I see and it is forgotten. Only that is brilliant which is there, there. Everything else, good and bad, is slipping away, taught by the anguish. But that which is there—it is without memory and without pain. My life is an effort to avoid memory; an escape. Fasten I will upon the thing, there outside the window, that lives without pain and without memory. It were idle now to remember. She is gone. Only two days since I had her in these arms.

Dev grew sleepy and slept. All day long they were in the train, going. It took a solidity away from them all, train goers. They became fluid from the excess of their passage and flowed together—the lines between them as individuals melting, only to be redefined later.

Those that got out at noon were not of the same cast with those going on. The panorama of the day. More than half Switzerland, east to west, they saw.

All day, since five in the morning, the struggling and rolling train had moved with the sun through valley after valley, in mountainous passes until the mountains had seemed to enter the train possessing it so that it became a mountain train, a thing belonging to the rocks and snows. All, nearly all day, the window had been pelted with these sights. Evans felt almost a mountaineer; he grew used to the melting winter of the Alps and their implications: Thus the world is and I am part of it.

Into a meadowy valley now the train swung, in a great curve, north then south, then over the river and, This is Switzerland! The train drew up at the silly station of Buchs and it was a new country!

Evans stepped down and got some new money. For several million Kronen he received a hundred francs or so. Now the passengers had paid their tolls and now the train was backing out—I thought they would go straight on—backing out and turning.

South turned the train, seeking to sense the way. No good striking in there. Then in the valley he saw a castle from a book, moated and turreted. All around, the country was a field of checkered green. The castle, once a fortress, spoke with an accent romantic and sad. Long Dev looked at the castle, trying to remember. Romance lived so long as he could see the pointed towers, he strained to see.

The castle spoke to him from the center of the valley, but the words were missing, just a sound; he saw—and could not recall. With an insistent drag the train wrestled with the castle. Gone, said Dev, still looking at the handful of deserted stones. Gone! It shot a pang into him, a bolt from Wartau—the ruined castle of Wartau. Well, we are the inheritors. They are better than the mountains anyway.—The long Rhine valley holding its story among the fields had succeeded the savage promontories of the uninhabitable Tyrol. Here we soften, the shell weakens.

So this is Switzerland. We have been riding for a thousand years. The evening is coming on.—They were ascending a stream that broadened in the reddening day into a still, long lake, quiet with evening. This is the *Walleen See.* Westward along the bank the train, lately out of Vienna, ran by rowboats while the mountains stole close—close to the water so that they could look down into it: it was clear. There were small houses by the banks and skiffs on the water. Dev saw a man rowing a boat, bending over and rowing. Whither? Why? Evening asks unimportant questions. The evening was entering the train as the lake was fading into the red light. Now it began to grow dark and the lake drew its banks together at the western end and dropped behind.

The trainmen switched the lights on in the car. Everyone was stirring now. Another lake had come up to the train purring along its side, a great broad lake—On this lake is Zurich, at the farther end. An excitement of the evening, of the lake, of pear trees, in blossoms here and there in the fading light, kept Dev on his feet, standing in the corridor with the rest. They were passing evening towns. Once they stopped, twice—close by the water. The trees and the houses became more and more huddled as the night grew quickly murkier. But a new feeling came into the train, a city. And there, out over the water at last they could see it, lights, seeming to move out over the water. Sparks of light they seemed, gathering, foregathering, spreading out over the quiet sheet of lake water. It had grown warmer, much warmer as the train circled, circled behind the city. Then, Here we are! cried someone.—For to-night I shall stay here, perhaps for two days, said Evans.

Alighting, he stood upon the ground and felt it solid under his feet. His legs felt as might a bird's after a flight. He carried his own bags. He hailed a taxi. He found his hotel by the rushing outlet of the lake. He found his fresh smelling room. He spoke French. Later he found the main street of Zurich and walked down it to the lake. He saw the lake, quiet and warm. He looked at the faces on the streets. He went to the hotel again. He undressed. He washed himself. He drew the window jalousies. He lay in the bed. Rising again, he opened the window. He turned out the light. Thinking of many things, finally he went to sleep.

XXXV

LUCERNE AND INTERLAKEN

THE little morning train from Zurich to Lucerne was so clean, so modestly patronized, so bevarnished, cane backed and seated, the windowpanes so shone, it seemed unfair to sit in it at all after this dirty world.

It was a dairy country: there were fruit trees and fields of hay uncut and full of flowers. Then in a little while they came into Lucerne.—I'll stay here a while, he said and found a hotel by the cathedral towers which, it being Saturday, began to toll their heavy bells.

All around to the south, Dev saw, beyond the quiet lake on which a white excursion boat was moving pleasantly, a ring of distant mountains while before him to the right across the water shot up a dark peak, Pilatus, by itself. I'll take that in, he thought. A horizontal cloud was spread across it near the top from which the peak itself rose into the sky as if cast off and floating. It was a still noon.

Miniature Lucerne amused Evans, it was a place to patronize. An amazing little chambermaid with cheeks flaming red and round had brought him the water at his ring. She spoke French of a gutteral peasant accent. Her smile was fixed, but so bewildering, bewildered, frightened, Dev laughed heartily to himself once she had gone outside and closed the door.—Good God, he said.

By the lake, on the broad graveled promenade by the Casino, he began to see the English, sitting about and walking up and down. He looked down into the warm lake in the warm sun under the blossoming horse-chestnut trees and saw the bottom. He walked in the sun, as the others also were doing and from there up to the *Drei Linden*. Then he went back and walked into the town. He read the names of the various hotels on the water front, the great and the lesser; there were greater and there were lesser. He saw the balconied restaurants.

Next day he rowed for two hours on the lake; he rowed out to the junction of the four lakes, a long row and he rowed back. But the best day was when he went up Pilatus—or rode up it with the others on the rack-and-pinion railroad.

In the valley at the foot the fields were butter yellow with the growth of buttercups. As the sloping train set out, an open car climbing through the woods, spruce branches came close to his hand. The ground was full of flowers; violets, clumps of them, anemones, purple hyacinths and low clusters of flowers, pink and white, with small waxy green leaves, of which he did not know the name. Up they went and as they went the flowers changed, and now the trees were left behind and they came out into a mountain pasture where great slabs of snow still lay white over the ground. Sticking through the snow were white and purple crocuses, masses—or clustered stars of them. Below a tiny trestle as the train crept over it, he could see them, on every side. But these gone, too near the top, nothing remained but snow or in one place, where the rock was split on a south wall a sprig of blossoming heather.

The top was wet with a great cap of slushy snow— sometimes it was ten feet thick—through which tunnels had been cut. The girls at the hostelry were out waving at the approaching train. No one had been to see them since the day before.

The next jump was to Interlaken. But here Spring had not yet come fully in. No one was there. There Dev rested—in the rain and mist. Interlaken pleased him. And here, he said I'll stay a few days anyhow. To the south; mist and rain. The streets were still, the great hotels were closed. It was higher here than at Lucerne; but grass in the yards and fields was rank.

He found a small hotel, the Hotel des Alpes, with only one other guest in it. So he got a fine room, and a nice girl to wait on him. This was better. The season is late, she said. Shall we see the Jungfrau? I hope so. When? Oh that depends on the weather.

I am a traveler, he said. So tucking his traveling things away, he walked down into the street and went up to see the town. The Casino was to open for the first time this season that same night. Standing by the municipal barometer, Evans read the weather news. Variable. The clouds were low, the Jungfrau was invisible in mist. Well—we'll wait for it.

Then he remembered that he had wished to see a chamois. That night he slept. There is seclusion here. I've been up Pilatus, I won't do the Jungfrau trip. No, not the Lauterbrunnen either.—I like this place at this season. He strolled—in the rain. It rained. He walked. The grass was dripping wet by the road and in the fields, wet and long and filled with masses of forget-me-nots and cornflowers, dandelions and daisies. There were other flowers, white and purple, and he came to the ruin of Malmfred's tower. He climbed about it in the rain. Romance. But at the bottom of the ruined keep it stunk, for a good reason.

Back he turned and on his way he came upon a modest brewery smelling sweetly-sourly of beer. All about it were the fields of long grass filled with flowers. It boiled up in his mind—America! The kind of visitors that come here are that sort—Switzerland is sickening —a strong prohibition party has sprung up: disease spreads.

But up a path he made his way hunting, solitary for a sight of a live chamois. He went up the hill, the Kleine Rüggen, and walked about under the trees in the rain looking for the chamois in the enclosure there. He went through deep woods. It was dripping wet. At his feet he saw the small white and yellow flower he had wondered over on Pilatus but could not descend from the car to pick. He picked some now from among their laurel-stiff tiny leaves. They were sweet as of strawberries, deliciously sweet. But the deer enclosure he found at the peak was empty—nothing in it. He sat in a broken shelter there and dug his cane down dismally into the piney ground. There he sat, dismally, in the rain.

At the hotel, he spoke with the girl, a fine, intelligent, self-possessed, comely girl.—In the winter I work at St. Moritz, she said. In the spring and summer here. Oh, the chamois have been moved to a safer place on the other side of town. The flowers? they call them *eiblumen,* for their color, egg flowers, orange and yellow.—They should have named them by their smell, said he.

In the evening he went back to the Barometer on the public square to see if he could see the Jungfrau. Still the rain fell. The amphitheater of the hills stretched before him, just the abutments of the mountains showing; all the tops were hid in cloud, a heavy cloud. Nothing of the Jungfrau could he see. *Sein de neige!*

For supper alone in the silly dining-room he was pleasantly served with talk and pretty smiles along with a good meal so that he felt at ease and said he would return to Interlaken some day. Why return? Are you not here now?—So he asked if he could have rhubarb for breakfast next day since he could see it growing in the yard.

That evening he went to the newly opening Casino, a broad balconied chalet, before which against the blue green side of a mountain in a park stood the greatest spruces he had ever known, dripping with the rain, and pansies as large as a man's palm. Evans played at the machines and lost ten francs or so.

The second day he went again to look for the chamois, in the new park, on the eastern side of the town. Rain was still falling. He found the park and saw ibex peacefully at their hay. Some were on the roof of their shelter. But there were no chamois. So back he went, crossing the canal on a bridge and saw the rushing water of the lake outlet. But at the Barometer, though the rain had stopped—the Jungfrau was as heretofore totally invisible. I'll leave to-morrow. That night he spent reading a book the girl had found for him. Five days more to Bess. He didn't care at all. As long as the cash holds out, let it run on.

And so he slept to the sound of a hard rain.

Where art thou?

In the morning, he was leaving at nine, the Jungfrau showed its white breast. O swan of rock and snow—new fallen, blizzard white. A mountain of snow he saw, the snow white mountain breast, the sun upon it.

Sein de neige! He woke as from a lethargy. The stupid lethargy into which he was falling, to some kind of feeling at that sight. Snow breast, white and icy: a pang of anguish.

Then he wanted to go. Damn Switzerland, it lulls you to sleep.—So that he fled now with a purpose to the next step. Eagerly now he felt the end of this slow journey.

XXXVI

GENEVA AND DIJON

It was Geneva, where as a boy of thirteen he had gone to school. His heart beat wildly seeing Geneva once more through those half-forgotten eyes.

And Bess cannot be far off now. Bess is here.

She had picked a quiet, decent-looking place. Wants to make that sort of impression on me. All right. But his heart was racing with the pleasure of it all.

He went in. Yes, there is a room reserved. Mademoiselle had left word. She would return at five.

At last.

Bess! he could feel her everywhere.

That and a boy, himself, just out of sight around the corner, upon the lake steamer that time; swimming under the raft at the old swimming place in the crystal blue water; on the train that afternoon when he had made the first team, when they told him they would pass the ball to him, left forward, at the kick-off. The violets back of *L'Orloge* by the *rouisseau;* the very branches from which he and Pont had stolen the goldfinch eggs.

Bess would not be back till five. He dropped his things in his room, ran out, down the street, over the Rhone bridge to the old Lancy steam-tram station. It was an electric car now.

He smiled to himself remembering the day he had run away from school and how M. Rommel had raised Cain with him on his return, speaking a blistering stream of French at him of which he had understood not one word.

And there was the old gateway with the enormous horse-chestnut trees over the entrance. But the school had ceased to exist, the town had taken it for a City Hall. He wandered about the grounds and lived again those old torments and delights—until he could endure it no longer,—it had worn so thin. He had to retreat at a run. Back he must run to Bess! She was there, she was there *real* once more. And so wildly as he had run to see the old haunts, so wildly he fled from them again—to find Bess, actual, living, going on with it. Bess! He could not wait.

But suppose the spell will not work.

He walked more and more slowly the nearer he drew to the Hotel du Lac. Only four o'clock.

Now he was no longer in a foreign country. The hotel was redolent of Bess. He had come definitely under a new influence which unconsciously he had been waiting now to test, to see what there was, as he had never done before, to see if it would do. For what? Now at least he realized fully what he had been looking forward to. He had come to Bess. Now he should see in, to ask of

her—What have you found? and to be asked and to
live again in the telling—maybe.

And Bess on her part. What would be her condition?
Would she too be asking? Many things must have happened. He grew excited as he laid away his few things
in his room, then smoking, he threw open the window
—more rain! to look across a court, over a graveled roof
below, upon which three pigeons were preening themselves in the light drizzle. He leaned on the window sill
and smoked. He looked at himself in the mirror over
the chiffonier to see what Bess would see. He brushed
back his graying hair. How much should he tell her?

His first impression of his sister was from the back as
she was mounting the stairs having missed him in the
lobby when he had gone down to look for her at half
past five. My God, she is young, she is exquisite. Bess!
he cried. She turned. Exquisite, severe—My own beautiful sister!

Bess came down again with a quick run and—in the
lobby—with a flashing smile, kissed him quickly,
squeezed his hand and saying, You dear boy, led him to
the stairs and took him at once into her room across
the hall from his own. There she threw her arms about
him and kissed him twenty or thirty times—with the
strong show of affection that had always marked the
relationship of the two when they had been apart for
any length of time.

After that, however, and almost at once an embarrassment came up between them which it was to take many

306

days to resolve. Both were reticent. Each stood back, watched the other intently—and was content to wait a while.

A sudden realization of what he had passed through since he had seen her last—and of all he would have to tell her if he told her anything—disconcerted the brother, and on her part, the sister presented an appearance very little different from his own. But they were glad to be near each other again, both of them.

Chase yourself, Dev, she said, I must change my dress. Let's have an early supper and get out of this. It is divine by the lake. It has stopped raining.

And so for the greater part of a week they spent these beautiful spring days together, buying a watch for "Sis," taking a trip to Ferny, old home of the divine philosopher. But the house was closed and the gates were bolted.

They explored once again the Salève where they literally bathed themselves in flowers on the short, sweet grass of the plateau. Such flowers! the blue columbine, acres of sky-blue gentians, yellow cowslips, and purple hyacinths, buttercups, until they gasped at it in bewilderment—nothing in their lives to give a word that they might understand it by. Nothing but the Greek could support such a wonder as this. Yet they had each other and it drew them somewhat nearer together to be thus employed.

They walked, they watched, they saw the men fishing at night from the lake bridges, they wandered in the old city and the new, they visited the Triano and fed the swans. They drank, they ate *patisserie* as he used to do when there at school. They had the same strawberry tartlets he had enjoyed thirty years before. They talked of the Riviera, of Italy, of Lake Constance where Bess had been for a time. But of their intimate lives for the past three months they said nothing at all. Geneva they both loved and resolving to come back to it SOON, presently the week had passed and they decided they must be going on. It was mid-May. Back to Paris! and then —Dev shut his eyes—home.

Of the trip to the great city the most striking incident was the halt at Dijon where they stopped at the famous Hotel de la Cloche, rendezvous of hiding lovers. All day, again, they had traveled; servants of the god-like train. Geneva, at the foot of the lake, though in the open, was still closer than Dev had remembered to the Juras, still bleak and snow-covered. But now they had gone through a gap in these, past flowery banks, poppies and fox-gloves, out into the great southern plain of France, the Dauphinée. It turned very hot.

France! blessed home of all wanderers. France! They looked hard at each other at the love they recognized each had for this haven of clean thought. Now indeed it was nearly summer, as out over the hot plain the train bore them past the grain fields, the slow streams with the yellow *fleurs de lis* of France growing on their banks. What a blessed relief! Both loved France as they loved the secrets of their own souls, to be revealed to no one.

France understood these without being told, it kept secrets and it offered its understanding—austere or abandoned, in return. A feeling of warmth, of release, of deep maturity came over the two children, for so they were, beside this old traveled, beaten country. Burgundy!

South they had gone at first until the Mediterranean seemed to be again near, then north with a château far off on some river bank. For an hour Dev had been glancing through a book he found in the rack, at the end of the train, a commercial guide to the region, interspersed with informative paragraphs on the various industries and business features of each place they would pass. Particularly he had read of the wine industry, Dijon, noting the difference between *gourmand* and *gourmet*—how to hold a glass expert-taster-style, sipping the wine, thumb and finger holding the base between them, puckering the mouth, *cul de poule* and gently sucking in air to make the beverage bubble over the tongue.

And there at length from the train window they saw the low hill, the famous barren plain of the Cote d'Or, home of those great wines, the Burgundies, the blood of this land, of which he had been reading. One passage particularly he pointed out to his sister handing the book to her that she might see:

Les grands vins joueront toujours un rôle prépondérant dans les relations sociales, ils seront toujours un trait d'union entre gens de bonne compagnie. Que d'heures enchanteresse nous leurs devons? Sous leur magnétique influence, l'âme s'ouvre aux sentiments généreux, l'ésprit devient plus subtil, la parole plus éloquente. Ils ont le bon de développer les délicatesses du gout et de spiritualiser les plaisirs de la table.

At Dijon he was overjoyed to find old Bill Jessup, his Parisian publisher friend. For one thing it broke up the alignment of the talk between brother and sister. Nelly, his wife, was with Bill and as a matter of fact the two men soon formed an alliance as did the ladies also, thus relieving the brother and sister at once of the false situation they had fallen into.

One of Bill's hobbies was wine. He knew wines, collected them and enjoyed the subtleties of their characters. Unlike us Americans who do not know that one half of an orange is sweet and the other sour, the genius of these people is to pay attention. They have discovered here the grape, said Bill. The Romans knew it. They have even found the imprint of the leaves fossilized in the rock of the place. It is a special soil for grapes, for wine —nothing like it has been discovered elsewhere in the world.

Marvelous, said Dev, the quintessence of the local virtue.

Oh shut up, said Bill. Are you interested in this?

Can't you see my eyes popping out?

I'm going to take you for supper to-night to a good *restaurenteur* here in Dijon, an old master of the *gourmets*. He'll show us something worth looking at. And to-morrow we'll make a wine-tasting trip to Baune.

Great.

Poor Ernest, they made him chief of the commissariat to provide for the Americans stationed here during the war. It broke his heart. All they wanted was whisky, whisky. They had no taste whatever for his rare vintages.

Damned good thing, I'll say, replied Dev.

Yes, but Ernest felt insulted, for the country's sake. He couldn't interest anyone.

All that day the four Americans wandered in the summer heat about Dijon, resting now over their drinks at some café or again seeing the curious façades of the twelfth century houses, built fortress strong, on what is to-day some back street; or again perusing, to shame-faced looks on the ladies' parts, some particularly gross praises in word and line to the perfections of one "Louise" scrawled in crayon on the wall of a house on the rue de la Jouissance.

That evening they had cocktails in their rooms and then betook them as promised, to Ernest's place, found only after a sharp appetite-enkindling walk of half an hour, round and about beyond the cathedral in the old city.

There was but one other party in the room, a strange party, as if at a family dinner a whore familiar with the *père de famille* should be invited to partake of it. The man himself was past middle age, but hearty. Their meal was nearly over when the Americans arrived. Bill asked Ernest about it. He said the gentleman was a doctor of the place and the little bright lady was his particular friend, to keep him going; the family knew it was she who kept him going and so she was permitted to be there.

And so the four Americans began to eat, and to drink *Richebourg,* 1915, *Chambertin* the same, *Musigny, Montrachet,* for two hours—until they could no more. Wow!

The science is exact. The grapes are not palatable; I told you that. Small and bitter. The soil must be poor, of a certain chemistry. They have tried them many places on earth but nowhere do they grow as here.

There was a map on the wall of the H. de la Poste at Beaune showing the famous vineyards. Here too the food was beyond compare: *Chablis, Corton.*

To Dijon, to Beaune must one go, said Dev to himself, from among all places "in the world," to eat and to drink well.

XXXVII

PARIS ONCE MORE

Dev, said Bess one day after they had been in Paris a week, I'm married. Don't be alarmed. It means nothing: What are we going to do now?

I'm going back home in ten days.

Without even a word?

Well, not now at any rate. Come on!

It was the night of Cocteau's *Romeo and Juliet* at the *Cigale*. Everyone would be there.

At the theater all seemed far, far off to Dev.—I should be quarreling with the rest around the bar or else leave in the middle of the performance.—He was interested; not in the play, however. The cult was strong, it was club night among the more heavily financed geniuses of Paris—and the most controversial. The orchestra had struck just before the show. The *Chambre* was represented there, in that little hall. For charity. Picasso, Dérain—and many more; all the lights.

Wearying of the play, which started well but grew tiresome later, the brother and sister went into the small salon which adjoined the auditorium, on one side.

To-morrow, Sis, we'll spend the day in the country, a canoe trip, the Seine, Ardennes.

Great!

How much has it cost you over here? How much have we got left? I've spent about five bucks a day, he said. I'm about at the end. Got to go back and get more. You've got the interest on Mother's bit. You can stay on.

No, dear, I'm going home, too; unless you—

Europe is poison to us Americans—delicious—distressing.

Dev, I want a baby.

Stupid. My God, what next?

I don't care.

You, with your chaste ability to—do what you please.

I'm not chaste.

I said your ability to be chaste, civilly. You're no American. Stay here. You don't want a baby.

A baby and never to be far from you.

This frightened Dev.—God help me.

Oh no, I do not want to censor you, or protect you. —Dev sensed that she was getting ready to question him—but it passed. That's better.

I can never be at home here, said Evans, there is a deep loss in me that comes of my inheritance. Years ago I was lost—I am not of this club. That is what I am, a great zero.

You are a great fool to talk that way.

I belong to the sea, Evans continued.

Oh Dev, you are ridiculous. You can't even swim, can you?

Suppose we should go home?

Lets get a place somewhere up in Jersey—with a sassafras tree on it—at least twenty years old—that's old enough in our country. If I share the interest with you, you can quit your job, said the Sister.

No, you keep it. Stay here.

I will not—not for long anyway. I insist that you quit work. I insist.

Dev was disturbed. Sis, what in hell is the matter with you? We came out here—

Well? Speak, or I shall—

—He would not.

Then you must listen to your silly sister. Live here with me, we have two thousand a year certain. Live here with me. Oh Dev, you've got to stop idling. You've got to work. We can do everything together, everything there is to do in this world. You need me—and you are mine, blessed man. Is it saddening to you to hear me say nobody knows you but I? You are my—secret.

Explain me, advertise me—will you?

Don't be a silly baby. We can come out in you.—Dev was amazed. I can't do it—and, Dev, you'll never do it going back there to that desert. Stay here. Listen. You don't know anything of yourself. Do you know you have five times the ability of these people, these great men you admire over here? But you are going nowhere; they *are*. That's just it, Dev. Their very slenderness is where

they beat you. They have made a virtue of their poverty
—and that is what it all is. Your silly profusion—our
silly profusion defeats us. Dev, you've got to quit fool-
ing—quit your cash job and study it out.

Like Eliot?

Who is Eliot? Like nobody. You've got to sit down
to it. Somebody must and few will get anything even
if they do. But I know that you can. It is their devices
with their poverty that you are admiring—not refinement
in the sense of slenderness, but shelling away, shelling
away to the core. You've never done that. You are
spoiled; you are a baby. You've always got to hit something.

What has been telling you all this?

But they are poor and they work at it and work at it
until it shines like a poverty-stricken door knob or a
peasant's lamp—if he be industrious.

I can do that in America.

Nonsense, Dev, no one can. You've written a lot of
stuff, dear, to break all our hearts that love you. You
don't care about success. No, because you don't even
know what success is—the place has tainted you so.
No one does there. It is too blocked off out of embarrassment to be appreciated. No one would recognize it if
it were before him and so you are pouting and indifferent
but—it's making you sick. Dev, you've never let yourself
go: Down inside you—

For God's sake, Bess, quit it. Down inside me is a
small piece of slime full of worm's eggs.

Oh shut up, said his sister gently. She thought a moment then went on, All right, then, America, but where? We can't live in New York.

I've told you. Let's go up into Sussex.

And starve like proper martyrs, among the copperheads and rattle-snakes—we two Parisians—how entertaining.

Well, you insist on rescuing me. We can get fifty acres for a song and grow our own vegetables. Live on five hundred a year. There I'll write.

You mean you'll actually give up twiddling with money; you'll quit your practice?

We'll see.

Dev, you're not serious. You never are. And you think you can be an artist that way. The only decent thing about art here is that they begin with poverty and work and work seriously at it until—Look at the post-impressionists—three silly tricks and yet they made everything anybody has ever made out of them until it's given up a bounty. Answer what that is. America doesn't need that. You are just deceived. You want to, Dev, but you're not doing it.

Well, Bess—as I said before, where in hell has this come from?

You, you lover, and—my own misery. It's our baby, a pure American.

Siegfried—

Live with me here, Dev.

I won't be your cathedral—

You are—

A nun, are you?

A Parisian patroness. I think I shall organize a coterie.

Oh, come on, let's get out of this.

No, you shan't. Listen to me. You must. Out of their poverty they have made something. I don't know anything about your technique—but I love you and you've got to do it because I can't. Out of their onions, their potatoes, their dandelion leaves, their snails and sparrows. I've spent my months, most of them, thinking, while you have been gadding around. But I've come to my limit.

Would you prefer a concrete road or just macadam—and what if someone should show up and take me away?

I'd kill her, that's all.

Within the auditorium there burst out a great hand-clapping. All the doors to the salon were opened, through them the throng from the theater poured in among the refreshment tables and found seats. The brother and sister watched them in silence. All kinds of celebrities were there, most of whom neither of them knew, painters, international women, and many lesser fry.

An orchestra began to play. The crowd danced.

There were many Americans, many South Americans, people from all over the world. Bess turned her back, her brother stared.

There is no way. There is no way.

When Bess suggested it he went willingly by her side

for their wraps and out into the lights of the Boulevard de Rochechouart.

Where shall we go from here? asked Dev of his sister.

Home, we are getting up at six to-morrow, aren't we?

The first taxi refused them a ride. No, he didn't care to cross the river. He was looking for a fare going to his own part of town.

Across the street were posters of the famous Fratellini Brothers, the international clowns.

Nobody is interested in them any more, said Bess.

XXXVIII

SEINE SISTER

SOFTLY the motion of the skiff—Spring. As though it had been spring forever—now again.

America, said Evans musingly, There are some things there—still some things there I want to gather—

Your æsthetic duty to the Stars and Stripes?

Where in the world have you stolen all this new smartness?

Dear brother, from you. I have done as you have preached—I am a woman of shame, she laughed.

You are happy?

Who can be unhappy?

Dev did not answer. She was shrewd—this sister, when she wanted something.

Where have *you* been these months? he countered.

Not out of Paris, save a week or so after you left—when I wrote you.

Hm, have you been so quickly successful?

I have discovered that I do not need it—with your success as my example.

What do you want?

Seine Sister

You.

After a year in Europe, Kitten, kidding?

I don't want you to go back to America.

Look out, you'll dump us into the river.

The river and again the yellow *fleurs-de-lis*. Dev picked one and marveled at the color. A yellow lily, a wild yellow lily. At home it's blue. The blue flag, yellow-striped.

How I hate to think of leaving it, said Evans.

The flowers or your peers, old dear? Do you like them?

Come on, Bess, what have you been up to?

Oh, I have had a lover, Dev. You would know him if I told you. One of the ones you admire.—She smiled.

Of course, you can't blame me if you picked some damned fool, but the best of them do know their onions.

My dear, of course they know. You are a barbarian beside them: you know nothing.

Stop kidding me.

They know everything, and they—are all Americans, they imagine.

Why did you bring me out here?

To get away from Paris. And to tell you about my baby.

Dev grew angry.—You want a baby, hell. You want to make me keep you here, that's the kind of a baby you want. I'm not it. You're a beauty, I see that now. I never did at home. But don't come any of your clever schemes with me. Stay here if you want to. I'm not sold to you.

321

Bess was taken aback.

Brother, *dear!*

Oh hell, Bess, I'm unhappy. That's nothing, I'm not so unhappy, nothing that's happened has made me so, but I'm not selling out to anybody, not even to you.

You need a wife.

Do you want the job?

If you'll stay over here.

Um. If I could quit work.

You can.

Oh, Bess, you're a downright idiot.

Don't be rude, brother, it doesn't become you and besides, you're broken-hearted, dear: anyone can see it but you.

What do you mean?

I mean what I say. Don't look at me as if I were a fool. I am, that's why I see so well. I've broken twenty walls down from around Saint Sulpice since I saw you last, said Bess.

It hasn't taught you much.

All right, but you've got to tell me what it is I should see then or I'll tell you what I *do* see and you'll have to accept my statement.

Dev was not pleased.—Stop trying to buck me up. I don't want to be saved.

It's not what you want, old dear, in this case, but what you are going to git, she laughed.

Some damn fool has been trying to get at you.

All right, I am that she of whom **A.** wrote the poem
that you admire.

But did you—?

Yes, he tried—

And so now?

She laughed. How wonderful it is to be a writer. Oh,
I wish I were you. The marvel of writing! Pick up a bit
of paper—and find a message upon it—a communication
from a distance: nothing so delightfully simple and exalt-
ing: but the art lies in what is being communicated,
doesn't it? the difficulty and the art—

Most forget what it is, though, said Evans, interested,
most forget what it is in the first place.—

Somehow, here in this small boat, lolling in this
morning sunshine, alone on the quiet foreign river,
Evans—for the first time in his life—had a feeling of
real fear before his sister which he could not understand. Or was it admiration? It was fear, mixed with an
admiration that was fast overpowering him and against
which he fought a quickly failing battle.

But most of all he wondered at this strange woman
before him out of whose mouth such unaccustomed words
were falling. And inside his heart, somehow, he was
being moved, *he* was being moved, that chronic sleeper,
himself. It was this that frightened him. He was curiously
elated.

There were things about Bess, **Dev** felt, that he had
never felt about anyone in his life before. From this
beginning, peace finally reigned between the brother and

sister and Evans began to tell her much of his last two months. She listened intently. Speaking only to make herself clear on certain details. When he had finished, it was noon.

Bess gave a sigh of relief when it was done. Then she began to sing the first bars of the Aria from Manon. She trailed her right hand in the cold water, made a face at its coldness but kept the hand there grimly nevertheless.

Evans was steering for the shore. If the water was cold the day was growing sultry—his brow was sweaty from paddling. Bess had not made a single comment upon his story save to sing aloud.—I wonder what she's thinking, he said to himself.

Mine. Mine. Mine!

What's that?

No sooner had he stepped on the grassy bank and begun to pull the canoe up behind him than she cried, Oh Dev, you old darling, and pretended, laughing, to pull him up also by the hair on top of his head. As she did so, it had flashed through his mind, looking down: Leaves of grass. As a symbol how tasteless, but as a fact how delightful.

There on the bank they spread newspapers and commenced to set out the things they had brought.

I am a sensual savage, Dev, do you know it? said his sister, I could,—do anything. I want to bite.

Go ahead.

Ugh—no, I couldn't, not now.

He joshed her.—I came out here for a holiday with my little sister before sailing for Vinland, the famous —and not to be eaten—but to enjoy this voluminous, voluptuous spring season.

Well, dear, I want to sell you your little Sis—in spite of all that.

Suppose then, now that I have bared my soul, he said, suppose that *you* tell *me* how you have spent *your* time *really*.

So she told him of her week-long unhappy journey to San Moritz with her poet lover.—Winter sports, Dev, that's what they were, but now it's spring again; thank God, that's over.

But, is it?

Sweetheart, laws are made to be broken—by and for the proper person. I have done that. There are other things to be done now. Isn't that enough told for one sunny afternoon?

Dev said nothing but he fondled his sister's slender hand for a moment while his love and loyalty came quickly forward to support her.

So that's what you were up to?

Crying and gnashing my teeth.

Bess, you are a cathedral in which all the pagan gods have come to hide to live secure there forever. I never had such an excited feeling about anyone in my life as I have had about you to-day.

Very pretty, Mister, but what does it mean? Wind up your affairs. Get out of it. We'll go it together. I don't want anything. There'll be enough, just enough. A small place there and the rest of the time here. You'll earn something in time with your writing.

But what about—?

We'll adopt a baby, a war orphan. I will domesticate myself.—He laughed uproariously.

I love you, brother. She embraced him in play. I've had a queer time. Let's spend a winter telling each other of it. I've had enough.

Dev did not answer. Meanwhile she was going on with preparations for lunch—rather elaborate they were. They picnicked on the grassy bank with the violets.—Imagine brother, violets and trees and a river and a grassy bank just like Ophelia's.—She had brought a delicious lunch, with wine, brandy and liqueurs.

To celebrate the ceremony, she said.

What ceremony?

The marriage of spring and the river! Booby!

You are very sure of yourself.

I've waited for this, after the first week, two months, and two months in sackcloth and ashes is too much. It is finished.

As the meal went on Bess made coffee at a little fire with three stones and a green stick as she had learned to do at a camp in the woods of New Jersey. Then she began to drink cognac. More, more!

You're going to get pickled, little girl, if you're not careful, said her brother.

Of course I am, that was one of the things I wanted you around for, I'm an awful baby.

And so she drank and talked, trying to win him.

Proteus, he squirmed, he twisted, he tried to browbeat her, he ridiculed her—My dear, I am not an artist—but shall I not possess even my own appendages—

But she would not let go.—I am a woman. No, dear brother, you are all I have left and—I will not release you, not yet at any rate.

Down with the damned country, she said at last, let's unite on that anyway.—He cared for her until she fell asleep, then covered her and went down and washed his face in the river and smoked—thinking.—Always, a woman tricks you—and it's always the one you don't think is going to do it.

She woke when it was already late in the afternoon—or he woke her for coffee which he himself had brewed.

She was surprisingly fresh. Dearest boy! She was up at once, rubbed her eyes and shook out her hair. Marvelous! A hundred years have passed from me. Dearest brother, you must never leave me again, never have I lived till now. But, if you go—I am finished. Tell me, dear, you will not return to America. You must promise me that.

Here it was out in the open once more. Evans felt it had come. Bess was staring at him now unsmiling, her hair hanging down. She was leaning forward, her hands on the grass, her mouth half-open—waiting for his answer.

His voice caught when he went to speak. Now or never. What should he do?

Don't say that, Dev. Don't say what's in your mind. I tell you you're killing me.

Why don't you come back to America with me then? —He knew he was hedging.

She shuddered a little and bit her teeth hard together. When she looked up she was smiling but it was not the smile Evans was familiar with in his little sister. This is a desperate woman, he said to himself, and prepared to combat her. But she was too quick for him.

You want to be a great writer, don't you, dear? she began. I sympathize with your instinct for writing.

Keep your dirty fingers off that—a wave of anger swept over him.

Oh, it isn't that—fight me as you will, I'm going to see you do it.

How to find a way to do it and not be beaten off, driven off or beaten or dirtied. Yes, that's my life, he replied.

They have learned a great secret of life here in France, she continued. Oh, the damned historical fools who only see the reverse of it in the abandon of this country, as if abandonment and devotion were not of the same fabric —She did not finish.

Oh, come on, let's paddle back.

No, Dev, I refuse to be put off. It's not that, that's just one of the things. It's your way and so I'm on it— but that's not it. There's something here in France any damned fool can learn and you haven't learned it. It's deep. It's moral—

Morality! I knew you'd get back to that sooner or later. Is there any cognac left?

It's in everything they do, right through the scale— You have no sense for it. It's not to make you out a success, Dev. But something's got to be done for all of us. I won't have you laugh. I refuse to become what I will become if you don't help me—without first a struggle. France has taught me. You and I have got to do something with ourselves. Americans. I want to do some good with myself. Oh *good,* Dev, in the French sense, the moral sense. To use well what we have, that's all. We are incurably Americans, you and I, but we can help each other—if we will. That offers us our only hope; to make a beginning, to make something useful out of that country where there's no honor left but a starved, thin, lying one—along the rocks. We've got to live with honor—not the way we treated your precious Indians, Dev, but like a Frenchman to whom France means something. It means something to them, Dev. They get a sense out of it whereas America means nothing to us at all—nothing but "patriotism" and cash. What a meaning! But with honor, the ground, France, can be used. They can retain a connection with original purity—with sources we have muddied away, just as our sorrow is that our purity— without morality—cannot be used.

Bess, you don't know what you are talking about. Art is a country by itself—A matter of learning how—

Without a moral core, it is as empty as—hell. You are unaware of this sense that I have, that we have got to make something moral out of what we have or we shall be just nothing. That's *la belle France*—fakers and all—but there it is. We are Americans and we've got to make something of it or we are just *nothing*. You don't see that. You think I'm a fool. I am. But I can see. You have got to find the words. I can't so I want you—or—I'm done. Can you see that?

And you want me to live here with you—

And let me teach you what morality means. Dev, you've got to listen—

Go on, then, I said I'd do it if you wouldn't—

What!

Finish what you were saying. Literature has nothing to do with life.

With truth? She was laughing like an *it*—damned fool. What the hell does she know? Yet, somehow he admired her crudity.

Dev, dear, listen to me. This means something to you, all this talk—you, I've got you, dear. I'm in love, dearest, with my brother—love, dear.

You've lived in Europe a whole year, Bess, quit that.

I tell you, it delights me. Criticize me, you fool, or I will and disgust you. You can or you can't—Fie, brother, or you won't. You must!

Bess was drinking steadily again now.

To hell with it. I love you all right, Bess, but god damn it, I'm not going to stay over in this country if I

don't want to, not for anybody. But I'll be damned if
I see why I should fight with you about it. Give me some
brandy.

She handed him the bottle.

Here's to love, he said.

Bess drank another, quickly, then leaned across her
brother's lap and threw her arms about his neck where
she hung desperately.

You're not going, dear; you're going, of course, you're
going. I'm not such a fool, Dev. I knew you weren't for
me. But I had to try for you. I feel as if they were closing
me alive into a tomb. But, I won't, Dev, and you can't
make me.

He didn't know what it was he couldn't make her
do, but he, too, was drinking—and it didn't matter.

Thus at forty gayly I celebrate *le printemps suzerain—*
à l'Americain—he said kissing her sister lightly.

But she, having drunk heavily, would not have it his
way. She clasped him ever more tightly round the neck
and pulled him down on the grass beside her.

She would not let him go, but burying her face in his
coat, over his breast she sobbed wildly, holding him
tighter, tighter.

He could not move her. She merely shook her head
and refused to budge. So he ended by letting her lie
there while he cuddled her tenderly.

At last, when it was quite dark, he got her into the
canoe and managed to feel his way back to the landing
whence they had embarked in the morning.

Clinging tight to him Bess insisted that they stay that night at the small inn of the place.

They were too weary for supper. There he put her to bed, kissed her and went down to the bar.

XXXIX

CHERBOURG

SHE insisted a week later on going with him to Cherbourg—Do you deny me my privilege as a mother to watch over my family at its advents and departures? Off to the New World!—She was with him at the Gare St. Lazare. It was cold, foggy, drizzling as the train slid almost noiselessly out of the station. They had not lit the lights; it remained pre-dawn inside the compartment.

So over the low dairy country of Normandie they rode, by the curious cathedral tower of Bayeux in the distance, the endless meadowlands, foxgloves on the railroad embankment. Going away! and toward noon they saw the slab roofs of the cottages near Cherbourg.

They had little to say to each other but sat and looked out of the windows.—I am glad you came. It was the least he could say.—Yes, I wanted to come.

At Cherbourg, they had several hours to wait before ship time. The tender was ready but the *Zeeland* had not come in. They were having difficulty to find conversation. They tried the binoculars Dev had bought for the

333

trip in Vienna, praised them, spoke of the ones they had lent to the Navy during the war. They could see a fishing boat rising and falling, far out.

Let's take a walk in the town.

Before them lay the great bare plaza on the wharf, with the statue of Napoleon, mounted and pointing toward England in the center of it. This was to have been one of the great ports of the world. Trafalgar spoiled it. Two lines of children, girls and boys, were coming from Confirmation, steadily streaming black and white out of the cathedral.

From the wharf, in a heavy wind, Bess took the binoculars, scanned the horizon for the ship, restless. She walked at his side. He was anxious to get away. She maliciously began teasing him about America. The land of promise! she called it.

At the fish market they saw two peasants, man and woman, kissing each other absorbedly, a farewell.—Perhaps he is going as far as Paris, who knows, said Bess, but she looked covertly at them several times.

A fellow went by with a handcartload of leathery, shining sand sharks.—I suppose they eat that stuff.

They passed by the barbed-wire enclosure of the naval air station; great hangars inside, power wires going in, radio aerials flaunted.

Then they walked aimlessly till they came to a little tea place with a few tables in the back room. Quite necessary. There a British naval non-com was sitting with two French women, one young, pretty and crying. The

Cherbourg

other had some English. The man was looking at the table top, making figures on it with his finger nail.—You can't do that. You can't treat us like that, said the older woman. You must do something for her.—The girl was crying in stifled sobs.—You come here and then you go away and leave us. No. You can't do that.

The brother and sister did not look at each other but listened intently.

A whistle was blowing. The ship! They jumped. Outside they started to walk swiftly down the street. Nothing in the windows worth buying for Bess. Can't offer her cash. Here, buy yourself something to remember me by. No? The bridge across the inlet was open. A fellow with a bicycle was on the draw.

Wait again, damn it. Dev felt Bess looking at him; he did not turn. At last he was on the tender. Bess seemed to waver. Guess I'll get on too, she said laughing. Show your tickets, please. All right. The gods are against me. Good-by, brother dear. Give my love to the New World.

Dev was feeling ill. But he couldn't help this miserable scene. Good-by, Bess. . . . He held her close and kissed her, not knowing why he felt so down. He kissed her hands.

She beamed with pleasure. Good-by, dearest, you're all I have left in the world. No, you are all there is. See you soon. Go on, and she pushed him toward the gangway.

Not over yet. He stood in the stern of the tender waving his handkerchief to her. She stood there unmoving until the head of the jetty cut her off.

Now he was on the ship—The sea! He felt better at once, but something was still there pulling him down.

It was a quiet day. The sea was oily, with a long ground swell. He was desperately tired and took a long nap on his bunk. He wakened, bewildered, gasping, a catch at his throat. Looking from the porthole he saw land not far off—One of the channel islands, I suppose. All that night he slept like a dead man.

Next day, now well at sea at last, he began to look around the ship. Few on board attracted him. But there was one man he delighted in talking to, a Scotchman with an Italian name, the son of an old time sailing master—himself a retired captain—who was returning from a leisurely knocking about in his old haunts round the world. An oldish man he was, powerful, straight-backed, red-faced and soft-spoken. He had a strong whisky breath to him in the early morning when Dev would meet him—waiting for breakfast.

—The country has gone to hell now for sure.—He seemed like one stunned.—But look at the English Navy and the German Army—two bodies of men not equaled on earth for hardihood and ability to give and take it—bred on beer; and the peasantry the world over on wine. When I was a young man on one of our trips, we made a stop at the Easter Islands—one of those small islands in the south seas where there'd be one or two men with the sheep during the growing season. Whisky doesn't touch those fellows. They take one of those cans they used to get kerosene in and put a couple of pounds of chewing tobacco in it. Then they'd fill the can with whisky and bury it in the ground for a month or two. I don't know what else they do with it after that. We were three men in our party, good strapping fellows used to an outdoor life and heavy drink. They offered us some of that stuff. I took one sup of mine and put up my hands but the other two downed theirs. It near killed them. But those fellows on the island drink it every day as a regular thing. Seems to make them strong. What are we coming to?

Approaching the Grand Banks, Captain Thomas had news of much ice ahead. Into the fog they plunged which, softly, silently lifting from time to time, Evans saw one, two, five, six sailless fishing schooners anchored in it, softened again now and disappearing. Twenty miles south they had had to steer in the night to avoid the ice. The foghorn had been going steadily. Toward noon the next day land again, Vinland! It was the long low shore of Newfoundland along which they coasted for several hours, ten miles out.

As they were approaching Halifax, Evans, on the side of the ship farthest from shore observed a humming bird, paralleling the vessel's course flying over the water.

At Halifax those in the ship bade some few of their companions adieu, then down the coast, now almost home. For the last night, Evans slept on the ship. In the morning they were in the waters off Maine, going south,

south. The shoal water was oily smooth in the half-sun, half-mist—and schools of fish, leaping by schools, ruffled the water in patches on all sides—a still sea seeming not more than just enough to float the ship—and a shore mist—seventy-eight miles away. A ship he saw, the Nantucket Lightship, anchored, rocking lightly in the smooth sea and men out upon it painting it a metallic red. What a life!

So this is the beginning.